Van ⟨✓⟩ P9-DMX-317
Decatur, MI 49045

DISCARDED

ROSEMARY REMEMBERED

ROSEMARY REMEMBERED

A CHINA BAYLES MYSTERY

Susan Wittig Albert

BERKLEY PRIME CRIME, NEW YORK

ROSEMARY REMEMBERED

A Berkley Prime Crime Book
Published by The Berkley Publishing Group
200 Madison Avenue, New York, New York 10016

Copyright © 1995 by Susan Wittig Albert

Book design by Rhea Braunstein

All rights reserved. This book, or parts thereof, may not be reproduced in any form without permission.

First edition: November 1995

Library of Congress Cataloging-in-Publication Data

Albert, Susan Witting.
    Rosemary remembered / by Susan Wittig Albert.
        p.   cm.
    ISBN 0-425-14937-4
    1. Bayles,   China   (Fictitious   character) —
Fiction.   2. Women   detectives — Texas — Fiction.
    3. Herbalists — Texas — Fiction.   4. Texas — Fiction.
    I. Title.
PS3551.L2637R67   1995
813'.54 — dc20   95-15062
                                                                CIP

PRINTED IN THE UNITED STATES OF AMERICA

10   9   8   7   6   5   4   3   2   1

ACKNOWLEDGMENTS

To all those herbalists upon whose assistance I so often rely and who are so generous with their encouragement, many thanks. To Sisters and Brothers in Crime, thanks and thanks again for advice, help, and support; without you, the business of murder wouldn't be half as much fun. And to my husband and coauthor, Bill Albert, who reads copy, repairs computers, and remains calm when the roof is tumbling down around our ears—well, what can I say?

AUTHOR'S NOTE

This novel is set in the imaginary Texas town of Pecan Springs, which incorporates a variety of fictitious elements, such as the campus of Central Texas State University and The Springs Resort Hotel. If you're familiar with the central Texas Hill Country, please don't confuse Pecan Springs and its inhabitants with such real towns as San Marcos, New Braunfels, Wimberley, or Fredericksburg, or CTSU with any local university. You will also forgive me, I hope, for inserting Adams County between Travis and Bexar and adding the Pecan River to the eastern edge of the Edwards Aquifer. The fictional characters and events of this book are created entirely for pleasure; the occasional references to real people, places, and events are intended only to lend depth and verisimilitude to the fiction and fool you into feeling that Pecan Springs is part of the real world.

CHAPTER ONE

Most of the herbs we use every day have a wonderful tolerance to heat and drought. In fact, it is often claimed that a dry, hot climate is ideal for herbs. The heat and aridity concentrates and intensifies the aromatic oils in the plants' foliage, so that the fragrance is clearer, the taste sharper.

China Bayles
A Book of Thyme and Seasons

For the past couple of weeks, Pecan Springs had been sizzling in a Texas-size heat wave. The red-orange sun skittered like a ball of flame across the cloudless morning sky, afternoon temperatures nudged one hundred, and the night air was a smothering blanket, hot and heavy. In this kind of weather, you never know what will happen. People burn down to a short fuse.

Take Constance Letterman and Ruby Wilcox, for instance. On this Thursday morning, Constance was standing at the counter in my herb shop, fanning her rosy face with a piece of junk mail and complaining about the heat. Constance is short and round, a Hershey bar or two away from Weight Watchers. She's usually as bouncy as a beach ball, but on this hot morning her tight brown curls were coming unfurled around her scowling face. She wiped her forehead with the back of her hand.

"Hot 'nough to toast the toes off a horny toad." She

spoke accusingly, as if Ruby and I were somehow to blame for this persistent meteorological phenomenon. "How people're supposed to *live* in this heat is beyond me. Cooks the soul right out of you."

Ruby Wilcox looked up from the box of herb conference programs she was unpacking for me. "I never saw the day that got one degree cooler because somebody bitched about it." Her tone was snappish. "And there aren't any more horny toads in this part of Texas, Constance. The fire ants ran them off."

Constance fanned harder, and her rosy face got rosier. "No need to get your back up, Ruby." She raised her chin and addressed a chili pepper wreath hanging from the ceiling. "Far as horny toads go, some folks jus' take things too literal."

I put down a large, fragrant bowl of just-clipped mint on the counter next to the phone. My name is China Bayles. Ruby Wilcox is my best friend and tenant, and this was probably the first time in Ruby's life that anybody ever accused her of being too literal. Her Crystal Cave shares space with my Thyme and Seasons in the century-old stone building I own on Crockett Street, a few blocks from Pecan Springs' town square. As you might guess from the name, The Crystal Cave is a New Age shop, filled with incense and rune stones and space music and books on how to read your horoscope. As you might also guess, the Cave is Pecan Springs' *only* New Age shop, which makes Ruby something of a rarity. But she's a rarity on other counts, too. She's just over six feet tall (depending on which shoes she's wearing), with carroty, every-which-way hair, freckles, and wide eyes, green or gray or brown (depending on which contacts she's wearing). This morning, her eyes were green and her orangy frizz was snugged back from her forehead with a green band. She was wearing a loose, lacy top, cream-colored; a flowing, ankle-length skirt in various shades of green; and flat, green sandals. Her toenails matched her hair, and her fingernails matched her toenails. Ruby is a real treat.

Constance Letterman owns and manages the Craft Emporium, next door on the corner of Crockett and Guadalupe. The Emporium is housed in a huge old Victorian that somehow reminds me of an eccentric but charming maiden aunt, laden with bandboxes and wicker baskets, wearing a floppy straw hat heavy with cabbage roses, and smelling faintly of lavender and lilies of the valley. It's crammed to the rafters with craft shops and boutiques: Gretel's CandleWorks, Peter Dudley's antique dishes, The Vintage Boutique, and Blanche's Buttons & Laces. The next time you're in Pecan Springs, you really should stop and browse. And while you're in the neighborhood, drop in at Thyme and Seasons as well.

Even under the best of circumstances, Constance and Ruby are equally volatile, and when they rub up against one another, they heat up. Today, they were like a pair of prickly pear cacti trying to dance on a hot rock. I changed the subject.

"Did you go to the fireworks last night, Constance?"

Every Fourth, the Pecan Springs Chamber of Commerce sponsors a fireworks display at the Little League Park out at the end of LBJ, behind the fairgrounds. Families sprawl on blankets on the grass or relax in lawn chairs in the backs of pickup trucks that flaunt the Texas star and bars and bumper stickers that say, "Buy American or Go on Japanese Welfare." The Lions Club sells chili dogs and nachos blanketed with jalepeño cheese and sweetened iced tea in white foam cups, while carnival honky-tonk blares in the background and everybody oohs and aahs at the cascades of fiery sparks that shower through the night sky. When the last Roman candle scorches the stars, it's time to dance country-western to a local band. Last night it was The Possum Brothers. They started with "Blue Eyes Cryin' in the Rain." We wished. Anything to cool us down. A gully washer, a frog choker, even a hurricane.

Well, we got our wish. A passing shower had dampened us this morning, but the rain didn't bring down the temperature more than a degree or two. In fact, the leftover humidity was only turning up the scorch factor and making everybody more touchy.

"O' course I went to the fireworks." Constance answered me indignantly, as if I'd accused her of missing her mother's birthday. "Nobody stays away from the Fourth."

Constance is right. In Pecan Springs, the town turns out en masse for the holidays. Fireworks on the Fourth, the parade of homemade floats on Labor Day, the Pecan Festival every October, "Silent Night" around the Christmas tree on the square, taps at the cemetery on Memorial Day. If you come from New York or Chicago, these probably seem like small-potato pleasures. But people around here grew up on them, find them nourishing, and want to pass them on to their children. The Fourth and Labor Day and Pecan Festival Weekend are big events in the life of a small town, and we celebrate them together, knowing that we aren't really celebrating the occasion, we're celebrating each other and the hope that holds us together.

This sense of quiet community is a strong contrast to the competitive life I used to lead as a criminal defense attorney in a big Houston law firm. I once knew a famous defense lawyer who bragged that he went to court armed for hand-to-hand combat. When he walked out of the courtroom, he expected to leave the other guy stone cold dead on the floor. A metaphor, maybe, but not by much. Our adversarial system may not be literally bloody, but that doesn't make it any less murderous. As one of the adversaries, I whipped the prosecution in my share of battles, and got whipped in the rest. I lived like a junkie on the adrenaline rush of legal skirmishes and courtroom battles. But the job was a good one, the best in the city, at least according to my friends, who kept telling me how lucky I was to have it. My work pumped up my ego, paid *mucho dinero*, and promised to promote me to senior partner sometime before menopause.

I didn't quite make it. A few months short of forty, I realized that I was deeply disgusted with the whole thing, with the sleaze and the lies, with the criminals and, yes, with the courts.

Nine out of ten of my clients were guilty as sin, which meant that if I was good enough, smart enough, and aggressive enough to win ten acquittals, nine guilty people went free. I began asking myself whether I felt morally good about this, and when the answer began to come up no more times than it came up yes, I turned in my resignation and moved to Pecan Springs, where I used my ill-gotten gains to buy a small herb shop in a century-old stone building with living quarters in the back. I make a decent living, I love what I do, and I'm happy.

But I couldn't spend the morning congratulating myself for escaping the rat race. This was the weekend of the annual conference of the Texas Herb Growers and Marketers Association, which was being held at The Springs Resort Hotel just outside of town. I was on the planning committee, and there were still a couple of hundred loose ends to tie up. But before I could tend to any of them, I had to pick up McQuaid's truck, affectionately known as The Blue Beast. Yesterday evening, he had loaned The Beast to Rosemary Robbins so she could move a file cabinet and chair she had bought. I was driving over to her house this morning to get the truck so I could use it to haul rental tables to the hotel.

But first things first. I frowned at the stack of conference programs Ruby had unpacked. "That doesn't look like a hundred and fifty programs, Ruby. There must be another box somewhere."

Ruby shook her head. "That's it. The printer must have shorted you."

I sighed. Another problem to add to the list, as if it weren't long enough already. Setting up a conference for 150 people isn't a picnic. Other members of the committee were handling the awards banquet, the trade show vendors, the workshops, seminars, and round table discussions, and the herbal spaghetti sauce contest that was always the high point of the annual conference. I was supposed to handle the Herb Bonanza Bazaar, which would be open to the public on Saturday, and work with the hotel to make sure that everything went smoothly.

So, sometime in the next few hours, I had to check out a list of details with the hotel, pick up extra tables for the bazaar, and chase down a gross of green tee shirts bearing the guild's logo, last seen on the wrong UPS truck, heading into the sunset at top speed. And on a weekend when hordes of out-of-town herbalists would be stopping in to see Thyme and Seasons, the shop's ancient air conditioner had begun to gasp and rattle as if it were dying of pneumonia. But herbalists are an understanding lot, the air conditioner was still wheezing out a few asthmatic BTUs, and UPS had phoned to say that the vagrant tee shirts had been apprehended in Lubbock and were being extradited to Pecan Springs. I could see light at the end of the tunnel.

I turned to Ruby. "I have to get moving, Ruby. Will you watch the store until Laurel shows up?"

Laurel Wiley gives me a hand when I need her, which has been pretty often lately, what with the conference and everything else. She's more than just a store-sitter, though. She's an expert on Southwestern herbs, and I rely on her for a lot of things I'm still learning about. If you're puzzled about *Lippia graveolens* or *Poliomintha longiflora* or *Coriandrum sativum*, Laurel will clear away the mystery.

"Sure," Ruby said. "Anyway, I owe you one. You subbed for me a couple of times last week."

"That's what's nice about having two shops under the same roof," Constance said. "You can trade off."

"Yeah." Ruby stood up. "We can have a life while we make a living."

Until a few months ago, Thyme and Seasons was crowded into one twenty-by-twenty room and I lived in four rooms in the back. It was a large, lovely living space, but there wasn't much shop room. Then I moved into a house outside of town with my friend Mike McQuaid and his eleven-year-old son Brian, and expanded the shop into the space where I used to eat and sleep. I still have to own up to some fundamental uncertainty about living *en famille*, but if I've traded away some of my personal freedom, I've gotten some great shop space in return, not to mention a reliable relationship that's always there to come home to. I'm now trying to decide whether to turn my former kitchen into an herbal tea room.

With the added space, Thyme and Seasons is just about perfect — or will be, when the remodeling is finished. Wooden shelves along the stone walls hold large jars and massive stoneware crocks full of dried herbs, small bottles of herb tinctures, and tiny vials of essential oils and fragrance oils. There are herbal seasonings, vinegars, and jellies to bring new life to any cuisine, and herbal soaps, cosmetics, and aromatic oils to bring new life to body and spirit. Books line one wall in a cozy reading corner, baskets of pomanders and sachets sit in the corners, dusty-sweet bunches of yarrow and tansey and salvia hang from the ceiling, ropes of pungent peppers and silvery garlic braids festoon the walls, and wreaths of artemesia, sweet Annie, and delicate dried flowers are everywhere, lending a sweet, spicy fragrance to the air.

Outside, Laurel's sister Willow and I put in many long hours last spring transforming the entire yard, from Crockett Street back to the alley, into a collection of theme gardens: a silver garden, a tea garden, a butterfly garden, a dyers' garden, a kitchen garden. The work won't be done for a few more months—probably never, actually, since herb gardens have a way of inviting you to do just a little more here and a little more there. But the gardens are already paying off in increased plant sales, and they look lovely.

Constance stopped fanning and pushed her damp hair out of her eyes. "I'd better get back to the Emporium." She went to the door. "Rosemary Robbins is coming this morning to go over the books."

Rosemary Robbins. The same Rosemary who borrowed McQuaid's truck. She did my accounting work too, as well as Ruby's and Constance's and McQuaid's.

Speak of the devil. The phone rang as I was waving good-bye to Constance, and I reached for it, moving the bowl of mint aside.

"Hi," McQuaid said. "Have you collected The Beast from Rosemary yet?"

"I'm leaving this minute," I said.

"Okay." There was something different about Mc-Quaid's voice. "But be careful."

I laughed shortly. "Be *careful?* You're worried I'll put another dent in the poor old Beast?"

My half-sarcastic reply requires a bit of explanation. Mike McQuaid and I met when I was a defense lawyer and he was a Houston homicide detective—not exactly a match arranged by your average dating service. Although I was immediately attracted to him, I pushed the temptation out of my mind. I wasn't into relationships. They took too much time, and I was too busy being a defense lawyer, which made a relationship with a cop very much out of the question.

It wasn't long after I left my career and moved to Pecan Springs that I saw McQuaid again. He'd recently resigned from the police force, for some of the same reasons I had left the law. He was working on his Ph.D. and teaching in the Criminal Justice Department at Central Texas State University, on the north side of Pecan Springs. I still called him McQuaid, as I had when we worked on opposite sides of the judicial fence. But we weren't separated by our jobs any longer. One thing led to another, and we became lovers.

Our relationship has gotten stronger over the last three years, although I've dragged my feet hard enough to leave heel marks in the dirt. Love isn't the problem, for McQuaid is a gentle man with whom I share a great many mutual interests, some of them delightfully, deliciously sensual. The two of us are very good in bed together, and getting better all the time.

No, it wasn't my feeling for McQuaid that kept me from making a commitment. The problem was that I wasn't happy about the idea of a full-time, live-in relationship. I cherished my personal space. I loved having my own business and being my own boss. I refused to jeopardize either state of affairs, and McQuaid was double jeopardy. He was a single parent with a young son. What's more, he hadn't planned to stay at CTSU forever. He aimed at a full professorship at some big-city university that could pay him what he was worth. A long-term relationship with him meant not only becoming a mother but moving back to the city — neither of which I was prepared to do.

But last spring, McQuaid turned down an offer of a professorship at New York University and accepted tenure at CTSU. The same week, he and Brian lost their lease. After a lot of soul-searching on my part and some undue influence from McQuaid, I finally agreed to go halves with him in an eighteen-month lease on a five-bedroom house large enough for two adults and one child and their various belongings, including a fine library of herb books, one large gun collection, and an assortment of reptiles and spiders (including — you won't believe this — a tarantula named Ivan the Hairible). Not to mention Khat, a testy Siamese, and an irrascible basset hound appropriately named Howard Cosell.

Living with McQuaid has surprised me. There is the ordinary rub of small conflicts, day to day, but overall it's soothing, this cozy cocooning, this enfolding of body and spirit in the pleasant warmth of home and hearth. But another part of me — the independent China — stubbornly insists that it's too soothing, too cozy. *If the feminist movement taught you anything,* I hear her whisper, *it taught you that there are board rooms to be invaded, career ladders to be climbed, financial killings to be made. So what are you doing washing the dishes and changing the sheets? Haven't you got anything better to do?*

And then there's Brian, who's eleven. I'm forty-four,

I've never been a mom, and life under the same roof with a preadolescent male requires some major attitude adjustments on my part. What's more, Brian has lived alone with his father for the five years since his parents were divorced. He naturally resents having to share his dad with an uppity and intrusive female who's used to having her own way.

And one more thing. For all of my adult life, I've been responsible to nobody, with nobody responsible for me. Now, though, I feel responsible to McQuaid. Worse, he seems to feel he's responsible for *me*. For instance, his telling me just now to be careful. It may seem to you like a small thing, but it bothers me and I get sarcastic, as I did a second ago. It usually doesn't accomplish anything. It didn't this time, either.

His voice grew hard and measured: his pull-over-and-step-out-of-the-car voice. "I said *be careful*, China. Houston Homicide just called. Pardons and Paroles turned Jake Jacoby loose day before yesterday."

That got my attention. Seven or eight years ago, Jake Jacoby killed his wife and mother-in-law and barricaded himself in his house. McQuaid talked him onto the porch and into the arms of the police. Jake was not grateful.

"I thought he got twenty-five years," I said. It had been a crime of passion and Jacoby had hired a good defense lawyer—not me, thank God. I had plenty on my conscience, but not that one.

"Twenty-five years?" McQuaid's chuckle was bitter. "You know better than that, counselor. The prisons are jammed. The prisoners are getting two days' automatic good behavior for every day served." He paused. "Where's your gun?"

"Forget it," I said. My gun—a 9mm Beretta—was behind the paneling in the storage room behind the shop.

I'd only used it for real once, and somebody—who, it doesn't matter just now—was dead. I wasn't going to use it again. Ever.

There was a silence. When McQuaid spoke, his voice was controlled. "Be reasonable, China. According to the prison grapevine, Jake's sworn to get even. I've given Brian his orders, and now I'm telling you. If Jacoby comes around the shop—"

"If he comes around the shop, I'll call the police," I said, being reasonable.

"The police!" It was McQuaid's turn for sarcasm. "You think Bubba's going to be waiting around the corner for you to scream?" Bubba Harris is the chief of the Pecan Springs police, a good old boy with a cigar and a beer belly. He's tough and he runs a tight town, but he's short on manpower.

I had to concede that there was some logic to McQuaid's concern. But it wasn't logic we were talking about, it was control. The emancipated China rose up in me, the China who hates to be told what to do by somebody who thinks he knows better. She was indignant, and she spoke for me.

"Look," she said, "I'm going to pick up the truck and get started on the seven trillion errands I have to run before noon. If you want to discuss this over lunch—"

"I don't want to discuss it at all. Go get your gun and put it in your purse. Jacoby's dangerous."

"I don't have a license for a concealed carry."

"Since when did you let a little thing like that stop you?" His voice was crisp. "I want you to watch out for him, China."

With an exaggerated sigh I said, "Okay. Who am I watching for?"

"He's six foot three, black hair, black mustache, five-inch knife scar on his right forearm, snake tattoo on his right shoulder and the right side of his neck. He thinks he's naked if he's not carrying a knife or a gun." McQuaid was grim. "I want you to be careful, China. *Very* careful."

"I'll be careful," I said. I hung up, being very careful not to slam the phone.

"What was that about?" Ruby asked. She moved the bowl of mint next to the cash register, pausing to sniff its fragrance.

I fished the keys out of my purse. "A man with a snake," I said. "And an ex-cop with a father complex."

CHAPTER TWO

For you there's rosemary and rue. . . .
William Shakespeare
The Winter's Tale

It was still early, but the heat was waiting outside like a ferocious tiger ready to pounce. Parked in the sun, my twelve-year-old Datsun was an oven, the seat scorching, the steering wheel too hot to grip. The air conditioner made a valiant effort, but the air on my face was a dry blast off the Sahara. I rolled the window down and the humidity rolled in. Texas in July. How did people survive here between the time the settlers built their log cabins and the first air-conditioning salesman knocked on the door? Especially the women, swaddled in long skirts and crinolines and buttoned into bodices so tight they could hardly breathe. Sheer torture, being confined like that.

Just so I could tell McQuaid I'd been careful, I cast a cursory glance around. No sign of a six foot three, black-mustached ex-con with a knife scar and a snake tattoo. Shaking my head at McQuaid's paranoia (once a cop, always a cop, always on guard against something), I pulled out onto Crockett, made a left, and drove a block to the courthouse square.

The tourists flock to the century-old stone-and-timber buildings in the center of Pecan Springs like pigeons to a roost. (In fact, the City Council recently built a public potty behind the library to meet their basic needs, a move which is said to have been instigated by Henry Hoffmeister of Hoffmeister's Clothing & Dry Goods, who got tired of providing toilet paper and a flush for the masses.) They come to Pecan Springs not just for scenic beauty but for a nostalgic taste of small-town Texas, which the merchants ladle out liberally. The square is decorated with flags, red-white-and-blue bunting, and posters announcing that the streets will be roped off on Saturday evening for the square dance competition.

This morning, a small group of silver-haired ladies in summery dresses and white shoes were standing on the corner listening to Vera Hooper, the town docent. Wearing a denim skirt and yellow tee shirt hand-painted with green cacti, Vera was extolling the architectural wonders of the Adams County Courthouse, which was constructed a hundred years ago of 160 flatcar loads of pink granite, hauled in from Burnet County by rail. As I passed, Vera pointed across the street to the Sophie Briggs Historical Museum, which features (among other enticements) a dollhouse that once belonged to Lila Trumm, Miss Pecan Springs of 1936, as well as Sophie Briggs's collection of ceramic frogs. The Sophie Briggs Museum is a big draw in our town. It's amazing the interest people can have in ceramic frogs.

The square is the first stop on the Gingerbread Trail. After the ladies have admired the courthouse and availed themselves of the new public potty, they'll board an air-conditioned minibus, The Armadillo Special, and tootle south on Anderson Avenue to admire the fine old Victorian houses that line both sides of the street. Pecan Springs was settled by German immigrants in the 1840s, but the big building boom didn't come until the '90s. That's when the arrival of the railroad brought the money to build the courthouse, the gingerbread Victorians, The Grande Theater, and The Springs Hotel. An opulent era, but I'll bet the residents would have traded it all for central air-conditioning. I'll further bet that Vera Hooper's ladies wouldn't have been so enthusiastic about the Gingerbread Trail if they were required to hoof it, rather than riding the air-conditioned Armadillo Special.

I waved at Vera and headed down Anderson to Chisos Trail and made a right. A few blocks west, I drove into Pecan Park, a recently built development of expensive homes surrounded by synthetic green lawns, unnatural rock terraces, and landscaped garden pools. Pecan Park doesn't have much to do with Pecan Springs. As I drove along I was reminded of the Houston suburb where I used to live: green, serene, and empty. In fact, I'd be willing to bet that very few of the residents were around this morning to enjoy their upscale homes. Most of them probably had to work from before dawn to past dark to make enough money to pay their upscale mortgages.

Rosemary Robbins lived on a winding street a couple of blocks off Chisos Trail. Her house was set well back from the road behind a screen of cedar and yaupon holly, with a carefully arranged clump of purple crepe myrtle and plumy pampas grass surrounded by a bed of flaming red salvia, all heavily mulched with bark chips and without a single weed, compliments of Garcia's Garden Service. A cement drive looped behind the streetside clump of oaks and onto the street again. Through the trees, I could see McQuaid's Blue Beast, sitting sheepishly behind Rosemary's stylish gray Mazda. This was not the neighborhood where a battered old truck felt at home — or a twelve-year-old Datsun, either.

I swung into the drive, parked far enough behind The Beast to give myself maneuvering room, and got out.

McQuaid had asked Rosemary to lock the truck and leave the key in the magnetic box under the fender. I wouldn't bother to knock on her door. I'd just get in the truck and drive off. McQuaid and I could pick up my Datsun this evening.

As I stepped out into the heat, the cicadas began a loud metallic drone. Their high-pitched crescendo was counterpointed by the sardonic clucking of a yellow-billed cuckoo, the bird that Leatha, my mother, called a rain crow. When I hear that sinister clucking, I remember summer afternoons when I was ten, eleven, twelve, reading a book in my favorite tree, Leatha on a chaise longue beneath me, her gin glass within easy reach. The rain crow is a bad-luck bird, Leatha always said, in her soft Southern drawl. When you hear it, watch out. Warnings like that were her defenses against the random perils of a world over which she had little control. Look for cars. Keep your hand on your purse. Lock the car doors. Don't let him touch you.

Perversely, I left the Datsun unlocked. I walked toward The Beast, wanting not to think of Leatha's warning — or of McQuaid's. Sure, Jacoby was a bad actor, and what he had done to his wife and mother-in-law was enough to curl anyone's hair. But Jacoby could be anywhere, Dallas or Houston or El Paso. Anyway, I reminded myself — or rather, the independent China reminded *me* — Jacoby wasn't the real issue. I slipped my hand under the fender and took out the magnetic key box. The real issue was a power issue. The real issue was —

No key. Well, no problem. Rosemary had probably left it under the seat. And if the truck was locked, I could knock at the door. Her Mazda was here, so she was still at home.

But the truck wasn't locked. What's more, it wasn't even shut. I pulled the door open and saw her.

Rosemary. On her right side across the vinyl seat, face turned up, empty eyes open, glassy, sightlessly staring. A neat, smooth, black hole under her left cheekbone, the seat under her head rusty with dried blood, furry with flies. Dark blood, like red ink, spattered all over the passenger side of the cab, the dash, the windshield. Blood and bits of something. Bits of the inside of Rosemary's head.

I gagged and stepped back. The cicadas were a hundred buzzing rattlers, the heat a hard, sweaty hand pressing on my head. I grabbed the door to steady myself, then yanked my hand back, hoping I hadn't smudged whatever prints there were.

After a minute I forced myself to look again, but not at Rosemary. The keys were in the ignition, Rosemary's purse on the floor, the wallet visible. A plastic grocery sack beside the purse spilled bars of soap, a carton of milk, a head of cabbage, all polka-dotted with blood. A Handy Jack Dry Cleaners bag full of clothing hung from the hook over the passenger door, blood-spattered. In the back of the truck I could see a gray metal file cabinet and a chair. Groceries, the dry cleaning, used furniture. Ordinary artifacts of ordinary, everyday life.

But for Rosemary Robbins, there was no more ordinary life, no life at all. The brassy rattle of the cicadas was suddenly swallowed up in her stillness. A sour sickness curdled in my throat. I swallowed it down and leaned over her body, clad in expensive beige slacks, creamy silk blouse, paisley scarf, to feel for a pulse at her throat. Nothing. Her skin was cool, her stillness utter, complete, final.

I looked down, feeling her separateness, sensing the absolute distance between us. Who had she been, this woman I had admired but barely known? What had empowered her, brought her pain, brought her peace? What had brought her to this terrible end? And I knew with sad certainty that it was only here, only now, in this last, quiet moment, that Rosemary Robbins could be whatever woman she was. In a little while, she would be the coroner's corpse, the cops' homicide, the DA's murder victim, the media's crime of the hour. Each of us, the living, would dissect her, construct her, imagine her, compose her as it suited our purposes, our needs. It was only in this moment, her death just discovered and not yet acknowledged, that she could be simply and purely herself, whoever she had been. Here, on the sly verge of death, I wished I had known her better.

I stepped back and took a deep breath, coming back to myself. Then I turned away and left the body in peace for the time it took to find a neighbor at home and call 911. When the PSPD showed up, I was beside the truck again, waiting, pacing, collecting observations: the door had been unlatched, the window was rolled up, unbroken, her wallet was still in her purse, there was no sign of a weapon. Unless the gun was out of sight beneath her, she hadn't committed suicide. If she'd been murdered, the killer must have shot her through the open door while she was sitting behind the wheel — last night, probably, just as she got home with her furniture, the groceries, the dry cleaning. I wondered whether she'd known what was about to happen. And wondered *why*, in God's name. Why Rosemary? My eyes, of their own accord, went to the spattered blood, the bits of flesh. Why, why?

The first cop on the scene was a slight, nervous brown-skinned man with large spaniel-brown eyes and a name badge that identified him as Gomez, H. He took one look at the body and ran back to the car to radio for assistance. A few minutes later a second cop arrived, Walker, G., a broad-shouldered woman with a competent jaw, a gritty voice, and a look of twitchy impatience, like a second-string offensive tackle with something to prove — Grace Walker, promoted a couple of months ago from prisoner attendant at the jail to patrol officer. Grace's mother, Sadie Stumb, works at Cavette's Grocery, on the corner of Guadalupe and Green. "That girl," Sadie always tells me proudly, as she rings up my fresh produce, "that Grace, she's goin' far. Ever'body better git outta her way."

Grace looked at Rosemary, then back at me. "Friend of yours?" She turned once again to peer closer. "Sister?"

"Sister?" I was surprised. "What makes you say that?"

Grace raised her heavy eyebrows in a facial shrug. "You look kinda alike. Brown hair, square sorta face."

"Not a sister," I said. "A friend." But that wasn't true, either. Rosemary Robbins and I hadn't been close enough to be friends, except in the most superficial sense. "A business associate, actually," I amended.

I glanced at the still face once again. I hadn't even known Rosemary well enough to know who would be sad, now that she was dead. Who would find the world empty, now that she wasn't in it?

"What kinda business?"

"She was my accountant. She did my taxes, handled my business accounts, stuff like that." I could hear a siren in the distance. More police were on the way.

"Taxes, huh?" Grace moved her shoulder in an economical gesture, expressing understanding. "Maybe somebody didn't get what they thought they had comin', and they took it out on her. I read the other day that accountants are always gettin' threats from people who think they been ripped off. Like lawyers, you know? Lawyers are always gettin' theirselves killed. Somebody just busts into the office and starts shootin'." She sighed and lifted her cap off her head, wiping her sweaty forehead. "Doesn't hardly pay to get ahead, does it?"

The police car pulled up at the curb, and we both turned. If this had been Houston, the vehicle would have been a Mobile Crime Scene Unit, a large white van equipped with state-of-the-art portable forensic technology and manned by a half-dozen criminalists. But this wasn't Houston, and Police Chief Bubba Harris had brought only two uniforms with him. One of them began to loop yellow crime-scene tape across the drive while the other unpacked camera gear. Bubba (his real name is Earl, but not even his mother uses it) conferred with Gomez for a moment, then with Grace Walker, putting them to work. Then he turned to me.

Bubba is in his mid-fifties, with hair going grizzled and a paunch that sags over his hand-tooled Western belt as if the last dozen plates of barbecue are still settling. His gray shirt was wet under the arms, and his unlit cigar—I've never actually seen it lit—was clamped in one corner of his mouth. He growled around it.

"McQuaid's truck, ain't it?"

I wasn't surprised that Bubba recognized The Beast. He and McQuaid, cop and ex-cop, have a fraternal relationship.

"I came to pick it up," I said. "Rosemary borrowed it yesterday evening about six to move some furniture she'd bought—what you see in the back of the truck. McQuaid offered to give her a hand, but she said she could handle it by herself." Typical Rosemary. She was the sort of woman who handled everything by herself. She didn't ask for a thing.

Bubba's heavily jowled face was dark, thick brows pulled down. Like most cops, he doesn't much like lawyers, even ex-lawyers. On the other hand, he likes

McQuaid, and the fact that McQuaid likes me compli-
cates the matter somewhat. Over the several years we
have known one another, he has grown more tolerant of
me.

"Any idea who might've done it?" he asked. "Assumin'
she didn't do it to herself."

I shook my head. A flash flared as the photographer
did his work. Grace Walker was hunkered down beside
the door, dusting for prints. Gomez was beginning a
search of the area around the truck. A fourth cop was
motioning to a passing motorist who had stopped his car
to gawk, directing him to drive on. Bubba turned to the
truck and Grace straightened up and stepped aside. He
felt rapidly and deftly under the body.

"Doesn't 'pear to be a gun," he said.

"Wouldn't hardly be, I don't reckon," Grace said dryly.
"Wound on the left side and the angle the way it is, she'd
almost have to hold it in her left hand. It'd be in her lap
or on the floor, and it isn't."

Bubba did not seem pleased that a mere female had
noticed these things, but he only grunted.

"Had her legs swung partway 'round like she was gettin' out," Grace went on. She was about to say something
else, but Bubba turned away. The EMS van had just
pulled up at the curb, followed by another car, a green
Oldsmobile. Maude Porterfield, Justice of the Peace, got
out of the Olds, conferred with the EMS techs for a minute, then came up the drive toward us, leaning on a cane.

In Texas, the law requires that a JP rule on every suspicious death. This requirement sometimes gives law enforcement officials heartburn, but not when the JP is
Judge Porterfield. At seventy-three, she has served the
county for forty-two years. Her white hair may be a little
thin, but her hearing and her right knee are the only

things about her that don't work at an optimum level. In addition to being a JP, she teaches criminal procedure in the seminars conducted by the Texas Justice Court Training Center, headquartered in the Criminal Justice Department at CTSU. Judge Porterfield and I had met at one of the center's social functions and hit it off immediately. As we say in Texas, she don't take no bull.

"Mornin', Earl," she said. "Hot as a pistol." She straightened the shiny belt of her red watermelon-print dress and nodded at me. "Mornin', China. How you been?" Without waiting for my answer, she switched back to Bubba. "Got a problem here, 'pears like."

Bubba plucked his cigar out of his face and raised his voice two notches. The judge wears a hearing aid in her right ear. "Mornin', Judge Porterfield. A shootin's what it is."

The judge, who isn't much more than five feet high, rose on her tiptoes to peer through the open door of the truck. She made a tch-tch noise with her tongue against even white dentures. "Suicide?"

"Murder," Bubba said.

"Domestic violence?"

Bubba looked at me. "The gal was married?"

"Her name is Rosemary Robbins," I said. "She was divorced, or about to be." Rosemary had mentioned the divorce in passing, but hadn't elaborated. Our encounters, while pleasant, had been focused on business and rather hurried. She was always checking her watch, as if she had to get on to another business engagement. It was a restless habit that had reminded me of myself, in my former life. "She was married to Curtis Robbins," I added, offering up the last bit of personal information I had.

Judge Porterfield pulled her sparse white eyebrows together. "Robbins? Manages Miller's Gun and Sporting Goods?"

Gomez came around the truck. "That's him," he said. "Too bad she didn't file a complaint when she had the chance."

"You been out here on a DV, Hector?" Bubba asked.

"Yeah. Back 'round Christmas. She phoned in a complaint, but by the time I got here, she'd decided not to press charges. Usual story."

The judge took a notebook out of her purse, which was red and shiny and shaped like a slice of watermelon. She looked at Gomez, obviously not accepting the "usual story" bit. "What did he say when you questioned him?"

Gomez colored. "He was gone, an' she didn't want me talkin' to him. Said she thought it might make him worse. She didn't want ever'body in town readin' in the paper 'bout her gettin' beat up."

Grace Walker shook her head gloomily. "Everybody'll be readin' about her now."

The judge looked from Grace to me. "She and Robbins have any kids?"

"Not as far as I know," I said. "She had a business. She was a CPA."

"Woman with a business probably doesn't *want* any kids," Grace remarked sagely.

Bubba gave her a warning look. "This their place?" he asked me.

I shook my head. "I don't think so. I got the impression she lived here alone. Her office is in the back of the house." That much I knew, because we'd met there to go over my tax stuff.

"Mebbe we better take a look at the office, Yer Honor," Bubba said.

Judge Porterfield sighed. "Right, Earl. It'll get us out

of this gol-durn heat." She and Bubba walked toward the house.

Gomez blinked. "Earl?"

"She used to teach the chief in Sunday School when he was a kid," Grace said. "Earl's his real name."

"Earl," Gomez mused. "How 'bout that."

Grace turned to me. "You wanta give me your statement now, Miz Bayles?"

When that was done, I promised to stop at the police station and leave my prints for elimination purposes, then got back in my furnace of a car. ABC Rentals would have to deliver those extra tables to the hotel, and McQuaid would have to rent a car. It'd be a few days before Bubba turned The Blue Beast loose. She'd done a lot of things during the course of her long and checkered career, but I'd bet this was the first time she'd been a murder scene.

By two o'clock, the temperature was an infernal ninety-nine, and the buildings and trees were shimmering under the blazing sun. I'd plowed through two-thirds of my list of things to do for the herb conference. Next was The Springs Hotel, where I needed to check on last-minute details. That's where I was headed now, the sun visor pulled low against the glare of the aluminum sky and the air conditioner turned up to gale force. Jeff Clark owned and managed the hotel, which had been a family business for several generations. I needed to talk to him.

But my heart wasn't in the herb conference any longer. I was remembering Rosemary Robbins, sprawled on the seat of McQuaid's truck, an obscene hole in her smooth cheek, flies buzzing in her hair. It was oddly intimate, this meeting in death, in contrast to the impersonality of our meetings while she was alive.

Tax accountants are a lot like doctors and priests. They

plumb the secrets of your innermost being, peer into your most private places, probe parts of you that nobody else is permitted to see. Rosemary Robbins had explored all my hidden places. She knew where I was succeeding with the store, where I was failing, and probably (damn it) why. She knew about my investments, smart and stupid, and about the financial aspects of my living arrangements with McQuaid. And since she did his taxes as well as mine, she had a pretty clear picture of the two of us and our relationship. Visiting Rosemary was like making a trip to the confessional, leaving my sins behind, large and small, and taking away none of the priest's.

That was the interesting part. Rosemary knew a great deal about me, but I had only vague impressions of her, the way you know a doctor as a crisp figure in white jacket and stethoscope, or a priest as a dim shadow behind the confessional screen. The times we had met, she'd impressed me as a woman who managed her personal life like her business, with such competent organization that it demanded very little of her.

But judging from what Hector Gomez had said, Rosemary Robbins's personal life had been deeply shadowed, her cool orderliness a camouflage for a relationship out of control. There isn't anything paradoxical about this, actually. A dozen years ago, I defended a wealthy woman who had confessed to murdering her husband, a well-known Houston optometrist. In her guarded self-control, that woman reminded me of Rosemary. For weeks, she refused to tell me why she had killed her husband, although she was perfectly willing to talk about *how* she had done it. At first I attributed her reluctance to some sort of confused consciousness of her guilt. But when she finally broke down and revealed the abuse that she'd undergone for over ten years, I understood why she guarded herself so closely. The woman was afraid of betraying her deep shame — not the shame of a murderer, but the shame of a victim. Had Rosemary Robbins been unwilling to reveal herself as a victim, fearing that this truth would compromise her public persona? Had her abuser become her murderer? Or was her killer someone else altogether, someone out of her past or her present? I was turning these questions over in my mind as I drove out to the hotel to talk to Jeff Clark.

The Springs Hotel is six miles north of town. It overlooks Pecan Lake, a three-acre man-made lagoon formed by a dozen crystal-clear underwater springs that geyser up out of the limestone of the Edwards Aquifer. The hotel was built by Nathan Clark as a resort for the wealthy back at the turn of the century, before anybody bothered to calculate the square-foot cost of air-conditioning and heating. The original building was a three-story Victorian wedding cake, decorated with turrets and towers and frosted with white-painted gingerbread. Mr. Clark owned and managed it for fifty years, adding a wing in 1916, another in 1925, and a nine-hole golf course and stables in 1928, on the theory that Texas oilmen and their families deserve to take a few days' respite from the tedium of pumping money out of the ground. The Depression took the starch out of the big spenders, though, and for a while it looked as if the hotel might not survive.

But with frugality and careful management, Mr. Clark — now *old* Mr. Clark — held on. He sold off forty acres of horse trails, shut down the stables, and closed a wing, and the hotel was still a going concern when he died in 1945. It went to his only son, Charles, whose tastes, unlike those of his frugal father, tended toward wine, women, and song, all in the pursuit of business, of course — or "bidness," as we say in Texas.

Over the next thirty-five years, Charles, or Big Chuck, as he was known, built a reputation as the most flamboyant host in all of Texas. He refurnished the hotel and reopened the wing his father had closed. He restocked the stables, built four lighted tennis courts, and piped the artesian water to a newly-built swimming pool. His friends and customers were wealthy, prominent, and legion. To suit their Texas tastes, Big Chuck threw dozens of Texas-sized parties: Superbowl parties featuring a half-dozen barbecued steers, rattlesnake canapés, and jalepeño-flavored vodka; political wingdings hosted by Lyndon and Ladybird, with country music by Willie and Waylon and the boys; a *Dallas* charity bash where guests came duded up in purple ostrich-skin boots, the caterer's crew were real Kiowas, and Larry Hagman auctioned off a Waterford cut crystal cowboy hat and a four-wheel-drive Land Cruiser rigged for the Ultimate Hunt with two phones, a stereo, and a wine rack complete with a magnum of Chateau Petrus 1961.

But even good parties come to an end. Big Chuck died and the hotel went to his son Jeff and daughter Rachel. The high-rolling days ended, too. By the late eighties, Texans were saying the R-word out loud and whispering the D-word in their sleep. The bottom fell out of oil, real estate, beef, high tech — everything but tumbleweed and fire ants. With $93 million worth of personal debts, former Governor John Connally and his wife Nellie took Chapter 11 and auctioned off their personal belongings. Socialites filled up their Neiman-Marcus shopping bags with excess glitz and sent them with their maids to the consignment shops. I remember a bitter joke that made the happy-hour rounds in Houston in those nail-biting years: How do you become a Texas millionaire? Start off as a Texas billionare.

With Big Chuck dead and the economy gone bust, The Springs no longer hosted outrageous parties. Jeff Clark had to struggle to keep the hotel alive — and it *was* a struggle, too, especially when his sister Rachel (who handled the advertising and part of the operations) was diagnosed with cancer. When she died, she left her half of the hotel to her husband, Matt Monroe. Matt had increasingly involved himself in the business as his wife's illness progressed, and by the time of her death, he had taken over a big chunk of the day-to-day operations. The hotel was now owned jointly by Jeff and Matt.

It was Jeff I had come to see. I parked my Datsun under a feathery mesquite tree behind the hotel, picked up my folder of conference plans and notes, and crossed the patio to the office entrance. I like Jeff. It's true that he has the temperament of a red wasp, the social grace of an armadillo, and the imagination of a slide rule. But in spite of his flinty personality, Jeff is deep-down fair. And he's a friend of McQuaid, who once did a small security job for him. They keep up the connection over late-night poker and on occasional early-morning or late-night fishing trips to Canyon Lake. Very occasional. Jeff doesn't seem to have much of a life except for the hotel.

I paused at the door to the main office. There were two desks, both empty. One belonged to Priscilla, the receptionist, the other to Lily Box, the office manager. Lily herself was at the Xerox machine, humming a tune while she filled the paper tray.

"Is Jeff busy, Lily?"

Lily turned around with a smile. "Oh, hi, China. He's gone fishing. Matt's around here somewhere, though. Or maybe I can help?" She pushed the paper tray back into the machine.

"Jeff's gone *fishing?* In the middle of the week?"

"Yeah. Surprised me, too." Lily raised the lid on the copy machine and put a paper on the glass, punching buttons. Lily is what every office needs. She's built as solid as a Mack truck, about as elegant and every bit as dependable. She was wearing black slacks, a white blouse, and an open vest that hung down over her hips, obscuring her actual size. "He went down to South Padre Island," she added, as the machine spat out copies. "Good fishing down there. Tarpon, red snapper, bonito, Spanish mackerel. My father used to go whenever he got the chance. Me, I'd settle for a beach-front hotel, a pool, and plenty of sun."

"South Padre?" The island's a nine-hour drive, as far south as you can get without bumping into Mexico. I began to feel frantic, thinking of the list of details and problems that needed immediate solutions. "I thought he'd be here for the conference. He didn't tell me he was going away."

Lily lifted the lid and deftly replaced the paper. The machine zipped out several more copies, fast. "Forgot, probably. The trip's been in the works for a couple of weeks now." She jiggled the copies to even them up. "What the heck, he's got it coming. He hasn't taken more than a few hours off since I've been here, and that's three years. Maybe a little relaxation will sweeten him up some." She glanced at my folder. "It's nothing to worry about. Whatever you've got, I can probably figure it out. And if I can't, Matt can."

"Sure," I said. Lily was right. Jeff could use the time off, and she could deal with just about anything. "But maybe I ought to check in with Matt. Where is he?"

"Right here," he said, from the door to his office. "At your service, ma'am."

Matthew Monroe is a charmer with a ready smile,

brown eyes, and brown hair—what little is left of it. There's a lot of shiny, freckled forehead between his eyebrows and his hairline. But surprisingly, his baldness isn't the first thing you notice. It's his easy amiability, his howdy-ma'am friendliness. Everybody says that big, beefy, back-slapping Matt, with his booming voice and hefty shoulders, takes after Big Chuck a lot more than Jeff does.

Matt thrust out his hand and I shook it. He was wearing an embroidered pale blue Western shirt and a bolo tie with a rattlesnake rattle tie slide, Western-cut blue slacks, snakeskin boots, and a belt with an ornamented silver buckle. He looked as if he'd just stepped out of *Texas Monthly*'s Twenty Texas Big Shots issue.

"Good to see you, Miz Bayles," he said heartily. "Sorry Jeff's not here. Everything shaping up okay for your big weekend?"

"More or less," I said. His face wasn't quite as ruddily affable as usual, and his grin seemed taut. I guessed that he wasn't entirely happy about Jeff's taking off to South Padre and sticking him with the work this weekend. I took my notes out of my folder. "I do have some questions about the table decorations for tomorrow night's reception."

"You'd like some herby-type stuff, I bet." Matt turned to Lily. "Hey, Lil, you got that list?"

Lily found a paper on her desk and handed it to him. He glanced at it. "Says here that Patty, over at Florio's Flowers, is making up wreath centerpieces with parsley, oregano, marjoram, lamb's ears, green and gray santolina, basil, and rosemary—all fresh, of course. Courtesy of the hotel."

I was surprised. "Hey, that's terrific!" Better than terrific, it was a lifesaver. "Where'd you get the fresh herbs?"

"From a grower in San Antonio." Matt frowned. "I didn't screw up, did I? You don't market the fresh stuff out of your shop?"

"Not right now," I said. "By next spring, I probably will." Until McQuaid and I moved to the country, I hadn't had room to grow fresh herbs as a sideline product. Now, I was considering planting a large herb garden in the backyard and marketing the produce to upscale restaurants and groceries in San Antonio and Austin. Basils, thymes, shallots, chives, oregano—they'll sell well, once people get used to having them available.

"Let the kitchen know when you've got some," Matt said. "Featuring local products on the menu is good business. Oh, and on your way out, take a look at the back corner of the patio. We're installing a new fountain— artesian, runs off a spring, with the help of thirty feet of pipe." He grinned. "And since the Herb Growers and Marketers Association saw fit to honor our little country hotel by having the conference here, Jeff thought we ought to plant an herb garden. He got Wanda Rathbottom to send over a bunch of plants from Wanda's Wonderful Acres. The garden crew is complaining that the heat is bad for the plants, but they aim to have everything in the ground by tomorrow."

"They're right," I said. "Heat's a killer for young plants. But it was nice of Jeff to think of putting in a garden. He actually took a few days off?"

"High time." Matt's pleasant laugh had an edge. "He's had the temper of a polecat lately. If this trip doesn't improve his state of mind, the staff's threatening to stage a lynching party." He paused. "No offense, but you look pretty done-in yourself. Bet you'll be glad when this conference is over."

"I had a nasty surprise this morning," I said, and told him about finding Rosemary. The news brought a cry from Lily.

"Rosemary! Oh, no!" Lily's face blanched and she sat down hard in her chair.

Matt stared at me, his jaw fallen. "You're kidding. Rosemary Robbins? Omigod!"

I looked from one to the other. "You knew her?"

"She's been working for us the past few months," Matt said. "I hired her to do an audit." He shook his head in disbelief. "God, poor Rosemary. Who could've done it?"

"I know who," Lily burst out furiously. "It was that ex-husband of hers. Curtis Robbins."

"Curt?" Matt pulled his eyebrows together. "He's a member of the Chamber of Commerce. Why would he—"

"Because he's a wife beater, that's why." Lily's face was puckered with anger. "He was here a couple of weeks ago, the day their divorce was final. He wouldn't leave her alone. She said he was always hanging around. Stalking her, was what she said."

"Oh, come on, Lily," Matt said soothingly. "Curt's a regular guy. Very pleasant, always a nice word for everybody. He's not the type to beat his wife."

I didn't say the obvious: that most men wouldn't know a wife beater from their brother. But Lily wasn't backing off.

"How do *you* know what he did and didn't do?" she demanded angrily. "Men don't beat their wives in public. They wait until nobody's looking."

"How come she didn't call the police?" Matt asked.

"She did." Lily hunched her heavy shoulders and blew

her nose into a tissue. "But she didn't press charges. She didn't want people knowing her private business." She wiped her nose. "If fact, she wouldn't have told *me* anything if she hadn't been so upset the day he showed up here. She just couldn't hold it in. Afterward, she acted like she hadn't said a word about it."

"It might be a good idea to phone the police department and tell Bubba Harris about Robbins coming here," I said. Bubba could add that bit of information to what he already knew about the husband's behavior. The outlines of the case were becoming clearer.

"You bet I will." Lily was fierce. "Robbins isn't going to get away with this." She darted an angry glance at Matt, as if he were a wife beater, too. "Chamber of Commerce or no Chamber of Commerce!"

Matt reached into his pocket, pulled out a slim address book, and turned the pages until he found what he wanted. "I'd better let Jeff know about this," he said, punching in some numbers on Lily's phone. "He and Rosemary were pretty good friends. He'll want to know that she — Pedro?" He slipped into a slurry Tex-Mex. "Hey, Pedro, *compadre*. Matt Monroe, up in Pecan Springs. Yeah, say amigo, my brother-in-law, my *cuñado*, went out with Charlie on the *Sea Lion* this morning. I need to leave a message for him. *Sí*, Clark. C-l-a-r-k. First name's Jeff. Short, not a lotta meat on him, kinda pinched nose, glasses." There was a pause, the flicker of a frown, then: "Well, okay. If he didn't make it this morning, he'll show up *mañana*. When he does, tell him to get back to me right away." He paused. "Yeah, sure, *bueno*, you too. *Gracias. Hasta luego.*" He put down the phone and stood with his hand on it for a moment.

"He didn't go out on the boat?" I asked curiously.

He looked up. "What? Oh . . . no." He rubbed his bald

spot as if he were polishing it. "Not yet, anyway. But he left pretty late last night. Probably checked into a hotel to get a few z's. Where's he staying, Lil?"

"I have no idea," Lily said numbly. "He didn't say."

"Well, Pedro works at the dock," Matt said. "He'll make sure Jeff gets the message." He pulled at his lower lip. "God, I can't believe she's dead. You say she was *shot*?"

"In the face. Whoever did it was standing beside the door of the truck."

"In the face!" Lily took another tissue. "It was him, I tell you." She wiped her eyes. "Robbins. You read about it all the time, men killing their wives."

Old habits die hard. I hate to hear somebody condemned without benefit of jury. "It could've been somebody looking for drug money," I said. "Or a couple of kids playing Rambo. Even a drive-by." But drive-bys don't happen in Pecan Springs, and the kids' pranks are still mostly kid stuff. Robbery hadn't appeared to be a motive, either. I had to wonder whether Curtis Robbins had an alibi.

Matt was scowling at Lily. "If you ask me, the guy's got a right to his day in court." He turned as a pale, pimply young man wearing a white apron came into the office. "What d'ya need, Skip?" he asked, transferring his scowl from Lily to Skip.

The pale young man cleared his throat nervously. "Sorry to charge in like this," he said, "but there's a gross of Cornish game hens just come for the Saturday night banquet. Cook's out for the afternoon and the walk-in freezer's locked. What are we supposed to do?"

Matt started. "Oh, yeah," he said gruffly. "Yeah, well, I'll come and unlock. I've got the key."

"The key?" Lily asked. "Since when has that freezer been locked?"

Matt was fishing in his pocket. "Since this morning," he said. "We've been having trouble with it staying cold. I locked it to cut down the traffic in and out."

Lily was perturbed. "If we're having trouble with the damn freezer, let's get Harold's Air-Conditioning up here to fix it. It's nonsense, messing around with a key."

Matt gave her a dark look. "Last time I looked, I was the boss here"

Lily muttered something under her breath. Matt ignored her. He clapped a hand on the pale young man's shoulder. "Come on, Skip," he said amiably. "Lily's upset. Now let's you and me get those chickens put to roost."

Lily blew her nose again, made herself a cup of coffee, and then called the police station and left a message for Bubba to call her. Then we got busy on my list. At the end of a half hour I felt better, at least as far as the conference was concerned. I thanked Lily, agreed for the third or fourth time that it didn't seem possible that Rosemary was dead, and left.

Walking across the patio to my car, I noticed the plumbing trench for the new fountain and the tidy area that had been dug for the herb garden. The setting was perfect, in a walled corner of the hotel grounds, although it certainly wasn't the best time of year for transplanting. Nursery flats of lamb's ears, santolina, yarrow, sage, thyme, and germander were sitting in the shade of the wall, along with several large balled plants, their burlapped roots covered with canvas. They had all been recently watered. Among the lot I noticed several silvery Powys Castle artemisias, a half-dozen lavender plants, some tricolor sage, a Cleary sage, and one absolutely stunning rosemary bush, nearly four feet high, lush, green, and fragrant.

Ah, rosemary, I thought, with a sharp sense of sadness. Ah, Rosemary. There's rue for you.

CHAPTER THREE

It's hard to overestimate the passion people all over the world have for eye-watering, mouth-searing, tongue-numbing, sweat-inducing chile peppers. Revered in ancient civilizations, nearly worshiped by some chefs, eaten daily by people from Mexico to Thailand, from Indonesia to Africa, the chile pepper is, for many, the *spice of life.*

> Jim Robbins
> *"Chile Peppers: The Spice of Life":*
> *Smithsonian, 1992*

To get to the house where McQuaid and Brian and I live, you drive west on Limekiln Road for just over twelve miles, until you see a sign with the fanciful name, Meadow Brook, done in fading calligraphy and decorated with bluebonnets. Turn left and follow the lane about a quarter of a mile until it ends in a gravel drive in front of the house. It's a big house, surrounded by a green lawn and separated from woods and meadow by a low stone wall, nearly obscured now by July wildflowers: lemon-mint monarda, which looks like purple pagodas and makes an effective insect repellent and a tangy tea; brown-eyed Susans, whose root juice the Cherokee used to treat earache; and buffalo gourd, its vines like hairy green snakes crawling over the rocks. A century ago, the Tonkawa and Waco tribes crushed the plant's roots to wash clothes, boiled and ate the green gourds, and painted the dried ones to use as rattles and ritual bowls. The meadow is a virtual cornucopia of useful plants, all of which thrive in the heat and less than thirty inches of rain we get each year.

This is the Edwards Plateau, commonly called the Hill Country. The rolling hills are covered with Spanish oak, live oak, cedar, and mesquite. In the spring, the meadows are gaudy with bluebonnets, Indian paintbrush, and the translucent yellow flowers of the prickly pear; in the fall, garnet red prickly pears, flaming sumac, and purple gay-feather brighten the fields. A couple of hundred feet beneath the stony surface lie the porous sandstones and cavernous limestones and dolomites of the Lower Cretaceous period: the Edwards Aquifer, an underground river that flows from northwest to southeast and emerges along the Balcones Fault as the Pecan River, the Blanco, the San Marcos, and the little creek that meanders through our meadow. It's also an endangered river, because the water demands of the residential and commercial development between Austin and San Antonio far exceed the aquifer's recharge capacity. Scientists at the Edwards Aquifer Research and Data Center at San Marcos say it will disappear in another decade or so. It's hard to imagine what this part of the country will be like when the springs have vanished, the rivers are gone, and the wells are dry. That's the trouble. Nobody wants to imagine it until they have to, and by that time it will be too late.

All three of us — Brian, McQuaid, and I — wanted Meadow Brook. McQuaid wanted it because there's a workshop and space for his gun collection. Brian wanted it because of the creek and the frogs. I wanted it because the sunny space behind the house is perfect for a large herb garden, and the round room at the top of the turret is perfect for Khat and me. And, of course, because of the five bedrooms. If push comes to shove, I can always move into one of those extra rooms. So far, that hasn't been necessary, but that's not to say that it won't.

It was McQuaid's night to cook and wash dishes. (It's a proven fact that if the cook has to wash, he or she goes easier on the pots and pans.) He was already in the kitchen when I got there, hacking at a charred poblano pepper. Judging from the rest of the ingredients on the table, we were having enchilada casserole. And judging from his assault on the roasted poblano, he had something other than enchiladas on his mind.

He looked up with a fierce scowl. "Why didn't you tell me about Rosemary?" he growled. Howard Cosell lying on the floor beside McQuaid's foot, gave me a reproachful basset hound glance.

"I *did* tell you," I said. I got two glasses out of the refrigerator freezer. "I left a message on your answering machine. I also said that you needed to do something about renting a car." I glanced out the window at the blue Ford in the drive. "Which I see you did, so you must have gotten the message."

McQuaid misses being handsome by a nose (his having been broken twice, once on the football field and once in an altercation with an incensed drunk). He has black hair, slate-blue eyes in a tanned face, and a pale scar (courtesy of a druggie) that zips diagonally across his forehead. His eyes turn dark blue when he's angry. They were dark now.

"Yeah, the answering machine. I had to hear about Rosemary Robbins getting murdered in *my* truck from an answering machine!" He slashed at the poblano. A hunk of it dropped beside Howard Cosell, who sniffed it and sneezed.

I stared at him, nonplussed. Was that what he was so

angry about? A simple telephone message?

"What else was I supposed to do? I had no idea where you were. I had a thousand errands to run, and I couldn't keep calling back. I did what I thought—"

"I was in the departmental library. You could've told the secretary. She would've come and got me."

"I didn't think it was that important." I put the glasses on the table. "I don't mean that. Of course it was important. I just mean—"

"Not important!" McQuaid is a powerful man, six feet, one ninety, muscular shoulders, deep voice. When he's upset, he's powerfully fierce. "You didn't think it was important that Rosemary Robbins was murdered in *my* truck, when Jake Jacoby is on the loose?"

Loud voices make Howard Cosell nervous. He lumbered to his feet, walked ponderously across the floor, and pushed his head and shoulders under my Home Comfort gas range.

"Excuse me for being dense," I said, "but I fail to see the connection."

McQuaid put down his knife, leaned on the table, and eyed me narrowly. "You're telling me that with all your criminal experience, it hasn't occurred to you that Jake Jacoby might have killed Rosemary?"

"Jacoby?" I rolled my eyes at this far-fetched theory. "I have to confess that the idea hadn't even crossed my mind." What had crossed my mind, tantalizingly, were twin margaritas, one for McQuaid and one for me. I opened the refrigerator crisper to look for a lime, but all I saw was a bunch of wilted cilantro, half an eggplant, a bag of carrots, and one very small, very dead fish, laid out on a saucer like a body on a slab at the morgue.

In my former life as a single person, my refrigerator harbored no surprises. The mayo and mustard routinely lived on the door shelf, the milk was top left, and Khat's fresh chicken livers were in a green bowl with a red cover on the lower shelf. Now, the lid to the mustard was missing, there were two open cans of dog food in the middle of the top shelf where the milk was supposed to be, and a dead fish in the crisper.

I was still staring at the fish when McQuaid came up and put both arms around me from the back and pulled me against him, my back to his front. He shoved the crisper shut with his foot and closed the refrigerator door so hard I could hear the catsup bottle fall over inside.

"Will you *listen* to me, Bayles?" he said gruffly against my ear as I struggled to pull free. "Rosemary Robbins looked enough like you to be your sister. She left here last night driving a truck that you drive a couple of times a week. When she got where she was going, somebody shot her. You damn well better believe it could've been Jake. He could've thought he was killing *you*."

I stopped struggling and stood very still. The room was loud with the humming of the refrigerator and the idiosyncratic tock-tick-tock of the hundred-year-old schoolhouse clock that hangs on the wall over it.

"*Me?*" I said finally. "You think Jacoby mistook Rosemary for *me?*"

His arms were so tight around me I couldn't move. "It's possible."

"It's also possible that her ex-husband killed her," I said. "In fact, it's very likely. She made a DV call last winter. He hung around the hotel where she was working. She thought he was stalking her."

He was stubbornly silent, still holding me tight. I was suddenly conscious of the strength of his arms around me. I felt the flash of warmth that comes with desire, and relaxed a little against his hard body.

"It happens, McQuaid," I said. "Read the papers. Spousal abuse is the leading cause of injury among women aged fifteen to forty-four. Three out of ten murdered women are killed by a spouse or a lover."

"It's also possible," he said quietly, "that Jake Jacoby killed her because he thought she was you. Seven out of ten murdered women are killed by somebody else."

I was leaning against him, wanting him, even in my anger—or perhaps the wanting was fueled by anger. That's the nice thing about living together. You can be angry and want somebody, and know they'll still be there and you'll still be wanting when the anger has passed. "But Jake's a free man," I said. "As long as he meets the terms of his release, he can go anywhere in the state. El Paso, Dallas, Lubbock—"

He kissed the tip of my ear. "New Braunfels."

New Braunfels was less than twenty minutes away. "Why New Braunfels?"

"Because that's where his mother lives." He cupped my breast with his right hand. "Because that's where he's supposed to live under the terms of his release."

I twisted in his arms until I could turn and face him. There was a deep worry furrow between his eyes, but they were light again. "We're lucky to find out where he is," he said. "Most of the time people don't get told when a criminal is back on the streets. But this is different, because—"

"Because you're a former cop," I said. "And cops look out for their own. Excuse me. Their *ex*-own." If it had been a lawyer who was threatened, you can bet your sweet bippy that the cop fraternity wouldn't have phoned to tell her about it.

"Put it that way if you want to," McQuaid said. "But you and Brian aren't safe as long as Jacoby's within spitting distance." He reached up to brush the hair off my forehead. "Rosemary's murder—it's just too coincidental, China. You've got to be careful."

My mouth tightened. "A case of mistaken identity. Isn't that a little far-fetched?"

McQuaid dropped his arms. "Bubba Harris thinks it's possible."

I wasn't surprised that McQuaid had talked to Bubba about the murder, and about Jacoby. Bubba belongs to the fraternity, too. Ex or no ex, they're still blood brothers.

"What about Curtis Robbins?" I asked dryly. "I don't suppose he's been questioned yet."

McQuaid ignored my sarcasm. "Robbins ate at his sister's house last night, and the two of them watched the late movie. He didn't get home until nearly one." He paused. "The man is well-known around town, China. Somehow I can't quite picture him doing this."

"Oh, yeah?" I laughed shortly. "Where is it written that well-known people lead blameless lives? And since when has Bubba Harris started buying alibis from relatives?"

McQuaid stepped back. "Did anybody question Rosemary's neighbors?"

"The woman across the street said she heard a gunshot around nine-thirty. She mentioned it to her husband, but he thought it was a firecracker. Last night was the Fourth, remember?"

I went back to rooting for limes. "Who's doing the autopsy?"

"Travis County was backed up, so the body went to Bexar." McQuaid was chopping another poblano.

I made a face. Adams County is too small to have its own medical examiner, so it buys autopsy services from neighboring counties. The Bexar County medical examiner's office is understaffed and overloaded. This was Thursday. If somebody worked over the weekend, Bubba might get an autopsy report by Monday. That would fix the time of death — more or less. I hadn't found the body until nearly ten, and the truck had been sitting in the sun. It would be hard to get the TOD down to less than a ninety-minute range. Until Bubba had something better, he'd use the neighbor's statement about the nine-thirty gunshot as a reference point.

"They found the spent bullet on the floor of the truck," McQuaid said. "A .38. Oh, and the truck was covered with prints." He pushed the chopped poblano into a neat pile. "Ours. Fortunately, we have an alibi for the time of the murder."

"No other prints?" I averted my eyes from the block of Velveeta McQuaid was cubing. The rule is no carping when the other one cooks, even when they're doing something unspeakable.

"Rosemary's, of course." He dumped the cubes and a can of evaporated milk into a bowl and added the peppers. "But nothing else." He stuck the bowl into the microwave and pushed some buttons.

"I wish I'd known her better," I said thoughtfully. I found a wizened lime in the bag of carrots and went to the cupboard to look for the salt. I found it, but the box was empty. "I might have a clearer idea who killed her."

"You still don't get it, do you, China?" McQuaid banged the heavy black cast-iron skillet onto the front burner of the Home Comfort, which has at least a decade on me but still bakes an admirable soufflé. "I am telling you, *you* were the mark. Jacoby aimed to get to me by killing you, but he screwed up and got Rosemary instead." He poured olive oil into the skillet and dropped in some chopped onions.

"That's speculation." I picked up the salt shaker, but it was empty, too. "I hope you don't mind margaritas without salt. Brian must have used the last of it to make dinosaurs." Back in the old days, I never ran out of salt.

"Just so there's tequila," McQuaid said, pushing the onions around testily. He tossed in four garlic cloves. "Maybe it *is* speculation. But I'm not willing to take a risk." He glanced at the clock. "Where *is* that kid, anyway? It's nearly six."

I got out the tequila. I thought I knew McQuaid pretty well, but I'd never seen him like this: edgy, irritable, nervous. He was acting like a stranger, and it made me uneasy.

"It's Thursday," I said. "He went to the matinee at the movie with some of the kids from the cadet corp."

For the past year, Brian and his father have been members of the Austin chapter of the Star Trek fan club, the U.S.S. Rhyanna. McQuaid is a security officer on this starship, and Brian is a cadet lieutenant. The activity seems to be a variant of the Boy Scouts, with a heavy dose of space and science. Being a Trekkie is certainly a lot better for Brian than belonging to a street gang.

"Oh, yeah, the matinee." McQuaid took the bowl of cheesy stuff out of the microwave and replaced it with a dozen corn tortillas. "Is somebody giving him a ride home? Maybe we should go pick him up."

I stepped close behind, wrapped my arms around him, and laid my cheek against his broad back. "It's okay," I said soothingly. "Brian will be home in a few minutes, I am making a margarita that will mellow you out, and your enchilada casserole will be *maravilloso.*" I slipped my hand under his belt. "So just relax. Okay?"

I felt him untense a little.

"That's good," I murmured, and stood on tiptoes to

nibble his earlobe. He turned, put his arms around me, and gave me a long, deep kiss that made me glad I'm living with this guy, in spite of the bad moments.

He rested his chin on the top of my head, still holding me. "I guess this Jacoby business has brought out the cop in me. I just need to know you're safe. You and Brian."

"We're safe."

He held me closer. "Oh, no, you're not. Somebody who looked a hell of a lot like you was shot dead, in *our* truck."

"And she could have been killed by her ex-husband, who was stalking—"

"Robbins has an alibi, for God's sake." McQuaid lifted my chin so that I had to look into his eyes. "It's not just you. Brian's easy game. I'm going to tell him to stay home until this is over."

"But that's *prison*," I objected.

He turned to stir the onions and garlic in the skillet. "More like protective custody."

At that moment, Khat strolled through the hallway door, whiskers twitching, tail held high, a gourmand inquiring delicately about the progress of dinner.

I put my hands on my hips. "If protective custody isn't prison, I don't know what is. And what do you mean, 'until this is over'? When will it be over? Jacoby did his time. He played by the rules, such as they are, and he earned his freedom. If he wants to drive from New Braunfels to Pecan Springs, you can't stop him. It's his constitutional *right*."

"Spoken like a goddam defense attorney," McQuaid said through his teeth.

"Well, somebody sure as hell has to speak up for people's rights," I snapped.

McQuaid was about to reply when he was preempted.

Khat saw Howard Cosell's butt sticking out from under the stove and succumbed to temptation. He unsheathed the claws on his right forepaw, took aim, and fired. Howard yelped and turned, teeth bared belligerently, to defend his left flank. Khat hissed and struck again. The fur, as they say, flew.

McQuaid had just put the dog out and I was trying to coax Khat down from the top of the refrigerator when Brian came into the kitchen. He looks a lot like his dad: blue eyes, dark hair, dimples. He sniffed.

"Something's burning," he said.

"Oh, shit," McQuaid said. He grabbed the skillet, burning his thumb. "Ow! How come you're late?"

"I'm not late," Brian said reasonably. "We just got out of the movies." He wrinkled his nose. "Are onions any good if they're burned?"

"Absolutely," McQuaid muttered, holding his thumb under the cold water. "Charcoal's good for you."

"That's a crock," Brian said with cheerful insolence.

"Don't be insubordinate," McQuaid thundered, raising his voice over Howard Cosell's indignant baying. "Now, go upstairs and start your homework. When I get this casserole in the oven, you and I have something important to discuss."

"It's summer," Brian said. "I don't have any homework."

"Upstairs!" McQuaid began to scrape burned onions off the skillet.

Brian stomped off, McQuaid went back to his cooking, and I cut off a piece of aloe vera for his burned thumb. Then I finished the margaritas, thinking nostalgically about the old days, the halcyon days, when I had no one to take care of but myself, a cat, and a small, undemanding herb shop surrounded by tidy gardens. Why had I joined this circus?

While Khat and Howard Cosell ate their dinners (one in the kitchen, the other in the backyard) and McQuaid and Brian conferred upstairs, I took my drink out to the porch swing, where I pushed myself back and forth, watching two squirrels chase one another around the pecan tree. Reluctantly, I considered McQuaid's theory. Rosemary and I looked alike; even Grace Walker had mentioned it. Rosemary had been driving McQuaid's truck. And Jacoby was living less than fifteen miles away. Even if I didn't buy McQuaid's conclusion, I had to acknowledge that it had a certain logic.

But my theory was just as logical. Rosemary's ex-husband had a history of abuse, and abusers can turn murderous, especially when the victim has the temerity to get a divorce. Robbins had showed up at the hotel and raised a ruckus; he might just as easily have waited for her in front of her house and shot her. His alibi? Well, I've heard plenty of trumped-up alibis concocted by family members. My theory seemed every bit as plausible as McQuaid's.

But it was only a theory, with no hard evidence to back it. Unfortunately, it reminded me of a faulty form of argument that one of my philosophy professors had labeled the "undistributed middle." Abusers murder; Robbins is an abuser; therefore, Robbins is a murderer. But while that kind of fallacy would have earned me an F on a logic exam, it's constantly used in subtle and devious ways in the media and even in court—*especially* in court. I've used it, too, more times than I can say. I'm not proud of it, but there it is. Guilty, Your Honor. Guilty of the undistributed middle.

The heat got to me after a while and I went back inside. Brian and McQuaid came downstairs to set the table. They didn't say anything about their conversation, but I could tell from Brian's sullen face what he thought about his father's restrictions. Still, as we sat down to eat, we were decently polite to one another. The meal was peaceful. But not for long. The enchilada casserole was just making its second round when the phone rang.

"I'll get it." Brian knocked his chair over as he bolted from the table. A minute later, he was back with the cordless phone. "For you, Dad," he said, handing it over. "It's Mom."

"Oh, shit." McQuaid dropped his fork as he took the phone. "Hello, Sally," he said in a guarded voice. There was a long silence, while he listened. Then he got up and carried the phone into the kitchen, closing the door behind him. Whatever he had to say to Sally, he didn't want to say in front of Brian. Or me.

Sally and McQuaid's ten-year marriage had been a casualty of his profession, at least as McQuaid saw it. I'd never checked with Sally, whom I barely know. As I understood it, she had never wanted him to be a cop, and the uncertainty, danger, and low pay—especially the pay—eventually got to her. After a long bout with depression, alcohol, and tranquilizers, she fell apart. When she came back from detox, she sued for divorce. It was a good thing she didn't want custody of the boy. Given her history of emotional instability, McQuaid would've fought it, and the conflict would have been terrible for Brian. As it was, she didn't contest, and the court awarded him custody.

That was five years ago. Sally sees her son a couple of weekends a month, when she can take time from her work as a sales representative for a multinational firm based in

San Antonio. She still has problems with alcohol and depression, but she's seemed better recently. So much better, in fact, that she's begun to talk about Brian coming to live with her. McQuaid doesn't seem to take it seriously, but I do. After all, she's Brian's mother. It's natural for her to want to spend more time with her son.

Brian turned to me and I noticed once again how handsome he is, like his father. "She's bugging him about me living with her, ain't she?" he said, serious now.

"Isn't," I said automatically, and added, with caution, "If you want to know what they're talking about, you'll have to ask your dad."

It's odd. Before McQuaid and I moved in together, Brian and I enjoyed an easy, uncomplicated familiarity. We high-fived when we met and bestowed the Vulcan blessing when we said good-bye and even occasionally hugged each other. But now that I'm in loco parentis, as it were, things are different. I'm never quite sure what to do, how to act. Am I too strict, or not strict enough? Too affectionate, or not affectionate enough? Too much mom, too much four-star general, too much pal? What exactly *is* this thing called mothering?

This issue isn't a new one, of course. It has its roots deep in my past. As a mother, mine left something to be desired: an alcoholic who drank to forget that her lawyer husband hated her because she drank. As a father, mine was occasionally present but always absent: a workaholic who substituted the law for a life and money for love. As a child, I yearned for each of them, for both of them. For a mother to hold me, a father to teach me. For a normal family. Not too much for a kid to ask.

But now that I've got a few decades under my belt, I'm not too sure whether there is any such thing as a normal family. Maybe every family is a circus. My mother eventually got counseling, sobered up, and last year married a guy who seems pretty decent. But there's no real bond between us. How can there be, after all those lonely, separate years? Anyway, with all this stuff behind me, it's pretty tough to be a decent mother to Brian. I feel like I'm inventing it as I go along, with no idea what the hell I'm doing.

Brian mashed a hunk of cheese with his fork. "What if I decided to go live with Mom?" He wasn't looking at me.

This was a big Catch-22. If I said, "Yes, do what you want," he'd think I didn't want him, and that would be wrong. You can harm a kid for life by letting him think he's not wanted. But if I said, "No, stay here with us," he'd think I was trying to tell him what to do, and that was wrong, too. Kids need to make decisions on their own. My perennial parental dilemma. Damned if I did and damned if I didn't.

After a moment I said the only thing I could think of. "That's something you'll have to take up with your dad." Over to you, McQuaid.

The dark hair fell across his forehead and into his eyes, slate-blue, his dad's eyes, and I leaned forward to smooth it back, gently. I haven't learned any easy way to show affection to this boy, but I feel it, and not just because he's a miniature version of his father. Brian has his own way of warming my heart. I wish I knew how to show it better.

He gave me his Mr. Spock look, eminently reasonable, logical. "I already know what Dad thinks. What do *you* think?"

I put my fork down. Tonight, of all nights, was not the best time for this conversation. But we needed to ease the strain that had grown between us. I put my elbows on the table, opened my mouth, and heard the clichés fall out like wooden blocks.

"I think we ought to shoot straight with one another, Brian. I know it's been tough, getting used to living together. It's been plenty tough for me, too. I haven't had a lot of practice being a mom. But we both care about your dad, and we want to see him happy. And I know that you love your mother and want to be with her as much as you can. Maybe we ought to try a little harder to . . . to . . . ."

To what? Here I was, with a reputation for putting the most complex case in terms that the least sophisticated juror could relate to, and I was tongue-tied by a reasonable, logical eleven-year-old whose direct look and honest question splintered my easy answers.

"To understand each other," I finished lamely, embarrassingly conscious of how little I'd said. It had sounded like a bad script for the longest-running American sitcom.

He looked back at his plate. "Maybe living with her would be better," he muttered.

His dilemma was as sharp as mine and I could hear it in his voice. He hadn't had a full-time mother for five years, and he wanted one. I knew how deeply, how painfully, a child could long for a mother. I remembered my own empty, unfulfilled yearning for my mother, a longing that was never satisfied, and I felt it echoed in him.

"If I was living with her, I wouldn't have to hang around the house all summer." He gave me a sideways glance. "Anyway, *she* wants me."

I leaned forward, the impulsive words, "But *I* want you!" on my lips. But they didn't get said. McQuaid strode into the room, his mouth tense, and the opportunity was gone.

Brian looked at his father. "What's up?"

"Your mother," McQuaid said stiffly, "has a new lawyer."

"What does that mean?"

"It means we're going to court." He sat down.

Brian rubbed his finger in the cheese on his plate, not looking up. "Would we still have to go to court if I just went and lived with her?"

McQuaid's eyes came to me, went back to Brian. "You're here because a judge said you could live with me. If you want to live with her, we have to ask the judge to change the order. Which means yes, we still have to go to court." He frowned, realized he was frowning, and smoothed his forehead with an effort. He made an effort to lighten his voice, too. "Is that what you want, Brian? To live with your mom?"

Brian squashed the cheese between his thumb and forefinger. "How do I know? I've never lived with her. At least not since I can remember. She's so sad all the time. Maybe if I lived with her, she'd be happier." He opened his fingers, pulling the cheese into a yellow string.

The child taking responsibility for the mother's health—that was something I understood, too. As a kid, I believed that if I could make my mother feel better, she'd stop drinking. Brian couldn't pull Sally out of her depression, but that wouldn't keep him from trying.

"Don't play with your food," McQuaid said.

Brian looked at him. "Do *you* want me to live with her?"

"I want what's best for you," McQuaid said very carefully. "We don't have to decide what that is right this minute. There's plenty of time. Eat that cheese."

Brian jammed the cheese into his mouth. "Excuse me," he said. He pushed his chair back.

"Where are you going?" McQuaid asked.

Brian stood up. "I'm riding my bike to Arnold's house."

"Oh, no, you're not. Remember what I said about that creep Jacoby?"

I stared at McQuaid, wanting him to stop this. I knew he was worried about us, but there had to be something better than summary ultimatums.

Brian screwed up his face. "But Dad, it's only a mile. Arnold's got some new hologram cards from the Episodes set, and the Rhyanna newsletter with all the stuff in it about the Star Trek Con in Austin next weekend. One of the dealers is bringing a Mr. Data card, and we have to figure out how to get to it before anybody else."

Star Trek cards, it seems, have replaced baseball cards. The male children of our culture pursue them avariciously, paying up to thirty dollars for a single card. Which boggles my mind. When I was a kid —. But there it is again. The perennial parental tone.

"Mr. Data or no Mr. Data," McQuaid said, "you're staying home."

"But Dad," Brian said, "it won't be dark for a couple of hours yet. Why can't I —"

McQuaid lost it. " 'But Dad' nothing," he roared. "I want you *home*. Not at Trekker conventions, not riding around country roads where Jacoby can jump out of a bush and grab you, but *home*. Got that?"

Brian threw me a desperate glance. "China, can't you —?"

This was another lose-lose situation, and I wasn't getting trapped in it. I shook my head. "This is between you guys. I'm only a bystander."

Brian glared at me, then at his father. "You're *mean!*" he cried. "*Both* of you!" And ran out of the room.

McQuaid shook his head. "Sometimes I just don't

know. I guess I'm too hard on him. But how else am I going to make him listen?"

I didn't say anything for a moment, hoping he might find an answer in himself. Finally I said, "What's this about Sally going to court?"

He pushed his plate back, his meal unfinished. "She's asking for a rehearing. She doesn't want Brian living with us because we're not married." His mouth was hard, bitter. "It might warp his morals."

I stared at him. "Of all the narrow-minded—!"

McQuaid held up his hand. "I know, I know. But she's the mother, and we're living in sin. All she needs is to find a sympathetic judge, and she gets the kid." He rubbed his eyes with his fingers. "Shit," he said. "There's no justice."

I got up and went around the table and massaged his shoulders for a moment in silence. "I'm sorry, McQuaid," I said. "But maybe she won't go through with it. And even if she does, there's no guarantee she'll win."

He picked up his fork and turned it in his fingers. "She's a mess. She's a total disaster as a mother."

I didn't say anything. Who am I to criticize the quality of Sally's mothering when I don't have a clue? I straightened up. "Want me to help with the dishes before I head for the shop?"

"The shop?" McQuaid was immediately tense. He swiveled to look up at me. "You're going over there tonight? Alone?"

We were back to the control issue again. "I was running errands most of the day," I said, as patiently as I could. "I've got a jillion things to catch up on before the conference opens tomorrow, and I need to do some work on my newsletter." *China's Garden* comes out three or four times a year, and it takes a lot of work. I was already overdue with the summer issue. "I won't be late," I added persuasively. "I promise."

Inside, the liberated, emancipated part of me was surprised. *You promise? Since when did you start punching a time clock?*

McQuaid looked at me a minute, thin-lipped. Then he began to gather up the dishes. "Give me five minutes to load the dishwasher. And five minutes to call Jeff Clark. I expect he's upset about Rosemary. They were pretty serious, you know."

I stared at him. "No, I didn't know. I didn't even know they knew one another until Matt Monroe told me this afternoon."

He shrugged. "It's not something Jeff wanted other people to know just yet."

"How long have they been seeing each other?"

"A few months, I guess. I don't know. He only told me a couple of weeks ago."

"Well, Jeff's gone fishing at South Padre," I said. "Matt was trying to get him this afternoon. He might not even hear about Rosemary until tomorrow morning." I got back to the immediate subject. "You're coming to the shop?"

The other China sneered. *Sounds to me like protective custody.*

"Yeah," he said. "And so is Brian." He picked up his plate. "Jeff went fishing, huh? I wonder how come he didn't ask me to go with him. He didn't even mention it."

I was scowling. "*Both* of you are coming?"

"That's what I said," he replied grimly. "You don't think I'm going to let you spend an evening in that shop all alone? With a killer on the loose?" He handed me the empty casserole dish. "Take this. And that salad bowl, and those glasses. I'll get the other stuff." He filled his hands and nudged me in the direction of the door. "Come on, Bayles, get your ass in gear. We don't have all night."

The sneer got louder. *You idiot. You gave up your independence so some ex-cop can tell you to get your ass in gear? What a dolt!*

CHAPTER FOUR

HERBAL PROTECTION BATH

In many cultures, herbal baths are an important ritual. The bathers believe that when certain herbs are steeped in bathwater, they release not only their scent but their "virtue," their special energies. The bath based on the protective herb rosemary, for instance, is thought to make the bather safe from the forces of negativity and evil. To recreate this ritual for yourself, put into a quart jar a cup and a half of rosemary leaves and one-half cup each of bay leaves, basil, and fennel. Pour boiling water over the herbs and let them steep. Strain into a warm bath. As you relax, allow yourself to feel safe and cared for.

Ruby Wilcox
"Personal Herbal Rituals"
in *A Book of Thyme and Seasons*

"Robbins did it," Ruby said. She poured hot water over a mint teabag. There was a plate of sesame seed cookies on the far end of the counter, and she took one. I always set out tea and cookies for customers, and Ruby helps herself.

"You're excused for cause," I said, retrieving the cash drawer from the box of cleaning supplies where I hide it at night. I figure that the last place a burglar will bother to look for money is under the dust rags.

"Excused for cause?" She bit into the cookie. "What does that mean?"

"If you were a prospective juror, you'd be disqualified in voir dire. Pretrial questioning. You've made up your mind before you heard the evidence. Hell, before there *is* any evidence."

Ruby tossed her head. She was all in white this morning: skinny white calf-length pants, loose white top, sandals that were no more than two white straps between her toes, white hair band subduing, more or less, her Orphan Annie frizz. "I'm not a juror. I'm a citizen, and I have the right to my opinion."

"And Robbins has the right to be considered innocent until the jury says he's guilty. Anyway, he's got an alibi."

It's interesting. When McQuaid and I debated Robbins's guilt yesterday evening, I was on the other side. But that's no surprise. It's almost instinct for me to take up the cause of the accused.

Ruby gave her tea bag a scornful swish. "His sister? We know where *her* loyalty lies."

I put the cash drawer into my vintage brass register and changed the date stamper. It stuck, as usual. The darn thing always malfunctions when the humidity's high. I got out my nail clipper, flipped out the little metal file, and tinkered with the stamper. Maybe someday I'll break down and get a register that really works, one of those electronic jobs that don't make any noise. But I'd miss the old-fashioned brassy *clang* that celebrates every sale.

"You know Curtis Robbins's sister?" I asked.

"No," Ruby admitted. "I don't know Curtis Robbins, either." She dropped her tea bag in the wastebasket. "But any sister worth her salt would lie for her brother, wouldn't she?"

"Not unless she wanted to go to jail for perjury," I said

evenly. The date stamper finally clicked into place and I closed the register. Behind me, I could hear the air conditioner whimpering. It didn't sound at all good.

"I still think Robbins did it," Ruby said. "He manages a sporting goods store, doesn't he? They sell guns, don't they?"

"That's an undistributed middle," I said.

"What?"

"It's a fallacy."

"What?"

"A faulty argument," I said. "But never mind — everybody does it, even lawyers." I got out the lemon oil and a cloth and began to wipe the wooden counter. It's only cheap pine sanded smooth, but polished, it looks very nice.

Ruby shook her head, musing. "It's hard to believe she's dead. I just keep remembering Rosemary the way she was. She really had it together."

I thought of the Rosemary I had seen lying on the seat of McQuaid's truck, blood and bits of the inside of her head splattered all over. I shivered. *I* didn't want to remember Rosemary the way she was, at least not the way I had found her. "I wonder if she really did have it together. Anyway, I'm not sure that any of us knew her well enough to know."

"Of course we knew her." Ruby was indignant. "She did our taxes, didn't she?"

"That gives us some magical insight into her personality?" I unlocked the front door, flipped the Closed sign to Open, and trundled the rack of potted herbs outside. I was putting down a clay pot of aloe vera when Sheila Dawson came up the walk.

"McQuaid told me about Rosemary Robbins's murder," Sheila said. "What a rotten shame."

"Yes," I said. Sheila's in her thirties, with shoulder-length blond hair, creamy skin, Jackie's style and Hill-ary's chutzpah. In her slim pink suit, dyed-to-match pumps, purse, and pearls, she looked like a Dallas Junior Leaguer on her way to lunch at Daddy's club. But under that feminine frivolity, she's all cop. Last March, she was hired as CTSU's chief of security. Before that, she was assistant chief of security at UT Arlington, and before that, a sergeant with the Dallas PD. You have to wonder about somebody who looks like a homecoming queen and thinks like the regional director of the FBI.

Ruby came out on the step behind me with the broom in her hand. "Hi, Sheila. I didn't know you knew Rose-mary."

"That gal was one sharp tax lady," Sheila said. Her smile was sad. "She knew every trick in the book, even some that weren't. But who cares how she did it? She got me a refund."

"She got me one, too," Ruby said. She began to sweep with short, hard strokes. "A *nice* refund. Not to mention straightening out all my tax problems. I didn't owe the IRS as much as they said I did." She swept harder.

Sheila turned to me. "Have you talked to Bubba? Has he turned up any leads?"

"Her ex did it," Ruby said, still sweeping. "He was abusing her. He manages a sporting goods store, you know. He could use any gun he wanted and put it right back on the shelf, and nobody'd be the wiser."

"Did Rosemary say anything to you about being abused?" I asked Sheila.

She shook her head. "No, but I did get the impression that she was afraid of him. The husband, I mean. Rob-bins. That was before they were divorced, which I think happened pretty recently." She started to say something else, but changed her mind.

"The cops aren't tough enough on abusers." Ruby was halfway down the walk, sweeping violently. "Neither are the courts. A slap on the wrist—that's all those fuckers get. Pardon my French."

"Ruby," I said gently, "you are destroying my broom."

"Oh," she said, and stopped sweeping. "Sorry."

"What about leads?" Sheila repeated.

"You probably know as much as I do," I said, picking yellow leaves off a curly-leaf parsley. Hot weather is hard on potted plants. If these didn't sell pretty soon, I'd give them away. There's nothing worse for a shop's reputation than selling tired, root-bound plants. "They recovered the spent bullet from the floor of the truck—a .38. The only prints were Rosemary's, McQuaid's, and mine. A neighbor heard a gunshot about nine-thirty, although it might have been a firecracker. And Robbins has an alibi—his sister. That about covers it, as far as I know."

"Well, I'll keep my eyes and ears open," Sheila said. "Sometimes Bubba tells me things." I had to smile at that. When I first met Sheila, I nicknamed her Smart Cookie because of her ability to get people to do what she wants. She'd known Bubba Harris for a total of two minutes when she had him eating out of her beautifully manicured hand. Talk about the politics of pretty. She looked at me. "I hear McQuaid has a different theory."

"When did you hear about that?" News travels in nanoseconds around Pecan Springs. Sometimes I think the grapevine's gone on-line on Internet.

"We're both on the Traffic Committee," Sheila said. "We had a meeting late yesterday and he gave me an earful. Mistaken identity, huh?"

"Yeah." I was skeptical.

"An ex-con?"

Ruby looked at me. "McQuaid thinks somebody *else* did it?"

I nodded. "Jake Jacoby. Somebody McQuaid sent up. He got out last week on early release." I laughed. "McQuaid thinks he's out to get Brian and me."

Sheila gave me a glance. "It happens, you know."

"Yeah, sure." I pulled several dried leaves off a rose geranium, which is a pelargonium, actually, discovered in mountains of South Africa by English and Dutch explorers in the 1630s. The dried leaves are wonderful in potpourri. Yellowed parsley isn't good for anything but compost.

Sheila was taking it seriously. "McQuaid says you and Rosemary could pass for sisters, and that she had his truck. He seems pretty well convinced it was Jacoby."

"He's also convinced that I need protection," I said. I picked up the hose and turned it on the plant rack. "I had work to do here last night, and he insisted on coming along. He brought Brian, too, so he could protect both of us at the same time. Between the two of them, I didn't get done half of what I needed to do."

"I sympathize with McQuaid," Sheila said thoughtfully, "but he's got to learn to let go. Dan had the same problem." Dan was Sheila's former fiancé. She broke their engagement a couple of months ago because she wanted to live her life her own way, and he couldn't give her enough room. "He wanted me to change careers because law enforcement's too dangerous. I kept telling him that I'm only a campus cop. My most dangerous assignment is convening Student Traffic Court."

I grinned, thinking that Sheila wasn't telling the whole story. "You did bag a real criminal a few months ago, as I recall." My friend Dottie Riddle had been accused of murdering one of her colleagues, and Sheila and I had collaborated to get the matter straightened out.

Ruby was leaning on the broom. "All men are into this protection thing," she said. "When they were kids, they watched all those big strong TV cowboys with six-guns protecting the frail, helpless women. Now that they're grown up, they get a testosterone rush from taking care of us."

"Yeah, sure," Sheila said with a laugh. "The same frail, helpless woman who walked across the Great Plains with a kid on each hip and her kitchen on her back. Right?" She shook her head. "If you ask me, men don't learn it from John Wayne. It's genetic. They can't help themselves. I remember my daddy trying to teach me to float. He wouldn't let go. How was I going to learn to float when he had his hand under my butt?"

"It's a power thing, in my book," I said. "They're strong, we're weak. We need them to look out for us because we're not strong enough and smart enough to do it ourselves."

"I'm not sure that's always true," Ruby objected. "A person can be responsible because he *cares*. Like Sheila's daddy teaching her to float. He was doing it because he loved her."

Sheila snorted. "Sure he loves me. He loves me so much that he'll never let me go. You should've heard him squawk when I moved into my first apartment. And when I became a cop? He wanted to ride in the squad car with me. Would you believe?" She turned to me. "Do you have any lavender soap? The last stuff I got was wonderful."

"I think so." I turned off the hose. "Ruby can show you where it is. I've got to get out to The Springs—registration for the herb conference starts in a couple of hours." I turned to Ruby. "Keep an ear out for that air conditioner, will you? If it dies, call Harold's Air-Conditioning and Refrigeration. The number's next to the phone."

"Laurel and I will take care of everything," Ruby said. "You just have a good time at the conference."

"Stay out of trucks," Sheila said, "and watch for Jacoby."

I laughed shortly. "I thought protectiveness was a guy thing."

"Not when *we* do it," Ruby said. "Go on to your conference, and don't worry."

"Yes, go." Sheila waved me away. "Have fun with your herby friends. Don't give a second thought to ex-cons or murderers."

At the conference that day, everything went beautifully. I ran around getting things organized while the other members of the planning committee conducted registration for the early-comers, convened the preconference seminars, and got all the vendors sorted out. The hotel staff did everything right, too: the meeting rooms were set up the way we'd asked, room registration went without a hitch, and even the herb garden was completed — all except for the big rosemary bush, which was still balled and ready for planting, sitting next to the trench that had been dug for the new fountain, which wasn't hooked up yet either. The newly transplated herbs were looking droopy, though, and the rosemary definitely ought to be in the ground, keeping its feet cool.

But herbalists don't wilt. We did what herb lovers always do when they get together. We talked nonstop herbs: planting and cultivating and harvesting them, buying them, marketing them, crafting with them, cooking with them. We talked about medicinal herbs, culinary herbs, decorative herbs, fragrance herbs, speciality herbs, landscape herbs. We traded recipes, merchandising tricks, names of reliable wholesalers, and horror stories about the Food and Drug Administration. It was a great day for herbs, and it went on being a great day into the late evening. At ten o'clock, I left the night owls to their late-night drinks and headed for home, bone weary but cheerful. It had cooled off slightly, and there was a breeze from the south. We'd be able to sleep tonight with the windows open.

My cheerfulness faded when I walked into the kitchen.

"I didn't think you'd be so late," McQuaid said crossly. He was in jeans, barefooted and barechested, his dark hair wet from the shower. McQuaid is remarkably sexy in bare feet and no shirt, but the appeal was spoiled by his scowl.

"It's only ten-twenty," I said. "I had a lot of people to talk to. I hung around after dinner to catch up on the gossip." The real business at herb conferences, like anywhere else, goes on in the hallways and elevators and over coffee—or herb tea, if you're a purist.

"You drove home alone?"

I tried for a little humor. "I should have brought a bevy of dancing boys?"

McQuaid's mouth turned up at the corner. "Sorry. I was worried. I guess I've been pacing."

"You guess?" I looked at the floor. "You've worn a path."

"You ain't seen nothin' yet." McQuaid thrust something at me. "Here. Take a look."

He had given me two eight-by-ten glossies, mug shots. An unshaven face with bulging eyes scowled defiantly out at me. The neck was sinewy and thick, and above the tee shirt and onto the throat curled a rattlesnake tattoo. I shuddered. "Not my type."

"That's Jacoby." McQuaid was terse. "You see this character around here, run, don't walk, to the nearest phone and call Blackie."

Blackie Blackwell is the Adams County sheriff. He and McQuaid went to grad school together at Sam Houston State, and they're still friends. In McQuaid's opinion, Blackie's a more effective lawman than Bubba Harris. He's educated, up-to-date on new techniques, likely to rely on the brain as well as the gut. McQuaid's kind of lawman.

I looked at the photos again. Jacoby's mouth was angry, the brows threatening, the eyes murderous. An ugly, ugly man. "You've shown these to Brian?"

"Yeah."

I handed them back. "Scared the shit out of him, no doubt."

McQuaid pinned the photos to the corkboard beside the phone. "That's what I intended. He needs to know that he can't go bopping around, having a good time—"

"Being a carefree kid on summer vacation."

McQuaid's answer was a growl. "This is an extraordinary situation."

"You're right, there," I said. It *was* an extraordinary situation, one with which I was scarcely prepared to cope. What would I do if Brian were my child? Would I show him the pictures? Would I confine him to the house? Maybe I would. Maybe I'd opt for the safe thing, even if I wasn't sure it was the right thing or the best thing. Glancing at McQuaid, I saw that he was caught in the same quandary, and my heart softened.

"Here's something else," McQuaid said. He tossed me

a small can about the size of a pocket flash. I grabbed it out of the air.

"Bug spray?"

One eyebrow went up. "You might call it that," he said. "For a bug with a nasty bite."

I looked at the label. *"Pepper* spray?" Capsaicin spray, more precisely. Capsaicin is the quintessence of the chili pepper, an alkaloid found in no other plant.

"Yeah. *Muy fuerte.* Disabling, in fact."

The can fit into the palm of my hand. "Is this the same stuff the Dallas PD adopted last year?"

McQuaid nodded. "You won't use your Beretta, but you can't object to cayenne. The ultimate in protection. If Jacoby won't stop, this'll stop him. Not kill him, mind you, just put him out of commission for the time it takes you to get away. Put it in your purse."

I put the can on the table. "Anything new on Rosemary's murder?"

McQuaid shook his head. *"Nada."* He padded to the refrigerator and took out two Coors. A dead mouse lay on the refrigerator shelf.

"What about Robbins?" I asked, not looking at the mouse. "Is his alibi still good?"

"So far." McQuaid popped the top on a can and handed it to me. "According to the sister, they were together from six-thirty to after midnight. She lives in San Marcos, so you can add twenty minutes drive time both ways."

"So the time of death will be critical," I said. I sat down in the rocking chair by the open window and sipped my beer. "If it's on the late side, Robbins could still be a suspect. He might have killed her after he left his sister's. Any sign of the weapon?"

"None." He was half-sitting on the window sill with

the cold beer can against his cheek, one bare foot propped on the chair seat beside me. "Jacoby killed her, China. By now, he knows he wasted the wrong woman. He knows we know. He's pissed at himself. He's pissed at us. Next time he'll get it right."

I shook my head at the way he was stretching his theory into fact. "So what am I supposed to do?"

"Let somebody else handle your part of the conference. Stay home this weekend. All the area police are on the lookout for the guy. They'll pick him up in the next day or so, and you can go on about your business."

I thumped the Coors on the arm of the rocker. "No way, José! I've been working my butt off for nearly a year to make this conference happen. It's important to me. It's important to my business."

His eyes softened and he reached for my hand. "But you're important to me, China."

I pulled my hand back. "Then stop interfering and let me do what I have to do." I spoke more crossly than I intended, but I wasn't about to apologize.

He straightened up and stood looking down at me for a long moment, his blue eyes dark and unreadable. When he finally spoke, his voice was flat and toneless.

"Keep that pepper spray where you can get it when you need it," he said. He drained his beer, tossed the empty into the recycling can, and left the kitchen. A moment later I heard the upstairs hallway floor squeak, then the sound of the bed sagging under his weight.

I turned off the light and sat in the rocker beside the window. The moon silvered the gray pillows of lamb's ears and santolina along the old stone fence, the mounds of silvery artemisia and fragrant nicotiana and the lacy dusty miller. The woods beyond were dark, still. Shadows flickered, then vanished, solid shapes dissolving into the black void.

And I continued to rock, remembering Rosemary, wondering about Jacoby, brooding about McQuaid. Was the threat real and serious, or was McQuaid exaggerating? If this was a one-time situation, I could live with it. If it was a taste of life with an ex-cop's paranoia, I couldn't. It was as simple, and as difficult, as that.

Somewhere in the woods a poorwill cried, his shrill loneliness shattering the dark. Khat came in, sat on the floor in front of me, and eyed the rocking chair with a firm and unmistakable intent. When I lived alone, he slept with me, curled against my back, purring deep in his throat, warm with fellow-feeling. Now that I slept with McQuaid, Khat slept in the rocking chair. I missed him. Maybe in the winter he'd join us in our bed. If we were still together.

As I got up and relinquished the chair to Khat, I saw the pepper spray. One more reminder of McQuaid's worry. I dropped it into my purse and went upstairs. I brushed my teeth, pulled on an oversized tee shirt with a sunflower on it, and climbed into bed. McQuaid, already asleep or pretending to be, was well over on his half. I was careful to stay on mine. There was a wide space between us, bridged only by shadows.

Saturday morning seemed cooler. At nine, the planning committee convened on the hotel patio, fortified with iced herb tea and breakfast croissants, to make sure we were still on track. It was a good time for a photograph, so I herded them over to stand beside the new fountain, in front of the rosemary that had been planted since yesterday—and planted rather hastily, and inexpertly I noticed, with the burlap wrapping still intact. The poor rosemary wouldn't be able to stretch out its roots and was crooked, to boot, leaning at an angle. I made a note to mention it to Lily. The shrub deserved better treatment. It ought to be replanted.

But the new herb garden — crooked rosemary and all — made a lovely background for the photograph. The herb-alists were smiling when I clicked the shutter, and they kept on smiling, right through the weekend. Saturday's conference sessions were even more successful than Fri-day's, and Sunday's were better still. The trade show in-cluded most major vendors, and the herb bazaar drew customers from as far north as Waco and as far south as San Antonio. Most of the booths sold out of merchandise by two o'clock — a sure sign of a successful bazaar.

In fact, as far as I could tell, the only things that went wrong the whole weekend were relatively minor. A grower from Denton slipped on the stair and twisted her ankle. A Lubbock retailer backed into the double doors of the loading dock. And the walk-in cooler — the one Matt had locked to keep down the traffic — went on the fritz Friday night. Matt wasn't anywhere to be found, and Lily had to arrange for dry ice to be trucked in from Austin until it could be repaired. I ran into her on Sat-urday morning when I was looking for Matt to tell him about the loading platform doors, which looked to me like they could be repaired without much trouble. Lily was harrassed and irritated, muttering something about both big bosses picking a fine weekend to take a vacation.

"Where did Matt go?" I asked.

"He's just gone, is all I know," Lily said. "Makes me mad, because I was planning on spending the day with my grandkids." And she huffed off.

Still, considering the size of the operation, the casual-ties were amazingly light, and when the last session ended on Sunday afternoon, I was exhausted but satisfied. While people packed up and checked out, I caught up on last-minute things and said a flurry of good-byes. By five-thirty, all the conference participants had gone. I finished up, dropped off my film at Fox Foto, and headed for the shop. Laurel had opened at one and closed at five, as usual on Sunday, but I wanted to check the register and find out what kind of weekend we'd had.

When I got to the shop, Laurel had already left, but next door, Ruby was just turning out the lights. "How did the conference go?" she asked, checking the front door. She retrieved her purse from under the counter and followed me through the connecting door and into my shop.

"It was great," I said. "But don't ask me to manage another one anytime soon. I've done my bit." I looked at the yellow Post-Its stuck all over the counter, notes from Laurel about things that needed my attention. I noticed one: the air conditioner had gone critical. Harold would be there on Monday morning to render an opinion on the cost of resuscitation or replacement. It didn't take a rocket scientist to figure out that the AC was in-op. In spite of the high ceilings and thick stone walls, the shop was sweltering. The other thing I noticed was the cash register tape, neatly rolled and fastened with a paper clip, the total circled in green ink with a happy face drawn beside it.

I whistled. "Hey, not bad." Next to January, when I close for a couple of weeks, July and August sales are the lowest in the year.

"There were a lot of herbies in town," Ruby said, "in a mood to spend money—regardless of the heat." She wiped her forehead. "I sure hope Harold can fix the AC. I had three fans going in the Cave all afternoon." The Cave and Thyme and Seasons share the same air-conditioning. She looked at me. "What are you doing this evening?"

It was on the tip of my tongue to say, "I'm going home," because that's what McQuaid was expecting. But the liberated woman in me spoke up. "I don't have any plans. Want to have dinner together?"

It had been a while since Ruby and I had done anything unconnected with the shops. When I moved in with McQuaid, the center of my life seemed to shift to what we shared together, while Ruby—along with my other female friends—gravitated to the periphery. I hadn't intended this to happen, and now that I thought about it, I didn't intend for it to continue.

Ruby was looking pleased at my invitation. "Actually, I was about to ask *you*," she said. "Ondine Wolfsong dropped in unexpectedly this afternoon, on her way from New Orleans back to Berkeley. She'll be here for a day or two. Several of us are having an early dinner across the street at Maggie's. We hoped you could join us."

I glanced at the telephone. It would probably be politic to call McQuaid and tell him where I was going. But I could just as easily call him from the restaurant.

"I'd love to," I said. "Being with Ondine Wolfsong is always a unique experience."

Ruby pushed out her mouth. "As I remember it, you weren't very polite the last time she was here."

"I promise to behave," I said, putting the register tape into the cash bag and stashing it with the cleaning supplies. "I'm hungry. What with one thing and another, I didn't get much lunch."

Ruby was right about Ondine. She meets some very weird women at the New Age conferences she goes to, and they drop in from time to time on their travels. Each one has an unusual name—Starfire, Moon Bear, Spider—

and what Ruby calls a "gift." Some cast horoscopes, some do tarot and rune stones, some read auras. Ondine Wolfsong is the spokeswoman for a disembodied entity named La Que Sabe, She Who Knows.

I am very fond of Ruby, but when you get right down to it, the two of us aren't much alike. I'm short, Ruby is statuesque. I have nondescript brownish hair, an unremarkable face, and my hands always look like I've been digging out rocks with my bare fingers. Ruby's hair is red (exactly which red depends on which particular tint she's using just now), her skin has all the suppleness of a model's, and her hands and nails are perfection. More to the point, Ruby accepts without question the idea that a spirit can speak through the mouth of a living person, while I question whether La Que Sabe is anything more than an entertaining scam. The last time Ondine stayed at Ruby's, La Que Sabe told us that she created women by sewing them out of the skin of the soles of her feet. "This is why women have such a deep knowledge of all things," she said in deep oracular tones, "because we are made of sole skin. We walk intimately on the earth."

I snickered. Later, doing dishes in the kitchen, Ruby bawled me out.

"The trouble with you, China Bayles," she said sternly, "is that you've cultivated your left brain at the expense of your right. The light of your inner life has been darkened by your cynicism and pragmatism. Your feminine soul has shriveled." Ruby talks this way every now and then, especially when she's under the influence of one of her California friends. "You need to make a special effort to rekindle your spirit, or it will forever be snuffed out."

"I thought La Que Sabe was making a pun," I said, trying to defend myself. "You know, sole and soul. I thought we were *supposed* to laugh."

Ruby put the last dish in the dishwasher. "La Que Sabe was speaking," she said with dignity, "about the Wild Woman archetype. Only fools laugh at the Wild Woman."

There had been a lot of conversation around the dinner table about the Wild Woman. I gathered that everyone but me had read a book about her. "I guess I've kind of missed out on this Wild Woman thing," I conceded. "She seems kind of . . . well, mysterious. Like nobody knows exactly what she is."

"The Wild Woman stands on the cusp between the rational and the mythical worlds," Ruby said, waving the dish towel like a banner. "She is ineffable, indefinable. She collects bones, bones of the heart, soul bones. She cooks them into soul soup."

I choked down another snicker. "That's all wonderful," I said, "and very clear. Except for one thing."

Ruby looked at me. "What is it?"

"Where does she buy her soul bones? I don't know of a butcher who—"

Ruby threw the dish towel at me.

CHAPTER FIVE

Anise. *Pimpinella anisum,* a member of the carrot family.

Foxhounds are familiar with anise. . . . The trend in drag hunting is to lay an artificial scent by saturating a sack in anise oil and having a horse and rider lay a trail by dragging the artificial scent a mile or two across the countryside. Two leader hounds are taught the fox scent as well as the artificial scent. The leaders are used to train the pack for the drag and the real hunt.

Elizabeth S. Hayes
Spices and Herbs: Lore & Cookery

Maggie's Magnolia Kitchen is across the street from Thyme and Seasons. The dining room has white plastered walls, a green pressed-tin ceiling that matches the green floor, and lattice panels hung with vines and pots of red geraniums. The tables are white, centered with fat terra-cotta pots planted with thyme and basil and oregano, and the wooden chairs are painted the same green as the floor and the ceiling, with magnolia-print seat pads. Through the open French doors on the right, you can see onto a flagstone patio shaded with a wisteria arbor and landscaped with pots of culinary herbs. Beyond the patio is a garden with clumps of tall herbs growing against the cedar fence: the feathery shapes of anise and lovage and dill, the arching leaves of lemongrass, the bronzy lace of fennel. I have a personal acquaintance with every herb in that garden, because Maggie Garrett and I planted them there.

Sometimes I reflect that almost all of my friends used to be somebody else before they came to Pecan Springs. Maggie, who has owned the Kitchen for the last year or so, used to live at Saint Theresa's, a community of Catholic nuns a half-hour's drive north of town, where she went by the name of Sister Margaret Mary. For part of her stay there, she managed the kitchen. Maggie says it's easier to cook for thirty nuns than for three customers: nuns are schooled to accept everything — underdone or charred, insipid or tasty — as a gift from God, while customers send it back if they don't like it. Enjoying Maggie's herbal omelettes and breads and especially her soups, I have been known to offer up a special thank-you to whatever mysterious forces, divine or otherwise, compelled her to leave the community. But I do often wonder why she abandoned the serene silence of Saint Theresa's. Someday I may ask.

Ondine Wolfsong, Pam Neely, and Sheila were already gathered at a back table around a carafe of zinfandel and a basket full of cheese and garlic twists. Pam teaches psychology at CTSU and has a private practice as a therapist. She's a petite black woman with skin like chocolate mousse, a cultured drawl that slips across the ear like French silk, and the wiry stamina of her field-hand grandmother. This evening she was wearing a loose caftan patterned in red and blue and orange. Next to Pam, Smart Cookie was dressed to kill in a lavender Liz Claiborne jumpsuit. She and Pam were reading the newspaper, their heads close together, Pam's darkly glistening cornrows threaded with exotic, colored beads, Sheila's Aryan blond pageboy satin-smooth.

Ondine sat on the opposite side of the table, a thin, darkly tanned older woman dressed in a long black gauzy dress. Her coarse silver gray hair was parted in the middle and worn long, her pale gray eyes were silver-flecked and deep-set beneath straight gray brows, and her only makeup was a silvery lip gloss. The combination of pale eyes and pale lips in a darkly angular face was dramatic, and when she said hello, her voice was deeply resonant, almost a man's voice. She said very little, seeming to watch us with a secret amusement.

A few minutes later, Maggie Garrett appeared, bearing a plate of her famous stuffed mushrooms. Maggie may have left the nunnery, but she still has the composure of a nun. Her graying hair is cut crisply; her square face is beautifully plain, without artifice; her gray eyes are straightforward and clear, holding no guile. She wore her working clothes: dark slacks and a tailored white blouse, with a green scarf, a green apron hand-painted with a magnolia, and crepe-soled black sandals. A minute later she was back, taking off her apron to join us.

The appetizers were followed by a second carafe of zinfandel, a crisp Caesar salad and anise seed bread, zucchini with clams in a lemony dill sauce, steamed carrots and cauliflower with thyme and basil, and Maggie's marvelously decadent pecan pie. The conversation rippled happily across the table and back again, ebbing around Ondine, who sat like a silent rock on a tidal beach, until we came to the subject of Rosemary — or came back to it, rather, for what Sheila and Pam had been reading in *The Enterprise* was a follow-up story on her murder. The article said that the body would be taken to Tulsa for burial by relatives, the closest of which appeared to be a cousin. There was no mention of a memorial service, and when

Maggie asked if we ought to organize one, we looked at each other questioningly.

"I don't think so," Sheila said. "I really didn't know her. Did you?"

Maggie shook her head. "I didn't know her at all." She glanced at me.

I caught myself thinking that I knew more about Rosemary now that she was dead than I had when she was alive. Something was drawing me to her. Perhaps it was the fact that we resembled one another, or that I had found her body. Perhaps—

Ruby cleared her throat. "Now that I've thought about it," she said, "there was something almost . . . well, crafty about Rosemary. About the way she did her work, I mean. I'm not saying she did anything wrong, and I'm certainly happy with my tax refund. But she knew every angle. Even some that weren't . . ." She twisted a corkscrew of red hair around her finger, a little embarrassed to be speaking ill of the dead.

Pam nodded. "It's hard to describe, but I certainly felt it when she set up the books for my practice. She said I ought to take advantage of all the loopholes. I asked what would happen if the IRS decided to audit, but she said not to worry, she'd take care of it." She made a wry face. "I think I'd better go back to doing things the old way. At least I understand it."

I knew what Pam and Ruby meant. I'd admired Rosemary's skill in manipulating numbers and interpreting the rules when she used it to cut my taxes, but was it so admirable after all? Maybe I wasn't entitled to the moral high road, though, since I'd hired her to use that talent on my behalf. I expected her to wring the last deduction out of my tax records, and if she'd missed any, I probably wouldn't have hired her again. I was jolted by the thought that Rosemary and I had something else in common in addition to a similarity in appearance. My former clients certainly expected the best defense money could buy, whether that was morally right or wrong. That's why people hired professionals — to help them beat the system.

Ruby turned to Pam. "Did the paper say anything about her ex-husband abusing her?"

"Only that the police questioned him." Pam pushed her plate away, shaking her head. "You know, I'll bet that the spousal abuse I see in my counseling practice has tripled in the last few years."

Sheila nodded. "I read the other day that one out of three women will be physically assaulted by their partners during their lifetimes."

We traded uneasy glances. There were six of us. Which two had been slapped around?

"And something like three-quarters of the women who are killed by their abusers are murdered when they move out or get a divorce," Pam said. Her eyes darkened. "One client actually told me that his girlfriend deserved to die if she left him."

"What did you do?" Ondine asked in her resonant voice. It was almost the only thing she'd said all evening. She leaned forward intently. "Whom did you tell?"

Pam lifted one shoulder, let it fall. "I couldn't say anything. The court sent him to me for mandatory counseling as part of his sentence for battery. Therapists are required to protect client privilege." She gave me a half-smile. "Just like lawyers."

Ondine looked steadily at Pam. She did not speak, but her glance said it clearly. *Privilege or no privilege, you should have intervened. If the woman died, you'd be guilty.*

I shifted uncomfortably. Ondine's unspoken indictment suggested that Pam was somehow responsible for what her client might do. But that wasn't right, any more than I was responsible for what my clients had done. Once we started accepting responsibility for other people's actions, where would we stop? Wasn't this just another version, hardly disguised, of McQuaid's taking care of me? People have to be responsible for themselves, damn it!

Ruby, as usual, saw the other side. "It's tough, Pam," she said sympathetically. "Knowing that somebody's in danger and not being able to help. But what *can* you do with somebody like your client? Or with Robbins, who'll kill a woman before he'll let her leave him?"

Sheila set her glass down carefully. "That bothers me, Ruby. What you just said, I mean. Robbins may have had a motive, but there's no physical evidence to tie him to the crime. No gun, no prints, no blood drops, no witness, nothing. And he's got an alibi. Rosemary was killed while he was with his sister."

"His sister!" Ruby exploded angrily. "I keep telling you, you can't trust a sister!"

"Ruby!" Pam and Sheila and I protested, and Ruby subsided. "Not *our* kind of sister," she muttered. "You know what I mean."

Maggie crossed her arms on the table and leaned on them. "If her ex-husband didn't kill her," she said softly, "who did?"

"I wonder if she was involved with somebody," Ruby mused. "That would've made Robbins see red." When Ruby gets her teeth into something, she holds on.

"She was seeing Jeff Clark," Sheila said, almost reluctantly.

"Jeff Clark. That's the man who owns The Springs Hotel, isn't it?" Pam asked. "I met him when our department hosted a seminar there."

"Jeff Clark?" Ruby asked. "No kidding. I went to high

school with Jeff." Unlike the rest of us, Ruby was born and raised in Pecan Springs.

I looked at Sheila. "I guess you and McQuaid are the only people who knew about that," I said. "How did you find out?"

"She told me. We went out to happy hour a few weeks ago, to celebrate finalizing my taxes. She'd just come from—" Sheila hesitated. "She was, well, sort of excited about something. Otherwise, I don't think she would have told me about Jeff Clark. She never talked about her personal life."

"Kind of late filing your taxes, weren't you?" Pam asked teasingly.

Sheila grinned. "That's what accountants are for—to file extensions."

"What did she say about Jeff Clark?" Ruby asked, shamelessly curious.

"Apparently they met when he asked her to straighten out a few things in the hotel books. The relationship was pretty serious, but she was keeping it quiet. I gathered that she didn't want her ex-husband to know. Or maybe he wasn't her ex, at that point. I don't remember when they were divorced." Sheila paused and I thought she might say something else. But Ruby spoke up again.

"There, you see?" She pounded her fist on the table. "She was afraid of Robbins. She was scared he'd be violent."

"Well, maybe," Sheila said thoughtfully. "Or maybe she just didn't want to hurt him."

Ruby didn't pay any attention. "There's the motive," she said excitedly. "Robbins was already upset about her getting a divorce. When he found out about Jeff Clark, he came unglued and—"

"You're guessing, Ruby," Maggie said firmly. "As

Sheila says, there's no evidence. And you can't know what was in the man's heart. Nobody can know what's in *anyone's* heart."

I turned to Sheila. "Anything new from the PSPD on the investigation?"

"Nothing, as far as I know. If they've found the gun, I haven't heard about it."

Ondine stirred, and I turned to look at her. Her silver-flecked eyes were intent, her gaze turned inward, as if she were seeing something we could not see. We stopped talking, and the noise of the conversations around us seemed suddenly muted, as if somebody had lowered a glass dome over our table. Ruby leaned forward to speak, but Ondine made a gesture that established distance. Ruby sat back as abruptly as if she'd gotten an electrical shock.

"They will find it tomorrow," Ondine said. She spoke in the ringing oracular voice used by La Que Sabe, a voice rich in harmonic vibration and overtone, full of portent.

"Find what?" Sheila asked curiously. She had not yet been introduced to Ondine's supernatural buddy and had no way of knowing that this was supposed to be a Significant Pronouncement.

Ondine impaled Sheila with a long look. "They will find the weapon beside the river."

"How the hell do *you* know?" Sheila asked incredulously.

Ruby twisted. "Sometimes Ondine has . . . well, intuitions."

Pam put her hand on Sheila's arm. "I'll explain later," she said, sotto voce.

Sheila ignored Pam. "Intuitions are one thing," she said in a steely cop voice. "Flat-out claims are something else." She leaned forward. "You can't assert where and when something will be found unless you—"

"Well," Ruby broke in hastily, "I'm sure they'll find it *sometime.*" She gave an embarrassed laugh. "And the riverbank is as good a place to look as anywhere."

Sound was getting through to us again. Dishes rattled in the kitchen, and at a nearby table a woman laughed. We were awkwardly silent, and then all spoke at once, on different topics. Maggie asked Ondine how long she would be in town. Pam asked Ruby when her next tarot class was scheduled. But Sheila turned to me, not wanting to leave the subject of Rosemary's murder.

"We're forgetting McQuaid's theory," she said. "Does he still think his ex-con is the killer?"

"He's even more convinced than he was," I said. My eyes fell on my watch, and I gasped. It was after eight. McQuaid had expected me at six, and I hadn't called.

"Talk about domestic violence!" I pushed my chair back. "McQuaid will *kill* me."

"In a manner of speaking, I hope," Pam said.

"Maybe not," I said. "If I don't show up tomorrow, you'll know who to question first." I took out my wallet and dropped a ten and three ones on the table.

"Tell him you tried to call but the phone was out of order," Ruby said.

"Tell him we tied you to your chair so you couldn't get to a phone," Sheila suggested wryly.

"Tell him the truth," Maggie said, meeting my eyes.

I would have, but he didn't give me a chance. I will draw the curtain of personal privacy over what happened when I got home. It's enough to say that our debate was as savage and slashingly staccato as a championship hand-ball match, and we were both exhausted by it. We didn't speak or touch as we undressed, and when we were finally in bed, lying remote and apart, last night's shadowy gap had widened into the Grand Canyon.

The window was open to the warm, still darkness and the perfume of the golden rain tree beside the porch was heavy, almost suffocating. I lay for a long time with my eyes open, anger and despair like a hot, sour geyser in my belly, thinking of all the things I should have said to him and rehearsing all the things I was going to say in the morning.

And then, when I finally crossed the ragged, unquiet verge of sleep, I was once again standing beside The Beast's open door. Rosemary was lying on the seat, brown hair matted with blood and crawling with flies. But suddenly it was not Rosemary's face at which I stared in mounting horror, it was my own, *my* face, and I was lying on my back, my own blood splattered all around me. When I tried to protest that I was alive, that I could speak and breathe and move, the words were bottled up with my breath in my throat, and my body lay unmovable, while the shadowy figures of Bubba Harris and Maude Porterfield and Grace Walker and McQuaid—yes, McQuaid—stood laughing and trading jokes outside the truck.

Finally, with a gasp and a strangled cry, I wrenched myself out of Rosemary's body and sat upright, my eyes staring into the dark.

"Whazzat?" McQuaid mumbled. He came fully awake in an instant and reached for the gun he keeps in the drawer of his nightstand. "Somebody outside?"

I pulled in a shuddery breath. "No," I said. "I just had a bad dream."

He looked at me. "You sure? You didn't hear anything?"

"I'm sure I didn't hear anything."

I thought he might reach out and touch me, but he only

shoved his gun under the pillow and lay back down. Both of us lay awake for a long while, McQuaid flat and rigid, staring up at the dark ceiling, I lying apart, staring in at my heart.

By the next morning, we were speaking again, but only to the extent of trading guarded remarks about neutral subjects. It was difficult to say whether we had gone too far in last night's quarrel. The fabric of a relationship is fragile, and ours hadn't been tested in enough tough situations to know how sturdy it was. It might be ripped beyond repair, and neither of us knew it yet.

The shop is closed on Mondays. I pulled on shorts and an old tee and went down to the kitchen to make coffee, noticing that the thermometer on the porch already registered eighty degrees. The sky was a metallic blue and the sun a golden coin above a copper horizon. I turned on the ceiling fan. The day was going to be another scorcher.

Brian came down a few minutes later, wearing a sullen look on his face and his iguana, Einstein, on his shoulder. Without saying a word he submerged a shredded wheat biscuit in a bowl of milk, and disappeared up the stairs with the bowl, a banana, and the dead mouse. The mouse, presumably, would be breakfast for one of his snakes. Ivan the Hairible, a furry black tarantula, would get part of the banana. I had never asked what Einstein ate.

A little later, McQuaid came downstairs, gritty-eyed and unshaven. He gave me a curt nod that I returned equally curtly, and went out to the shop. I took orange juice out of the refrigerator, and three eggs. I was getting out the skillet when Harold, of Harold's Air-Conditioning and Refrigeration, called to ask what time he was supposed to meet me at the shop. We agreed on eleven, and

I went back to the eggs. I'd broken two into a bowl and was holding the third when the phone rang again.

"They've found the gun," Sheila said without preamble.

"No shit," I said, and immediately thought about Ondine and La Que Sabe.

"No shit." Sheila was grim. "You'll never guess who it belongs to."

I hate you'll-never-guess games, even when they're played by my friends. "Who?"

"Jeff Clark."

I dropped the third egg.

CHAPTER SIX

Raspberry leaves have a long tradition of use in pregnancy to strengthen and tone the tissue of the womb, assisting contractions and checking any hae-morrhage during labour.

David Hoffman
The Holistic Herbal

"Jeff Clark?" I repeated, stunned. Egg yolk was dripping off the edge of the counter.

"Yeah," Sheila said. "Ain't that a stunner?"

McQuaid, his tee shirt already sweaty, came into the kitchen and began to rummage in the cupboard beside the refrigerator. "I'm looking for the cleaning fluid," he said. "Do you know where it is?"

I held up the phone. "It's Sheila. They found the gun that killed Rosemary."

McQuaid's head snapped up. "All *right*," he said. "Where'd they find it?"

"Where'd they find it?" I said, into the phone.

"By the river, under the I-35 bridge. A couple of guys were bank-fishing. Around midnight, one of them relieved himself in the bushes. He peed on it."

"Under the I-35 bridge," I repeated to McQuaid.

"Where's the cordless?" McQuaid asked, and I pointed to the dining room. He came back with the phone to his ear, speaking into it. "What's this about a gun?"

"A couple of fishermen found it," she said. "They called Bubba. He figures it was tossed off the bridge, maybe out of a car window, with the idea that it would land in the river. He recognized it right away."

"Recognized it?" McQuaid was startled.

"Yeah," Sheila said. "Apparently you don't forget this gun, once you've see it. A nickle-plated Smith & Wesson .38 with an elaborate monogram carved into a rosewood grip. The initials are C. C."

"Damn," McQuaid said under his breath.

"Those aren't Jeff Clark's initials," I said.

"No," McQuaid said. "They're his father's initials: Charles Clark."

"Right," Sheila said. "Bubba recognized the gun because Big Chuck shot an armed robber at the hotel some years ago, and he impounded it for a while."

"Who says it's the murder weapon?" McQuaid asked. "If it was found at midnight, they haven't run ballistics yet."

"The chief himself took it up to DPS in Austin," Sheila said. "At six this morning. He dragged somebody out of bed. It's the gun that killed Rosemary, all right."

We were all three silent. I was thinking about Ondine and La Que Sabe and wondering how the hell she knew. McQuaid's face was working. I knew he was thinking about Jeff.

"Prints?" he asked finally.

"Plenty," Sheila said. "Whose, they don't know yet. Clark's aren't on file. He's been clean—until now."

"Just a damn minute, Sheila." McQuaid sat down abruptly on a kitchen chair, elbows on his knees, shoulders hunched, back turned to me. "You're saying that Bubba thinks Jeff Clark murdered Rosemary Robbins? That's ridiculous!"

"Tell *him* that," she replied. "He's up at the hotel right now, questioning Clark and taking prints. If it's a match, he's got his killer."

McQuaid pulled at his lip. "Where'd you get this information?"

"I ran into Bubba at the Doughnut Queen about fifteen minutes ago."

"I just don't see Jeff doing something like this." McQuaid rubbed his head and his dark hair stood up. "He'd asked Rosemary to marry him, and she'd said yes. They were only waiting until her ex cooled down some. Robbins was ticked off about the divorce."

"Jeff wanted to marry Rosemary?" I asked, surprised. "Why didn't you tell me?"

McQuaid jerked around, his eyes dark, narrowed. "Because he told me to keep it to myself. Is there a law that says I have to tell you everything I know?"

Sheila jumped into the breach. "Rosemary told me they were seeing each other." She paused, then added with greater deliberation, "She also told me she was pregnant."

McQuaid gave a startled grunt.

"Pregnant!" I exclaimed. "Why didn't you tell me before?"

"Because I haven't seen you alone. It wasn't something Rosemary would want blabbed all over town."

"How far along was she?"

"Almost three months. It was a month or so ago when she told me, the night we did happy hour."

There was another silence. I was trying to square the out-of-wedlock pregnancy with the cool, matter-of-fact businesswoman who had whipped my Schedule C into submission. It didn't seem like a mistake Rosemary would have made. Did that mean it wasn't a mistake? Was the pregnancy deliberate?

"Did Robbins know she was pregnant?" I asked.

"If he did," Sheila said grimly, "it might have given him a reason to kill her. I hope Bubba's taking a long, hard look at that alibi of his."

"But how could Robbins get his hands on Jeff's gun?" I looked up. "Have you ever seen it, McQuaid?"

"Everybody in town has seen it. It originally belonged to Big Chuck's cousin Cameron, who was a Texas Ranger. He used it to off a flock of bandidos down around the Rio Grande, some sixty, seventy years ago." He paused. "Come to think of it, there was a write-up about it in the paper a few months back, with a photo of the gun cabinet in Jeff's office. That's where he kept it."

"If lots of people knew about that gun, somebody could have stolen it," I said.

"I don't suppose there's any point in speculating," Sheila said. "We'll know a lot more when Bubba's questioned Clark."

"So he's back from South Padre?" I asked. From the way McQuaid swiveled to look at me, I knew he'd forgotten.

"Clark's been gone?" Sheila asked.

"He drove down Wednesday night to go fishing," I said.

"Rosemary was shot Wednesday night," Sheila said.

McQuaid's mouth tightened. Neither of us said anything.

Sheila cleared her throat. "Well," she said uncomfortably, "I guess that's a wrap. God, it's hot. Like living in a frying pan."

"Get back to us if you hear anything else," McQuaid instructed tersely.

"Yeah," Sheila said. "I will." She paused. "China, what's up with that Ondine character we met last night?

How'd she know about the gun?"

"Probably just a lucky guess," I said, not wanting to get into it with McQuaid on the line. He has enough trouble with Ruby and her tarot cards. Ondine and La Que Sabe would be beyond him.

But McQuaid wasn't deflected. "Who's Ondine?" he asked. "What's this about the gun?"

"One of Ruby's flaky friends," Sheila said. "She told us last night that the gun would be found today, by the river."

"Well, that's easy," McQuaid said. "She put it there."

"Nuh-uh," I said. "Ruby said Ondine just got in from New Orleans. She's not connected to this."

"You've got to admit that it's pretty strange," Sheila said. "I'll check her out."

"Yeah, do that," McQuaid said. "Keep me posted." He clicked off the phone and put it down.

"What happened after you got home last night?" Sheila asked.

"You don't want to know," I said.

"I told you to tell him we tied you to a chair."

"I should have. Thanks for calling."

"He's a great guy, but don't let him push you around," Sheila said, and hung up.

McQuaid spoke, his voice hard. "If Jeff wanted Rosemary dead, which I don't believe for a minute, it's ridiculous to think he'd use his father's gun for the job. And he sure as hell wouldn't toss it into the river."

It didn't seem very likely to me, either. Jeff Clark had a reputation for snapping at his employees, and I could see him exploding in a sudden burst of bad temper. What I couldn't see was Jeff crouching in a clump of yaupon holly with an heirloom gun, waiting for Rosemary to pull into her drive, then shooting her—and murdering his baby—in cold blood.

I stopped myself. I was only assuming that the baby was Jeff's, just as I was assuming that Rosemary had told Sheila the truth when she'd said she was pregnant. Maybe it had been a lie. Or maybe the child had been fathered by somebody other than Jeff—Robbins, for instance. The autopsy report would tell us whether she was carrying a fetus when she died. And if the ME was smart enough to take fetal tissue samples, DNA testing would reveal the father.

Still thinking, I got a paper towel and began to clean up the egg that had dripped over the counter and puddled on the floor. Kneeling, I said aloud, "If it wasn't Robbins and it wasn't Jeff Clark, who . . . ?"

McQuaid jerked his thumb at the mug shots pinned up on the corkboard beside the phone. "Him," he said roughly. "I tell you, China. He thought she was *you.*"

I turned to stare at the ugly face until I couldn't stand it anymore.

"If Jacoby killed her, how did he get Jeff's gun?" My lips felt stiff.

"His mother lives in New Braunfels. If he grew up around here, he knew about Big Chuck's .38. If he saw that newspaper article, he knew where Jeff kept it. It would've been easy enough to steal."

I forced myself to speak again. "That's a pretty long shot, isn't it?"

"Life is full of long shots." His look softened. "Are you fixing breakfast?"

Have you ever noticed how often it's the little things—cooking eggs, weeding the garden, changing the oil—that keep us going, keep us sane? It's ordinary life that steadies us when we suddenly bump into something unfathomably dark and huge, hidden like an iceberg under black water.

"I was about to make an omelette," I said in a voice that didn't sound quite like mine. "Should I make enough for two?"

He cleared his throat. "If it's not too much trouble. Or I can do it, if you need to take care of something at the shop this morning."

I glanced at him. "Should I plan to go under armed guard, or have I been paroled on my own recognizance?"

"Look, China," he said with an effort. "I'm sorry for what I said last night. You're not my wife. I can't tell you what to do or where to go."

"You couldn't tell me that, even if I *were* your wife," I said, then relented. "I'm sorry, too, McQuaid. I should have phoned to say I was having dinner with friends. It was rude of me."

A smile flickered and disappeared. "Rude and insensitive?"

"Yeah," I said. I got out another egg, a package of mushrooms, and some cheese. "Not to mention thoughtless and tactless. And inconsiderate."

He came toward me. "Is that an apology?"

"Yes." I took a step back. "But you're still not justified in setting a curfew, or in accusing me of—"

He put his finger on my lips. "You're right," he said humbly. "You're a grown woman. If you're dumb enough to—" He stopped. "Strike that, counselor. You're responsible for *you*. All I can do is warn you if I think you're in danger, and hope to hell you'll have the good sense to—"

I gave him a warning look.

"Sorry." He caught my hand. "I guess I'd better shut up." He put my fingers to his lips. "Am I forgiven?"

I pushed him back a little so I could look into his eyes. "You promise not to worry about me?"

He shook his head. "Of course I'll worry. But I promise to keep it to myself." He pulled his brows together. "Well, maybe not *entirely* to myself. But no nagging. And no curfews. Just phone so I know you're all right. Okay?"

"Okay," I said, and surrendered to his arms.

Was that what it was, a surrender, a capitulation? I silenced that question as we held one another tight, our bodies separate at first, then joining, knitting together, his hips firm against my body, his arms enclosing me, my arms around his neck, my fingers in the hair at the back of his head. He rested his cheek against my forehead, and we swayed together, our breath coming as hard as if we had just negotiated some deadly hazard—as perhaps we had. A heat grew inside me, a sweet softening that melted my belly, turned my bones to wax. I felt his hand under my tee shirt, his fingers light and easy on my breast, brushing the nipple, teasing it. His open mouth was on mine, urgent, his tongue going deep, searching. His murmured "Want to go upstairs?" was husky, aroused.

I pressed against him, cradling his face in my hands, kissing his mouth. "Oh yes, let's," I said breathlessly.

Brian cleared his throat from the doorway. "Does this mean I can go to Arnold's house?"

McQuaid dropped his hands and stepped back. I colored and pulled my shirt down. How long had he been standing there?

"Nothing doing, kid." McQuaid's casual laugh sounded forced. He jerked his head toward the corkboard. "You want to take a chance running into that creep on the road?"

Brian's chin trembled. "But I heard you tell China—"

"China's a big girl. She can take care of herself,"

McQuaid said sternly. "You're a kid, and I'm telling you—"

But he didn't have a chance to tell Brian anything. The boy turned with a sob and ran from the room.

"Shit." McQuaid appealed to me. "Where am I going wrong, China?"

I remembered Sheila's daddy teaching her to float in his arms, wanting to keep her safe, willing her to be *his*. I thought of my own father, who had never, as far as I could remember, even held my hand. I glanced at Mc-Quaid, his brow furrowed, his mouth strained with fear for his son—a fear that he might go out in the world and be harmed, a fear that he might be harmed by not being allowed to go into the world. Neither the careful holding-on nor the careless letting-go is right. How do fathers learn these things? Who teaches a cop to hold his child close but not too close, when he's trained to take responsibility for the safety of an entire community?

I had no answer, but somehow McQuaid's question made me feel a little easier. People aren't born knowing how to be parents. McQuaid might hold too hard, I might not hold hard enough. Maybe between the two of us, we'd get it right, or close enough.

The mood had been broken. We didn't go upstairs to bed. But we did share a mushroom omelette and some quiet talk, nothing special, just ordinary talk, steadying us, putting things mostly right between us. When we finished, McQuaid put the dishes in the dishwasher while I went upstairs to change into khaki town shorts and a blouse so I could go to the shop and introduce Harold the repairman to the comatose air conditioner. I was combing my hair when I heard the crunch of tires on gravel. I looked out the window. A blue Porsche had pulled up out front, and Matt Monroe was hefting himself out of the driver's seat.

I came into the kitchen with my purse and car keys just as McQuaid was pouring Matt the last of the break-fast coffee. Matt's white shirt was wrinkled, his tie was untied, and what there was of his brown hair was mussed. He stood up.

"Mornin', China. Sorry for bustin' in on ya'll like this. I wouldn't, if it wasn't important." At my nod, he sat back down again.

"Did Chief Harris have a search warrant when he showed up at the hotel this morning?" McQuaid asked, and pushed the coffee mug at him. I picked up the kettle and sloshed it to to see if there was any hot water.

"No. He just wanted to talk to Jeff, was all." Matt sat back down, his usually amiable face pale and drawn. "Wasn't the first time he'd dropped in, either. He was up at the hotel late Friday afternoon. That's when I told him about Jeff going fishing. He wasn't real pushy, then. Just wanted Jeff to let him know first thing he got back."

"He was pushy this morning?" McQuaid asked.

"You bet." Matt took a gulp of his coffee. "He made me go over it again about Jeff's trip, when he left, who saw him last. Then he told me to go see if Big Chuck's gun was in the case. It wasn't. He left. Said he was goin' to get a warrant, and he'd be back." He looked nervously at McQuaid. "What's going on?"

"The chief didn't tell you why he was there?"

Matt shook his head numbly.

"They found the gun that killed Rosemary Robbins. It was Big Chuck's .38. Somebody tossed it onto the river-bank under the I-35 bridge."

Matt covered his face with his hands. "Oh, Jesus," he said. It was nearly a groan.

I measured out instant coffee into two cups and added hot water from the kettle. "The gun cabinet," I said, putting a cup in front of McQuaid. "Where is it? Was anything else missing?"

"In the wall beside the bookcase. The guns aren't collectors' pieces, just sentimental stuff, mostly, family guns. There's a Model 94 Winchester, you know, the old .30-30 lever-action saddle gun. A single-shot .410 and a bolt-action .22, both of which belonged to Big Chuck's daddy when he was a boy. And a Springfield .30-06 Cameron brought back from the First World War. They were all there when I looked, along with a couple of Bowie knives. Nothing was gone but the .38."

"Was the cabinet locked?" McQuaid asked.

"Yeah. Jeff has the key." Matt looked at McQuaid. "He never showed up at the *Sea Lion.*"

McQuaid stared at him. "You mean, nobody's seen him since he left here?"

"You got it," Matt said. He pulled out a white handkerchief and wiped his shiny forehead. "I didn't tell Harris, you understand. I keep thinking there's gotta be an explanation." The sweat was popping out again before the handkerchief was back in his pocket.

McQuaid's voice was level. "What is it you want from me, Monroe?"

"I want you to find him, wherever in hell he's gone to, and bring him back. If he's killed this woman, he's got to come back here and face the music. If he didn't, he's got to fight it." He turned his head away. "It's not good for the hotel, him running away like this. People talk, they get ideas, the hotel gets a bad rap." His mouth twisted. "Fifty percent of that fuckin' white elephant is mine. It's not much, but it's all I've got, and I've put my life into it the past few years. I'm lookin' out for it."

"Jeff doesn't have it in him to kill Rosemary," Mc-Quaid said quietly.

"Maybe not." Matt shook his head and picked up his coffee mug. "If you're right, all the more reason for him to get his ass back here. He's got a lot of respect for you, McQuaid. You find him, talk reason to him, he'll come back with you."

McQuaid shook his head. "It's out of the question." He glanced over my head at Jacoby's photo, then at me. "There's a situation here that I—"

I put down my coffee cup and made him meet my eyes. "I can handle the Jacoby thing, McQuaid. If you want to bring Jeff back, I'll look after Brian."

McQuaid's mouth hardened. "I can't ask you to do it, China. Jacoby's too dangerous. And there's that business with Sally. We'll be hearing from her damn lawyer any day now."

I looked hard at him, challenging. "You don't *trust* me to do it."

McQuaid looked startled, then stung, and I knew I'd been right. Trust was at the bottom of this. He didn't trust me to take care of myself and Brian, any more than Sheila's father trusted her to float on her own. He hadn't realized this until just now, and the knowledge shook him.

"The business with Sally isn't that urgent, either," I said, pushing my advantage. "It'll be weeks before she goes to court."

"See?" Matt said. He gave me a thin-lipped smile. "Whatever you got goin', this pretty lady's sharp enough to handle it. Do it, McQuaid. Go get him. Make him come back."

McQuaid turned his cup in his hands, staring at it.

"He's not running. He's not the type. Something's happened to him."

I reached for his hand. "That's why you have to go, McQuaid. Jeff's your friend, and you have to help him."

Matt chimed in. "I don't see him killin' her, either. He wanted to marry her, for God's sake. She was goin' to have his kid. He needs to get back here and clear his name."

McQuaid's head turned sharply. "You know about the pregnancy?"

Matt shifted in his chair, and I looked at him. "Well, sure, I know," he said, coloring slightly, suddenly ill at ease. He held out one hand, palm up. "I gotta be honest with you, Mike. Jeff and I had our share of disagreements after I inherited his sister's half of the hotel. We didn't always see eye to eye. But we were partners, not enemies. Sure, he told me about Rosemary. Why wouldn't he?"

"Wait a minute," I said. "You're talking as if he were dead."

Matt pulled out his handkerchief and mopped again. "Yeah, well, this thing's makin' me crazy. It's a wonder I'm not talkin' like *I'm* dead." He appealed to McQuaid again. "Mike, you've gotta help me on this."

McQuaid shook his head. "I really don't think —"

"Maybe it's as simple as car trouble," I said.

"Yeah," Matt said. "Or maybe he took another boat, and he's been out on the Gulf for three, four days. Probably all you have to do is show up and break the news to him. He'll *want* to get back here and get this mess straightened up."

McQuaid's hand came up and tugged at his lip. After a minute he said, "How long had Jeff been planning this trip?"

Matt seemed to relax a little. "Couple weeks. He told me he wanted to get away for some fishin' and did I have any ideas. I told him about the *Sea Lion,* because I've been out on her myself a time or two and always did real good." He grinned. "Got seventy pounds of snapper last time I went."

"He left on Wednesday night?"

"Far as I know. That was the plan, anyway. I last saw him on Wednesday afternoon. He said he was going to work late, then drive down that night."

"He was driving the Fiat?" McQuaid asked. "You know what year?"

"Maybe '87 or '88."

"Has anybody heard anything from him since he left?" I asked. "Has he called in?"

Matt rubbed his shiny forehead. "Nope."

McQuaid spoke slowly. "I'd need his tags and the numbers of his credit card accounts. His telephone calling card, too, and a recent photo."

Matt leaned forward. "Calling card, social security number, credit cards—you got it, buddy. I don't care what it costs, either," he added. "Whatever seems right to you, plus expenses, of course."

"You sure you can handle Brian?" McQuaid asked me. "He's going through a pretty unpleasant stage right now, and this thing with Jacoby is making it worse."

Matt looked from one of us to the other. "Who's this Jacoby ya'll keep talking about?"

McQuaid gestured toward the corkboard. Matt glanced at it and raised both eyebrows. "Snaky critter. What'd you do to get *him* mad at you?"

"I sent him up," McQuaid said. "He's out, and threatening to get even." He glanced at me. "I've got the idea that Jacoby killed Rosemary Robbins. She resembled China, and she was driving my truck. It could've been a case of mistaken identity."

Matt looked at me, considering. "Sure could've. I never noticed it before, but the two of you do look quite a bit alike. You're both kinda hard-nosed gals, too. Not exactly the domestic type, if you know what I mean."

I knew what he meant, and I didn't disagree. It was unsettling, though, his easy confirmation of McQuaid's theory. Robbins had an alibi and Jeff seemed an unlikely suspect. That left Jacoby. Maybe I ought to take Mc-Quaid's idea more seriously.

"Jacoby's mother lives in New Braunfels," McQuaid said. "He might have connections in Pecan Springs. A girlfriend at the hotel, for instance." He gestured at the photo. "Have you ever seen him?"

Matt glanced again at the photo, then shook his head. "If I had, I'd remember," he said. "But I didn't start full-time at the hotel until after Rachel got sick. That gun's been in that very same case for forty years or better, except when the cops had it for a while. It's possible that your man worked there some while back and knew about it." He turned to me. "You bring that photo up and show it around, Miz Bayles. Somebody might could recognize it."

I nodded. "But Jeff's the big question now," I reminded McQuaid. "If you're so sure he didn't do it, you owe it to him to help him clear his name. I can handle Brian." I looked at him squarely. "You can trust me."

McQuaid rubbed his nose. "If there's a problem at night, you could call Blackie. But what about during the day, while you're at the shop? Brian can't stay here by himself."

"He can come to the shop with me," I said, and then wanted to bite back the words. What was I letting myself in for?

Matt pushed back his cup and stood. "Then you'll do

it?" He was excited, twitchy. "You'll go after him? You'll bring him back?"

McQuaid stood up, too, glancing first at me, then away. "I'm not wild about it," he said slowly, "but I'll do it. For Jeff, you understand. There's *got* to be an explanation"

"Sure there is," Matt said. "I can't figure him for a killer, either. But from the way Harris was acting, he's under suspicion. He needs to get back here and get himself a good lawyer." His eyes swiveled to me. "Say, you're a lawyer, aren't you? And didn't I hear you used to do criminal law?"

"*Used* to," I said. "Past tense. I'm in a different business now."

"If you're going to pick up the tab for the search," McQuaid said, "we'll need to write up a letter of agreement."

"Sure thing. Why don't you write something up and bring it by the office. You'll need an advance, too, I reckon. Just name the amount." Matt thrust out his hand and McQuaid, reluctant, shook it. It was a done deal.

CHAPTER SEVEN

Pennie Royall boiled in wine and drunken, provoketh the monthly termes, bringeth forth the fecondine, the dead childe and unnaturall birth.

John Gerard
John Gerard's Herbal, 1633

Monday is my day to do errands, have lunch with a friend, and treat myself to a haircut or a new book. But at eleven A.M. on this Monday, I was bent over the air conditioner, listening with half of my mind to a detailed explanation about relays and condensors while the other half wondered just how much this initiation into the esoteric mysteries of refrigeration was going to cost. At length, Harold hitched up his gray work pants, turned the bill of his red gimme cap to the front again, and announced that he'd be back that afternoon to start work, as soon as he finished repairing the walk-in freezer up at the Springs.

"Oh, yes," I said, "I'd forgotten about that. It went out on Friday evening, didn't it? It seemed like a big emergency. Lily had to send somebody to Austin for dry ice on Saturday morning."

"Yep," Harold said blithely, "failed *big* time. Weren't the first failure, neither. Went out here a coupla months back." He leaned forward, confiding. "Problem was, they din't call me. They called Tiny an' Tim's Plumbin', Heatin' an' Coolin'." He leaned back again, his snaggletoothed grin cheerful. "That was their mistake, y'see. Call Harold the first time, won't be no second. That's my motto." He said it again, with obvious relish. "Call Harold the first time, won't be no second."

"Mm-m-m," I said without conviction, studying the innards of my air conditioner and wishing I could be sure that Harold was the expert he claimed to be.

Harold scratched a scab off his sunburned nose. "Yep, that Mr. Mon-roe, he purt'near had a heart 'tack when that freezer went out. Phoned me up when I was sittin' down to supper, orderin' me to git my tail up there lickety-split, like I was one of his maint'nance men, 'stead of a independent perfessional." He chuckled. "Looked to me like he had sumpthin' in there he din't want thawed out."

"Chickens, probably," I said. "They got in a load of Cornish game hens for the banquet."

"Wasn't no game hens," Harold said, scribbling something on a piece of paper. "Side of beef, mebbe." He handed me the paper. "Here's what I figger this thing'll cost," he added sunnily, "plus or minus ten percent. How does that there number look to you, Miz Bayles?"

It looked awful. It looked like I could send Brian to college on what it was going to cost to repair the air conditioner, plus or minus ten percent. "Do I have any choice?" I asked bleakly.

"Well, sure," Harold said. "You kin call Tiny an' Tim fer a second opinion." He paused and screwed up his face. "Course, Tiny's in the hospital havin' his hernia sewed up, and Tim's took off fer a while, nobody knows where. Sad to say, but them boys're none too reli'ble. Might be a while before they git over here. Even then, chances are they'd come up with the same figger. Higher, prob'ly." He patted my air conditioner consolingly. "Ain't no two ways to deal with this here problem."

"Forget the second opinion," I said, resigned. Getting something fixed in a small town can be a big problem. "Let's just get it repaired. Today."

"Sure thing," Harold agreed happily, thrusting his screwdriver into his jangling belt of tools. "Right after I git that freezer runnin' up at The Springs. Like I say, call Harold the first time, won't be no second."

Harold left, whistling. I cut an armful of thyme sprigs and took them into what used to be my old kitchen, where I swished them in cool water, blotted the moisture with towels, and put them in the dehydrator, where they would dry until tomorrow morning. Then I poured myself a glass of red zinger tea out of the pitcher in the refrigerator, added some ice cubes, and surveyed the large, bright room, with its stone walls, original pine woodwork and ceiling, and red clay tile floor. I still hadn't decided how to use it. Certainly, it was great space for my occasional classes in wreath-making, herb-crafting, aromatherapy, and traditional folk remedies. But with almost no remodeling, the guest house at the back of the lot (once an old stone stable) was suitable for classes, and the kitchen could become a tearoom. It would mean more work, of course, and I'd have to hire extra help. But it had good income potential and wouldn't necessarily require a heavy cash investment. Maybe I should check with the health department and see what kinds of requirements I'd have to meet.

I dreamed for a few minutes. The space is an ideal setting for Victorian, which appeals to my softer side. Wicker chairs, even a wicker sofa with chintz-covered cushions over there under the window. Lace tablecloths and lace swags at the tall windows. Delicate glass pitchers filled with fresh hydrangea and cosmos and cabbage roses, with silvery lamb's ears and dark green leaves of tansy. Crystal and silver espaliers brimming with lavender potpourri. With a fairly small investment, I could turn my old kitchen into a lovely place for an herbal high tea on Sunday afternoon, a place where friends could linger together over cups of hot mint tea and cheesy twists in the morning and iced glasses of rosemary lemonade and plates of puff pastry in the afternoon. I could make an arrangement with Maggie's Magnolia Kitchen to handle the cooking.

I sat quietly, sipping tea and letting the images come into my mind, enticing, entrancing images. But what kept coming with them, like unbidden shadows, was a barrage of questions. Where was Jeff Clark, and why had he run away? Had Rosemary been murdered in my place by a revenge-crazy ex-convict? Or had she been killed by an angry ex-husband? After a while, I acknowledged that the questions were too intrusive to allow me to think about Victorian delights, and with no air-conditioning, the temperature was creeping upward. I took one last sniff of the sweet fragrance of drying thyme, locked up, and went home to see if McQuaid needed anything for his trip to South Padre.

I found him in the bedroom, stuffing socks and jockey shorts into a duffel bag. Men don't pack underwear the way women do. I count the days I'll be gone and take that many pairs of panties. McQuaid had dumped in everything he owned.

"How long do you think you'll be gone?" I asked, looking at the shorts.

He peeled off his shirt. "Your guess is as good as mine." He took an underarm holster off the bed.

"You're carrying?" I asked.

Dumb question. The evidence was right there in front

of my eyes. But I'd never seen McQuaid wearing a gun. Cleaning and repairing guns, yes, in his workshop. Shooting them, yes, on the practice range behind the house. Driving around with them, yes, in the window rack of The Beast. McQuaid is a gun person. But I had not seen him wear one, with the obvious intention of using it as a weapon. I was taken aback by the difference it made in him, and by my response.

His "You bet I'm carrying" was clipped and terse. He slipped into the holster, snugged it with a practiced motion, and took a plaid cotton shirt out of the closet.

I sat down on the bed. He hadn't wanted to go in the first place, but the excitement of getting ready was charging him up. The adrenaline of the chase was turning him into somebody I didn't know very well, into the hard, macho cop he used to be. A man riding into the wilderness to do a man's job while his woman stayed behind with his child. Some part of me was excited by this arming of the hero, by McQuaid buckling on his gun belt and sallying forth. This man in my bedroom was a stranger, and the fact aroused me, made me want him. My hand reached up and touched his arm.

But something about this scene and my response to it reminded the liberated woman in me of a worn-out myth. *Sorta like Penelope watching Ulysses strap on his sword and head out for Troy, huh? (Sardonic laugh.) Have you forgotten what happened after he left? There she was with that stupid loom all day, nothing to do but weave. So what do you think you'll be doing when your hero's on his way to the border and you're left to baby-sit?*

I dropped my hand. "What are you going to do when you get to South Padre?"

"Check the docks, the parking lots, the hotels. Talk to the local cops." He picked up a small snub-nosed revolver, swung out the cylinder to check the rounds, snapped it shut. His mouth was a firm, hard line. "Bubba's put out an APB for the Fiat." He looked at me. "The prints on the gun belonged to Jeff."

"Oh, no," I said—sympathetically, because Jeff was McQuaid's friend.

"Oh, yes." McQuaid was grim. He went to the closet for his new boots.

I picked at a tuft of thread on the green and white Irish Chain bedspread McQuaid's mother had quilted for our bed, bless her heart. She's an old-fashioned ranch wife who's lived with the same man on the same two thousand acres of Texas prairie for the last forty-five years, and she has deep moral qualms about our living together without benefit of clergy. But that doesn't keep her from wishing us happiness and making a quilt to cover us while we make love.

"Everybody knows Jeff can be hot-headed," I said quietly. "Maybe Rosemary told him she wouldn't marry him, and he got angry. Maybe he found out the baby wasn't his. Maybe—"

McQuaid came around the end of the bed and sat down beside me.

"Maybe he did kill her. Or maybe he didn't. Either way is beside the point, far as I'm concerned. I want to change boots. Give me a hand, will you?"

The liberated woman in me put up a squawk, but I knelt at his knee and eased the boot over his instep while he tugged. His voice was muffled, gruff.

"Whether he killed her or whether he didn't, it's none of my business. I don't want to know what he's done. I'm going down there to bring him back, that's all. It's not my job to make judgments."

Both boots on, I sat down beside him again. *I don't want*

to know. I recognized McQuaid's logic, for I'd used it often enough to shout down my own doubts. If you're worried about guilt, you shouldn't be in the business; if you demand that your client tell you the truth, you're only reducing your options. Innocent or guilty, it's beside the point.

"Did you let Bubba know you're going?" I asked.

"Bubba *and* Blackie." He picked up a dirty sock and began to buff the toes of his already-gleaming boots. "Bubba can't spare any warm bodies for a search, so he's glad enough to let Matt pay me to look. Blackie says to tell you he's adding a night patrol route past this house. A deputy will be driving that county road out there every few hours. Any noise, anything out of the ordinary, all you have to do is pick up the phone." He stood up and began to push his hand-tooled Western belt through the loops of his jeans. "I don't want you to take *any* chances, China. You hear? You get on the horn to Blackie at the slightest hint of trouble."

"I hear," I said. This was starting to sound like a lecture. "You don't have to worry."

He laughed, a brusque male laugh that showed just how far away from me he had already gone. "I'll worry anyway." He fastened his belt and sat down beside me again, pulling open the nightstand drawer. "I know all about you and guns, but I want you to forget that and pay attention."

"Yessir," I said with exaggerated deference, but he didn't notice. He had a gun in his hand.

"This .38 is loaded, and it's right here where you can get at it during the night." He put it back and closed the drawer. "There's also a pump shotgun behind the raincoats, in the closet by the front door. It's loaded with double-ought buckshot. All you have to do is pump once, point it, and pull the trigger. Don't bother to aim; the choke is set to cylinder for max spread. Your automatic is at the shop?"

There was a quick retort on my tongue, but I only nodded. I couldn't imagine using the .38, or the shotgun, or the Beretta. But McQuaid didn't want to hear that now. The hero was off to war, and he wanted to lead his woman armed and prepared to kill in defense of his child.

"There are other weapons out in my workshop," he added, "but they're locked up. Oh, and leave Howard out at night. He's not much of a watchdog, but he'll bark if he sees anybody moving around out there."

I sorted through two or three responses, and settled for one that seemed appropriately neutral. "The place is an arsenal."

"If you need to protect yourself, I want you to be able to do it. And Brian knows to leave the guns alone. That's one thing I've never had to worry about." He stood up, threw the dirty sock into his duffle, and zipped it.

I forebore to ask him why he was taking one dirty sock. Instead, I asked, "What about Sally? Are you going to let her know you're out of town?"

"Not on your life," he said firmly. "If she knows I'm gone, she might put pressure on you to let her take Brian. She's done a few things lately that make me think she's not very stable—quitting her job, for instance."

"If that's instability," I said wryly, "then Brian's in bad trouble. I quit my job. You did, too."

"That's different," McQuaid said. "Anyway, you should have heard her on the phone last night. Totally unreasonable. I don't trust her to keep Brian safe." He sat back down on the bed again and put his arm around me. His voice became tender. "You'll miss me?"

"Of course I'll miss you," I said. The other China whispered, *Will you?*

He nuzzled my cheek. "You and the boy are more important to me than anything else, China. I'd go crazy if anything happened to either one of you."

The other China whispered that we were talking in soap-opera clichés. I shushed her and kissed him, murmuring reassuringly, "Nothing's going to happen. We'll be fine." As my arms went around him, I felt the bulge of the holstered gun under his armpit and the wanting came up again in a hot, rushing wave that pulled me under. This time the other China didn't say a word. She just stood by and watched, shaking her head.

Sometime later, Brian and I stood on the porch, waving goodbye as McQuaid drove away in his rental car.

"Dad's going after a bad guy?" Brian asked, squinting up at me. "Just like in the movies?"

"You might say that."

Brian looked after the car. *"Awe-some,"* he said.

I spent the hour after lunch doing necessary domestic things like laundry and the vacuuming. Then I went outside to work on what will be a wonderful herb garden — this time next year.

A couple of weeks ago, in the center of the sunny backyard, I had staked out a large area. Now I hosed down the grass thoroughly, then spread black plastic over the ground. It would serve as a solar kiln to bake the grass roots and residual weed seeds. By the middle of August, everything under the plastic would be cooked to a crisp, the plastic could come up, and I'd start putting in paths and borders and shaping the beds. In September I'd turn the soil, then cover it again to catch any late sprouters, and in the middle of October, before the onset of fall rains, I'd transplant the basic biennials and perennials: rosemary, sage, thyme, catnip, parsley, lavender, artemisia, chives, yarrow, santolina, fennel. These I would compost and cover lightly with grass and leave until early spring, when it's time to sow the annuals: basil, borage, coriander, dill, nigella, sweet Annie.

Working in the backyard was hotter than making whoopee in woolens. Having spread the plastic, I went back indoors, washed off the sweat, and settled down at McQuaid's computer to work on the newsletter. You can write about herb gardens as well as dig in them. Writing doesn't tear up your hands.

Arnold came over early in the afternoon with the latest copy of *Card Collector* magazine, and he and Brian retired to Brian's bedroom to drool over pictures of the collector cards they coveted and play with a computer game Sally had given Brian last month. A couple of hours later they migrated downstairs and settled in front of the television for a rerun of *Star Trek: The Next Generation.* A little later, they came into the office and stood behind my chair, one on each side. Brian was wearing Einstein on one shoulder. Arnold was wearing a remarkable ridged plastic forehead, à la Lieutenant Worf, a vest that looked like it came out of the costume shop for *Die Nibelungenlied,* and a Klingon sash peppered with various fan pins, security badges, and the Karizan stella. I didn't even do a double take. I've gotten used to seeing Brian and his friends in Trekkie regalia.

Brian came straight to the point. "Arnold wants to know can I go with him to the Trekker Con on Saturday. It's in Austin."

I stopped typing and turned around. Before he drove off, McQuaid had laid down the law to Brian. He was to go to the shop with me. He wasn't to go anywhere else.

"You heard what you dad said, Brian. You and I have to stick together until he comes back."

"Well, then," Brian said, "*you* could take Arnold and me to the convention. That way, we'd be together."

Arnold's face was earnest under his formidable Klingon forehead. "There'll be plenty of other mundanes there, so you won't feel too weird."

I shook my head. "You heard your dad, Brian. If I said you could go, your father would kill me." Probably not, but it took me off the hook.

Brian gave a heavy sigh. "Well, then, can Arnold come to the shop with us tomorrow?"

I saved my file, turned off the computer, and stood up. "I'm sorry to keep saying I'm sorry, but the shop is a business."

There was the expected whine. "But China —"

I offered the expected compromise. "Why don't you stay for supper and spend the night, Arnold?"

The boys agreed as long as they could fix armadillo burgers (the recipe for which will definitely *not* appear in the newsletter). The compromise earned me a relatively pleasant evening, the high point occuring when Arnold came into the kitchen with a grimace of pain on his face and a huge nail through his finger. I had only to glance at it to realize that it must hurt like hell.

"Omigod!" I babbled. "How did you *do* that?" Without waiting for an answer, I grabbed my purse. "Come on, Arnold. We've got to get you to the emergency room! Oh, lord, where are my car keys? Brian, have you seen my car keys? Your dad didn't drive off with them, did he? Sit down, Arnold, while I try to find —"

My ballooning panic was punctured by a loud chorus of guffaws. The nail turned out to be one of those mail-order gotchas, stuck into a flesh-colored plastic sleeve that fitted on the finger. With their usual warped adolescent humor, Brian and Arnold thought my alarm was hilarious. When I calmed down and stopped shouting, we made popcorn and hot chocolate and they went to bed happy.

I sat down with a before-bed brandy and thought how little I knew about the psychology of preadolescent males. My mind went to McQuaid and what happened when he strapped on his gun, and I had to admit that I didn't know very much about male psychology, period. I went to bed remembering our lovemaking earlier that day.

The other China notwithstanding, it wasn't a cliché. I *did* miss him.

Tuesday was more trying. Brian insisted on bringing Einstein to the shop; I, feeling guilty for refusing to admit Arnold, finally agreed. When Brian and Einstein and I got there, the air conditioner was in pieces, a battalion of ants had invaded the former kitchen, and the neighbor's dachshund had dug up my carefully nurtured lemon balm for the second time in a week. I sent Brian out to annoy Harold, bagged the thyme that had been drying in the dehydrator, and replanted and reassured the lemon balm (dropping a chickenwire bonnet over it for extra defense). Then I sprayed the kitchen floor with Raid and flung the doors and windows open to dispel the aromatic evidence of my nonherbal, nonenviromentally-sensitive offense against the ants. When Brian got bored with bugging Harold, he and Einstein came in and bugged customers until I assigned him the busywork of inventorying the bookshelf, after which he bugged me with questions about how to write things down.

For a while, it got mostly quiet. Brian crouched on the floor, muttering titles and numbers over a yellow legal tablet. Ruby opened at ten, as usual, and there was a constant flow of traffic in the shop, which cheered me considerably. The more people there are, the merrier I am when I check out the register at the end of the day.

At eleven-thirty I left Brian counting cookbooks and went into The Crystal Cave to check with Ruby about lunch. We usually take it in shifts, one of us watching the stores while the other one eats. Today she was costumed in a gauzy red broomstick skirt, a red tunic embroidered with goddess figures, and red satin ballet slippers with ribbon ties. Ruby always looks right at home in the Cave, which is stocked with crystal balls, incense burners in the shape of pregnant goddesses, Tibetan prayer flags, South American rainsticks, and books on Wicca, women's spirituality, alternative medicine, tai chi, meditation, and astrology. Ruby is a wild, wacky, wonderful person who lives on the lunatic fringe, a little far out for Pecan Springs—and yet she was born here. Sometimes these things are difficult to understand.

It was my first chance to update Ruby on the discovery of the gun and the fingerprints, Rosemary's pregnancy, McQuaid's trip to South Padre, and Harold's confident prediction that the air conditioner would be functioning by three that afternoon. She was asking whether we should say prayers to the air conditioner goddess when Sheila Dawson came in. She was wearing elegant beige slacks, an ivory silk blouse with pearls, and a creamy white jacket.

"I just came from talking to Bubba," she said without preamble. "The autopsy report on Rosemary is back."

"What'd it say?" Ruby asked, putting down the smudge pot she was holding.

"The bullet entered the left lower maxilla and exited the lower right parietal, just above the temporal." This from a woman in a silk blouse and pearls.

Ruby gave her a questioning look.

"In the lower left cheek and out on the right side just above the ear," I explained gently.

Ruby put her hand to her cheek. "Oh," she said in a small voice.

"Sounds like death would have been instantaneous," I said.

Sheila nodded. "That's what the Bexar County ME thought, too."

"What time?"

"Bubba says she picked up the furniture at seven, and stopped for fried chicken at the KFC on Buchanan Street. From the stomach contents, the ME says she was killed no later than ten."

"Then the nine-thirty gunshot report pins it down pretty well."

"Yeah. But there's more. She wasn't pregnant."

Ruby shook her head sadly. "She must have had an abortion."

"Maybe she had a miscarriage," I said. "Or she lied. There's more than one way not to be pregnant."

Brian spoke from the doorway. "Is somebody pregnant?" He looked at me, interested. Einstein sat on his shoulder, his tongue flickering. "Did Dad make *you* pregnant, China?"

"No," I said coloring. Will I *ever* get used to the forthrightness of eleven-year-olds? "There's another box of books in the storeroom," I added hastily. "Why don't you go write down all the titles? When you're done, we'll get some lunch."

"It'd be okay if you were pregnant," he said. "As long as it was a boy." With that cheerful observation, he disappeared.

"I'm too old for this," I said.

Ruby sighed. "Why didn't she *tell* us she was having an abortion? We might have been able to help. You know, support her."

"She didn't tell us because we hardly knew her," I said crossly. "God, Ruby, just because we're women, it doesn't mean we have to bare the secrets of our souls to every casual acquaintance."

Ruby looked hurt. "Well, I just thought —" She paused reflectively. "I guess you're right," she said after a minute. "I mean, it's pretty easy to assume you know a lot about somebody, when the actual truth of the matter is that you don't know much more than they tell you or you figure out from looking at them or listening to them. I mean . . ." Her voice trailed off and she looked from one to the other of us. "Don't you think so?"

"Yeah," I said. "I was still getting used to the idea that she was pregnant. Rosemary didn't exactly strike me as the kind of person who went in for unsafe sex."

"I wondered that when she told me," Sheila said thoughtfully. "Here she was, all business, bawling me out because I hadn't kept track of my travel, and she'd forgotten her pill. She's the last person you'd think would get pregnant by accident."

"Do we know enough to say that?" I asked. "We don't know what she was *really* like, under all that professional stuff."

Ruby was pacing, her gauzy red skirt billowing around her legs. "Maybe it wasn't Jeff Clark's baby," she said. "Maybe it was Robbins's baby, and he found out she got an abortion and shot her. Or maybe he was beating up on her and there was a struggle and —"

"The only hard evidence points to Jeff Clark. His prints were all over the gun."

Ruby stopped pacing. "I don't understand that. Jeff

has a temper, but he's not that kind of person, whereas the ex-husband—"

"It's Ondine I want to hear about," Sheila said impatiently. "How did she know about the gun, Ruby?"

"*Ondine* didn't know about the gun," Ruby corrected her. "It was La Que Sabe. You see," she added earnestly, "Ondine is only a channel. The entity who comes through is called La Que Sabe. That's because she knows—"

"You and Ondine are so full of *shit,* Ruby," Sheila said. "How can you possibly believe that ridiculous New Age garbage?"

Ruby gave Sheila a pitying look. "Face it, Smart Cookie. There are more things in heaven and earth than—"

"Quoting Shakespeare doesn't prove anything," Sheila said disgustedly. "This is *reality* we're talking about, not something some dead poet dreamed up. Listen here, Ruby. I've got some questions for Ondine, and I want answers."

"It's too late. She's left already. She went to Austin to stay overnight with a friend. She's driving back to California tomorrow."

Sheila gave Ruby an accusatory scowl. "She shouldn't have been allowed to leave town."

Ruby was indignant. "Oh, come on, Sheila! You can't think Ondine had anything to do with—"

I intervened hastily. "What are we doing about lunch?"

There was a silence as Ruby and Sheila traded wary looks, trying to decide whether they were really angry with one another, or just momentarily pissed off.

"How about Bean's Bar and Grill?" Ruby said finally. "I'm in the mood for fajitas."

"We need to split up," I reminded her. "Somebody has to watch the stores. Brian and I could go across the street to Maggie's and get a quick soup and salad, and then you and Sheila could go to Bean's." Maybe they'd work out their disagreement over a beer.

"I need to get back to work," Sheila said shortly. Ruby looked hurt, but she only gave a careless shrug.

"I'd rather go to McDonald's," Brian put in from the doorway.

I turned to face him. "How long have you been listening?"

"Long enough to know that the woman who isn't pregnant is the woman who got shot. Do you 'spose she was dealing Mexican dope? Maybe Dad's working undercover for the Feds."

I was still trying to come up with an answer when he added, "Oh, by the way, there's an old lady with blue hair hangin' around over here. She wants to know if you're goin' to come and wait on customers, or does she have to give her money to me and my lizard."

I am *really* too old for this.

CHAPTER EIGHT

To summon minor devils, burn incense made up of parsley root, coriander, nightshade, hemlock, black poppy juice, sandalwood, and henbane.
A 16th-century formula, cited in
Herbs & Things: Jeanne Rose's Herbal,
by Jeanne Rose

I intended to spend Tuesday evening finishing the newsletter, but things didn't work out that way. I was checking out the register at closing time and feeling grateful to Harold for getting the air conditioner running again, when Ruby stuck her head through the door.

"Ondine just called," she said. "She wants you and Sheila to come over this evening."

"I thought Ondine went to Austin," I said, jotting the sales figure in the ledger. For a July day that had been hot as a two-dollar pistol, sales had been pretty good.

"She did go to Austin. But this afternoon, La Que Sabe told her to drive back here. Actually, it's La Que Sabe who wants you to come tonight." Ruby sounded uncomfortable. "She's got something to say about Rosemary's murder."

I rolled my eyes.

"She *did* get it right about the gun, China," Ruby pointed out, sounding injured.

I thought about this for a moment. I wasn't keen on

consulting La Que Sabe, but Ruby was right. She *had* zeroed in on the gun. If Ondine had anything else to offer, it wouldn't be the first time a psychic had helped with a murder investigation.

There was Lyle Biggs, for instance, who was struck by lightning during a golf game in 1968 and discovered shortly thereafter that the jolt had gifted him with an unusual ability. He solved a 1982 Harris County murder after the victim's brother brought him a picture of the dead man and a shoe that had belonged to him. Biggs visualized the circumstances of the man's death and the location of the body, which led to the discovery of a grave in a muddy field. The killer turned out to be a neighbor who had already passed a polygraph administered by Houston police. And there's Peggy Simmons, who was picking corn in her Kansas garden when she was hit by a bolt of lightning. The psychic insights awakened by this cosmic intervention are guided by a spirit she calls Samuel. Consulted by baffled police on a missing persons case, Samuel led them unerringly to the mutilated victim, stabbed to death by her boyfriend. I reminded myself that the world is full of enigmas. La Que Sabe might be another Samuel.

"I can't speak for Sheila, but I'll come," I told Ruby. "I've got to think of something to do about Brian, though. I can't leave him home by himself."

"Sheila will be there," Ruby said. "If it were only me, I'd tell you to bring Brian along. But I don't know how La Que Sabe feels about kids. She might not come through if he was there." She paused, thinking. "Maybe Maggie could baby-sit for an hour or so."

Brian came in from the garden carrying enough sage for a couple of big wreaths. Sage grows so fast here that I make four or five cuttings a year.

I took the sage. I'd hang it for drying tomorrow. "What would you say," I said brightly, "to spending an hour at Maggie's house tonight? You know, the woman who runs the restaurant across the street?" McQuaid couldn't object to my leaving Brian with an ex-nun, for heaven's sake. Anyway, Jacoby hadn't been heard from. The threat was probably a figment of McQuaid's imagination.

But Brian saw through my subterfuge in a flash. "I'm *eleven*," he said indignantly. "Baby-sitters are for *babies*, not for *me*."

I turned to Ruby. "You're a mom. How would you handle this?" Ruby is a mom twice over. One daughter, Shannon, is a junior at UT. The other, Amy, is a graduate student in journalism at CTSU. Therein lies a tale, too long to tell at the moment.

"Girls are easier to raise than boys," Ruby said. "Anyway, I had mine before children's rights. Back then, you could whack their butts and not get sued." She went back into her shop and shut the door.

I sighed. There must be options other than butt-whacking. Luckily, I thought of one. "If Arnold's parents plan to be home tonight, how would you like to spend the evening there? I'll take you and pick you up." McQuaid might not be too happy with the idea, but I didn't see the harm.

"All *right*!" Brian exclaimed, his eyes bright.

"Call Arnold and confirm," I instructed, "while I finish closing."

We were headed out the door around five-thirty when the phone shrilled. I was going to let it ring, but on a hunch, went back to pick it up. It was McQuaid, calling from the border town of Brownsville, a half-hour's drive from South Padre Island. I'd been too busy during the day to think much about him, but hearing his voice, I realized I'd missed him. Missed him quite a lot, actually.

"How's it going?" I asked. "Have you found Jeff?"

"Ask him if he's cracked the dope ring yet," Brian said loudly. I made shushing noises and shooing gestures, and he went to sit on the step.

"He didn't go fishing," McQuaid said. "I've turned up the Fiat. At the Brownsville airport."

"I'm sorry, McQuaid," I said with genuine sympathy. Brownsville is the jumping-off point for travel to Mexico City and points south.

His "Me, too" held the bitter betrayal of a kid whose best friend has just stolen his girl. "God, China, I didn't figure him doing this."

He *had* been betrayed. Jeff Clark wasn't the kind of person who'd run off to Mexico for the weekend — unless he was running from something. From a murder charge. And finding him wouldn't be a piece of cake. Safe houses are for rent cheap, and the local gendarmes don't take much of an interest in *norteamericanos* on the lam. If they do, it doesn't cost much to convince them to forget about it.

McQuaid cleared his throat. "I've got some information for Bubba and Matt. You got a pencil?"

I fished for a pen and paper, settling for the back of a paper bag. "Okay," I said. "Shoot."

His flat monotone held no hint of feeling. "Item one: The Fiat was unlocked. The parking ticket in the car indicates that it was driven onto the lot at eleven-fifty-four on Saturday morning, July 7. Item two: According to the American Airlines computer, Jeff used his Visa card to purchase a ticket on Flight three seventeen to Mexico City, departing Saturday at thirteen hundred hours."

"Wait," I said, scribbling to catch up. "Okay. Item three?"

"Item three: In the car was an unsealed number ten white envelope with Matt Monroe's name typed on it. The envelope has the printed return address of The Springs Hotel." He paused. "Got that?"

"Yes. What's in the envelope?"

"A sheet of white paper on which is typed a quit claim, by means of which Jeffrey P. Clark gives and conveys his interest in The Springs Hotel to Matthew L. Monroe, in consideration of services rendered. The document is dated July 7 and bears both the typed and the hand-written name Jeffrey Clark. It was notarized in Browns-ville."

"Christ," I said.

"Amen." McQuaid's voice had gone from flat to gruff. "Get all that to Bubba first, then Matt. Tell Bubba the Brownsville PD is faxing the quit claim and the airport parking ticket. They're also towing the Fiat to the im-pound lot where they'll go over it for prints. Bubba can call them for a report." He paused. "And one more thing. When you report to Matt, tell him first thing tomorrow to get in touch with the bank or banks that service Jeff's credit cards and ask them to notify him of all charges, as they are made. If Jeff's used the card again, they should be able to trace it. Matt can let you know, and you can pass it on to me."

"Jeff won't use the card if he's serious about hiding out," I said.

"Yeah, but it won't hurt to check." He paused. "I guess that does it from here, babe. Any sign of Jacoby? Any-thing new on the case?"

Babe? "Nothing on Jacoby. The autopsy report is back." I told him about the missing pregnancy and added Sheila's reconstruction of an abortion as a possible motive for murder. "I'm beginning to wonder if we knew Rosemary at all," I said. "She's a mystery."

"I guess I didn't know Jeff, either," McQuaid said, grim. "I should've figured he was capable of pulling a scam like this, though. The bastard bluffed me with a pair of tens once."

"What are you going to do next?"

"I couldn't find anybody at American who could give me a positive ID on Clark's photo, but I can't hang around until the shift changes. My plane to Mexico City leaves in about twenty minutes. It's a bitch to take my gun on the flight and Mexican cops are squirrely about armed gringos, so I've left it with the Brownsville PD. I'll get a hotel when I get in, start checking around, and call you at home about nine-thirty. If you've got anything new from Bubba and Matt, you can give it to me then."

"Wouldn't you rather check with them directly?"

I could hear his grin in his voice. "I'd a helluva lot rather talk to you than them. Anything else?"

I considered telling him about Brian's visit to Arnold's and my scheduled consultation with La Que Sabe, but I decided against it. McQuaid thinks Ruby and her friends are flakes. Anyway, as long as I was home by nine-thirty, it didn't matter.

"That's it for me," I said. "Is it hot down there?"

"Hot as hell's furnace," he said. "Is the kid around? Let me talk to him."

I handed over the phone and went to lock the windows. After a few minutes' conversation, Brian gave it back to me, looking glum. He sat on the step, dejected, Einstein on his lap.

"That certainly went over like a lead balloon," I said to McQuaid. "What did you tell him?"

"To stay home and do what he's told, and not to bug you about going to Arnold's." I was about to tell him that

I intended to take him to Arnold's tonight, but he became brisk. "They're calling my plane. Consider yourself kissed top to toe and places in between." He hung up.

The bored male voice at PSPD said Bubba had gone home for the day. When I called his house, Mrs. Bubba— Gladys, president of the Garden Club and collector of African violets—said that he was out back, tending his bees.

"Bees?" Somehow, I hadn't thought of a police chief doing anything besides being the law. But this is Pecan Springs, where people don't just work for a living.

"He's collecting honey." Gladys was exasperated. "It makes nice Christmas presents, but he leaves the kitchen in an awful mess when he's extracting it. Honey all over the floor. The flies think they've died and gone to heaven."

The image of Bubba Harris hovering like a huge moth over a vat of honey almost made me forget why I'd called. But not quite.

"Tell him I have a message from Mike McQuaid," I said, and she went to the back door to summon him.

"Take your shoes off, Bubba," she said, loudly enough for me to hear her. "I don't want you trackin' honey onto the carpet." When he came to the phone, I pictured him clutching it in sticky hands. All this was giving me a different view of the man I'd never seen without a wet cigar stuck in one corner of his mouth.

"Sonavabitch," he said warmly, when I told him about the Fiat in the parking lot. By the time I got to item three, he'd almost forgotten that he didn't like me.

"Tell McQuaid we'll fax Brownsville the prints we got from Clark's house this morning. Soon's we get a match, I'll rattle Chick Burton's cage for a warrant."

Chick (for Charles) Burton is the Adams County DA,

recently appointed to fill out the term of Larry Cannon, who died of a heart attack after sinking a birdie on the ninth hole at the Pecan Springs Golf Course. Chick and I are acquainted, although I haven't seen him for some years. His father was a senior partner in the Houston firm where I worked, and we dated occasionally. Sometimes I think it's a very small world.

"McQuaid's phoning at nine-thirty tonight," I told Bubba. "If you've got anything for him, call the house before then. I may not be there, but you can leave it on the answering machine."

"Roger," he said. He cleared his throat, and his tone changed. "About that fella McQuaid's been worried about. Jacoby."

I glanced at Brian sitting on the step, his chin in his hands, and felt an apprehensive shiver between my shoulder blades. "What about him?"

" 'Pears he got himself in a mite of trouble in New Braunfels last night. Cut up a woman with a knife."

My apprehension turned to relief. Cutting up a woman with a knife certainly violated the terms of Jacoby's early release. "Well, I guess we can stop worrying," I said. "They're sending him back to Huntsville, I suppose."

" 'Fraid not," Bubba said, apologetic. "Slipped out the back as the depitty came in the front. We put a bulletin out on him, though," he added hastily, obviously to reassure me. "Prob'ly have him by mornin'." He paused. "Thought you'd wanta know."

"Thanks," I said, not knowing what else to say. I hung up and called Matt, who was still at the hotel. His response ranged from a grim grunt (at the news of the Fiat and the plane ticket) to exuberant amazement when he heard about the quit claim.

"Sweet Jesus," he breathed. "So he had a heart after all."

"Beg pardon?"

"What I mean is," Matt said, "that he hasn't left me holdin' the bag the way I figgered. We're in each other's wills, so the survivor gets the hotel if the other one steps in front of an eighteen-wheeler. Sounds crass as hell and Lord knows I don't wish Jeff any grief, but that quit claim's sure gonna make my lawyer 'happy. That little piece of paper is almost as good as a death certificate."

It did sound crass, but I understood the problem. Without his partner, there were a good many business decisions that Matt couldn't legally make. What's more, our system of justice is slow and expensive. Even if McQuaid located Jeff and brought him back, that was just the beginning. There'd be a hearing, an arraignment, and eight or nine months later, a trial. A first-degree felony conviction would carry five years to life, which would likely be appealed. However it turned out in the end, Jeff's defense would eat up his share of the hotel and more, meaning that Matt would either have to ante up fifty percent of the value or accept a new partner. Jeff had given his share to Matt before the lawyers could take it away from him. I could understand and forgive Matt's exuberance. I could also guess that Chick Burton would use the gift itself as another evidence of Jeff's guilt. You don't give away something handed down from your granddaddy to your daddy to you—unless you figure you've already lost it.

"Well, is that about it?" Matt asked.

"One other thing," I said, and relayed McQuaid's instructions about the credit cards. "If the bank officer gives you any trouble," I added, "tell him to check with Chief

Harris to verify that the trace is necessary to a fugitive search."

"I've already got that ball rolling," Matt said. "The bank faxed me a paper to sign about an hour ago."

I gave him the same instruction about calling before nine-thirty that I'd given to Bubba and hung up. I looked at my watch. Six-fifteen. I thought briefly about McQuaid's interdiction, about Jacoby cutting up a woman in New Braunfels, and about La Que Sabe's invitation. I went out and locked the door behind me. Brian was standing beside a large lemon verbena, where Einstein appeared to be enjoying salad.

· "Fetch Einstein," I said. "We're going to Arnold's."

"You got Dad to change his mind!" A joyful grin split Brian's face.

"You might say that," I said. And then again you might not.

Do all parents lie to their kids?

CHAPTER NINE

We exist on a plane in which we cannot perceive all the other beings sharing the earth with us, good guys and bad guys, spirits that might protect or harm us. It is just common sense to get the good spirits in our corner. This can be done with the pleasing smoke of the sage herb or other incense and with prayers left to us from olden times. . . . Here is mine:

> I invoke the Goddess of Protection, and my grandmother's and grandfather's spirits to shield me and my possessions with impenetrable power. My house will be safe from accidents, thieves, drunk drivers, and other cars. And I shall be safe in the Goddess's grace, like a child in my mother's arms. So mote it be. Blessed be.

> Zsuzsanna E. Budapest
> *The Grandmother of Time:*
> *A Women's Book of Celebrations,*
> *Spells, and Sacred Objects*
> *for Every Month of the Year*

The temperature had been in the upper nineties and the skies relentlessly blue all day, but by the time I dropped Brian off at Arnold's house, the sky to the southeast was heavy with rolls of black-bellied clouds, the air was sticky as hot glue, and the mesquite fronds hung limp and un-

stirring. Lightning flashed in the clouds, and I could hear
the distant rumble of thunder. On the drive over, I had
kept one eye glued to the rearview mirror. If Jacoby
didn't follow us to Arnold's house, I didn't need to worry.
Brian would be perfectly safe there.

"I'll be back by nine," I told Brian, letting him out of
the Datsun. "Your dad's calling at nine-thirty, and I don't
want to miss him. You guys stay in the house, you hear?"
I rubbed the back of his neck with rough affection, then
removed my hand quickly when Einstein flicked his
tongue at it.

He sighed loudly, but he gave me the Vulcan blessing
as he got out of the car — the first in a long time. Maybe
things between us were lightening up. I watched him until
Arnold's mother opened the door and let him in. Then I
drove back to town, fast, wondering if the storm would
bring a day or two's respite or just raise the thermostat
from broil to steam.

Ruby lives in a large, tree-shaded Victorian that was
once owned by a mutual friend who died a few years ago.
She painted the outside in gray, green, and plum, wall-
papered the interior walls, and scraped and refinished the
floors and woodwork. Over the last couple of years, she's
furnished the house with an eclectic mix of periods, cultures, and traditions that always reminds me of Ruby herself: a little bit of just about everything, tossed together
with a lot of panache and little regard for rules.

When she met me at the door, she was wearing a straw-
colored tunic, heavily embroidered with colorful folk figures. Her gingery frizz was pulled back with Oriental
combs, and she was barefoot. She led me to the living
room, which is furnished like an art gallery. Southwestern
paintings, African masks, and Appalachian textiles hang
on the cream-colored walls, Navajo rugs brighten the

glossy wood floor, and pottery and driftwood sculptures
are arranged in the corners, with tall cacti here and there.
An appropriately primal setting for La Que Sabe.

Ondine was seated on a white futon heaped with colorful pillows. She wore a black tiered skirt and silky black
blouse with a silver and turquoise Navajo belt and heavy
silver necklace and bracelets. She had the look of a Native
American wise woman: high cheekbones and flat facial
planes, shuttered eyes, coarse gray hair drawn in wings
on either side of her forehead and falling straight to her
shoulders. She responded to my greeting with a nearly
imperceptible lift of her lips that might or might not have
been a smile.

Sheila was already there, sitting cross-legged on a purple zafu in yellow shorts and a white blouse, looking as
if she had better things to do. There was an empty zafu
beside Sheila, but I can't imagine a worse torture than
being forced to assume the lotus posture, or even a half-
lotus, for more than thirty seconds. I sat on the other end
of Ondine's futon, to Ruby's right.

Ruby took a smudge bundle off the mantle and lit it,
then walked around the room, waving the smoking twigs
in the air and saying things under her breath. The room
began to smell pleasantly of smoldering sage and cedar.
Ondine didn't take any notice when Ruby made several
passes over her head, but Sheila glanced at me with an
I-don't-get-it look. I mouthed the words "purification ritual" at her, and she made a wry face. If the smudge was
supposed to cleanse us of skepticism and impure thoughts,
as well as to drive evil spirits from the room, it wasn't
doing much for Sheila.

When Ruby finished smudging, she went to the French
doors at one side of the room. As she closed them and
drew the heavy white drapes, there was a bright flash of

lightning and a loud clap of thunder that made all of us jump.

"I suppose you want the room dark," Ruby said to Ondine, and turned off the lights on either side of the mantel, leaving only a large pottery lamp lit on the table behind the sofa. Beside it was a clay statue of Coatlicue, the ancient Aztec Great Mother, sprouting two snake heads, a skirt of tangled snakes, and a horrific necklace of human hearts and severed hands. Not all goddesses are beautiful.

Sheila gave a hard chuckle. "I imagine it's easier in the dark," she said, her tone implying that darkness was a good cover for psychic fraud.

I smiled a little. Sheila may look sweet and pretty but she has the left brain of a cop. She's only interested in what she can weigh and measure. The rest is so much hokum. A few years ago, I shared that viewpoint. But after hanging around Ruby for a while, I am willing to stipulate that there are some things in this world that don't yield to quantitative analysis. A lot of it's hokum, yes. But some of it isn't. You have to *be* there to know the difference.

Ondine sketched a shrug with her narrow shoulders. "It isn't what I want," she said, "but what La Que Sabe wants."

"What does she want?" Sheila growled.

Ondine fixed Sheila's face with an impassive gaze. "We will know when she tells us," she said. She added, with a small smile, "You do not need to fear, Smart Cookie. She Who Knows, knows that your heart is good."

Sheila was about to retort when Ruby intervened.

"This isn't a séance, either," she said as she placed a beeswax candle on the table in front of Ondine. "It's a *channeling*. There's a difference."

"Oh, yeah?" Sheila demanded. "Like what? She goes into a trance, doesn't she? There's some weird supernatural being hanging around, isn't there? If it quacks like a duck, waddles like a duck —"

"Sheila," I said, "it's okay." I leaned over and patted her hand. It was cold, although the room was very warm. "It's safe. Nothing's going to happen."

Sheila cleared her throat. "I just don't like spooky stuff." She glanced over her shoulder at the shadowed corner.

The drapes closed out the gathering storm and what was left of the daylight. Ruby lit the candle, then turned out the lamp. The candle flickered, then steadied and burned brighter as she sank down on her knees on a tasseled paisley cushion and folded her hands in her lap, giving the impression that she consults the spirits every day of the week — as perhaps she does. Her tarot cards are in a wooden casket on the table, a bowl of I Ching coins sits on the table, and a large painted horoscope — Ruby's birth chart, rendered symbolically — hangs over the fireplace. Maybe it's fairer to say that the spirits consult Ruby.

"It's not spooky, Sheila," she said reassuringly. "It's just an ordinary room. Just take a deep breath and try to relax. You're sending out waves of negative *chi,* and your aura is awfully dark. Your stuff might keep La Que Sabe from coming through."

But the room didn't seem ordinary any longer. Nothing concrete had changed — the furniture was the same, the art, the candle in the dusky dark, the sweet fragrance of smoldering sage and cedar — but the room held an energy that had nothing to do with us. It wasn't anything I could see, anything I could touch or smell or hear, but I sensed it, nevertheless: a gathering urgency, a canny concentration of power as wild and unruly as the storm outside. I glanced at Ondine. Her hands were clasped, her eyes closed, her lashes dark against her pale cheeks. She looked as if she were asleep. Or dead.

A few moments—how many, I couldn't say—passed. Finally, Sheila cleared her throat. "Excuse me for interrupting," she said in a loud voice, "but can we open a window? It's getting stuffy in here."

It *was* stuffy. The air seemed to have an oppressive weight and texture, as if we were seated in the burial chamber of a pyramid and tons of rock were pressing down on us, compressing the air, making it soupy. Half-giddy, I realized how ancient our air is, millions, billions of years old, breathed in and breathed out by millions, billions of beings, human and otherwise. An ancient communion, a wordless, soundless liturgy, linking creatures with no common inheritance other than birth, death, and breath.

Ruby shook her head. "Leave the window for now, Sheila," she whispered. "It feels like La Que Sabe's about to come through. Anyway, it's raining too hard."

And suddenly it *was* raining, coming down in lashing sheets mixed with small hail, to judge from the sound as it hit the porch roof. The room was lit by a flash of blue-white lightning, flaring like a torch across our pale faces. An impatient clatter of thunder rattled at the window panes, as if the storm wanted to come in.

Ondine's eyes opened. "I see that we are all here," La Que Sabe said, her deep voice resonant and a little amused. "It is good that we are all here."

"*Really,*" Sheila said desperately, "I *wish* we could *open*—"

"Shush!" Ruby said.

Ondine turned toward me. Her mouth was shadowed,

pale eyes lit as if the lightning had set off an inner blaze. Her gaze transfixed me for a long moment.

"Your friend who is searching, he follows the wrong trail." The voice was taut, vibrating, a strummed wire. "He seeks the wrong man."

I blinked. "The wrong man?"

"It's Robbins!" Ruby yelped. "I told you so!" She clapped her hand over her mouth. "Oops. Excuse me."

Ondine was still looking at me — no, not at me, but *into* me, as if I were transparent. It was as if she had found something of interest inside me and was pulling it out, turning it over to examine it, approving it, putting it back.

"You are the one who will find the killer," she said. Her face was a flat, expressionless mask in the dimness of the room, but her eyes brimmed with light. "Tell the boy's father to abandon his search and come home at once. The child is in peril. You have much to fear."

"Brian's in peril?" I leaned forward, urgent.

Ondine's voice became hard. "There is a man who wears a snake."

A snake? Jacoby's tattoo! A cloud of black, unreasoning fear rose up out of the most primitive core of my being and blotted out everything else. I whispered, "Was it *Jacoby* who killed Rosemary? Is that why McQuaid's after the wrong — ?"

My question was silenced by a sudden jagged flash of lightning and the simultaneous roar of thunder as loud as a dynamite blast. Something like pebbles rattled in the chimney, and a fluorescent wave of blue-white sparks rippled across the floor, across my feet. I felt a jolt. My feet tingled.

Ondine raised her voice above the howling of the storm. "The man who wears a snake will lead you to the truth. You will find the answer by *el río abajo*."

For a moment I thought I hadn't heard her right. *El río abajo?* The river beneath? Beneath what? It wasn't enough to have psychics, now we had psychic riddles, *Spanish* psychic riddles, for God's sake.

"What river?" I demanded. A clap of thunder swallowed up my words. "What river?" I yelled.

Suddenly the wind and rain stopped and there was utter silence for the space of a dozen heartbeats. Ondine closed her eyes. When she opened them again, they were empty. The light had gone out.

"La Que Sabe has no more to say," she said.

I leaned forward, coldly angry. "Well, that's a hell of a note. Who does La Que Sabe think she is, coming on with a teaser like that and then—"

"She Who Knows will tell you nothing more." Ondine's expression was closed, her voice flat. "The rest you must learn for yourself."

I reached out my hand. "Nothing more?" I snarled. "Well, you tell that bitch—"

I was stopped by a blaze of absolute light, a clap of thunder loud enough to wake the dead, and a long, shuddery ripping sound that froze us in place. We were released from our paralysis by a splintery crash and the brittle chime of breaking glass. The French doors slammed open. A chill hurricane of pelting rain and pebbly hail. The acrid smell of ozone and burnt wood filled the room.

Sheila jumped to her feet and ran to wrestle with the doors. It took a moment to force them shut. "Get that sofa over here," she yelled. "The latch is broken. The doors won't stay shut."

Her command galvanized us into action. Ondine scrambled out of the way as Ruby and I shoved the futon against the doors.

"It sounded like a limb from the oak tree," Ruby said, her face white. "It must have been fallen onto the garage."

But when the rain stopped and we went outside to survey the damage, we discovered that it wasn't a limb that had fallen, it was the entire tree. Oaks are notoriously shallow-rooted, and this one had been pushed past the limits of its endurance. It had toppled onto Ruby's garage.

"Your insurance will probably cover the garage," Sheila said, "but it's really too bad about the oak. It was a nice tree."

"Actually, the poor thing was half-dead with oak wilt," Ruby replied. "It was going to have to come out anyway. But at least it missed the house and the car." Ruby's Honda was safe. There's no room for it in the garage, so she parks it in the driveway. She gave a rueful laugh. "I guess I should have smudged the garage, huh?"

There wasn't anything left to say. I gave Ruby a hug and said a strained good-bye to Ondine. Together, Sheila and I went out to our cars, parked on the street. The storm had rolled northward, and in the clear lemon-yellow light of the setting sun we surveyed the flotsam of branches, leaves, and loose shingles that littered the street. Ruby's next-door neighbors were out on the sidewalk, peering anxiously up at their roof, while across the street, another neighbor dragged a limb off a brand-new white van. All the damage looked to be pretty minor, compared to Ruby's garage.

"I hope you don't believe that weird stuff Ondine was dishing out," Sheila said. Safely outside, in the cool normality of the street, she had regained her skepticism. "All that nonsense about McQuaid coming home to protect Brian, and that stuff about the snake man. Ridiculous!"

I opened the car door and leaned on it. "It doesn't matter what I believe. McQuaid's not going to come home, whatever La Que Sabe says. He doesn't care whether Jeff is the right man or the wrong man. He's got a job to do and he's doing it."

"Stop calling her La Que Sabe," Sheila said tautly. "it was Ondine, talking in a funny voice. All those special effects, the lightning and thunder and stuff, that was just the storm."

"Was it?"

"You're not suggesting that—"

"I don't know what I'm suggesting," I said. I leaned over and brushed wet leaves off the windshield. "I just wish I knew how Ondine found out about the snake."

"What about the snake?" Sheila asked, and I told her about the rattlesnake tattoo on Jacoby's neck.

"Ruby didn't tell her?"

"Ruby doesn't know." Wearily, I opened the door and got in. "I've had enough excitement for one night. I've got to collect Brian and head for home."

Sheila put her hand on the door to keep me from closing it. Her gray eyes were serious. "I don't for a minute believe that there's a dime's worth of truth in any of Ondine's pronouncements, but—" She stopped. "I suppose you've got a gun."

I rolled down the window. "McQuaid left me enough firepower to defend the Alamo, if I wanted to use it. We'll be safe."

"Of course," Sheila said. "You can take care of yourselves." She bent over to look at me through the window. "You and Brian must really rattle around in that big old house out there. How many bedrooms did you say it has?"

"Five." I put the key in the ignition and turned it. "It's almost nine," I said. "I need to get home."

"I've got an idea," Sheila said. "I'm not doing anything

evenings for the next few days. Why don't you invite me out until McQuaid gets back? You know, sort of an extended sleepover. Just the two of us and Brian."

I squinted up at her, silhouetted against the last of the light. "Do you have any idea what you're letting yourself in for? Eleven-year-olds are beastly, not to mention their pets. This one has a bassett hound, an iguana, and a tarantula — at least. Lord only knows what else is lurking at the back of his closet."

"Sounds like my kid brother." Sheila grinned. "Mice in his pockets and lizards up his sleeve. I'll just zip on home and get my toothbrush and something to wear to work tomorrow, then stop at the liquor store and pick up a jug of wine. While McQuaid's away, the girls will play, huh? What'd'ya say?"

I grinned. "I'd say you're one smart cookie."

CHAPTER TEN

I have presented to view divers forms or plots for
Gardens, amongst which it is possible you may find
some that may near the matter fit, and shall leave
the ingenious Practitioner to their consideration and
use.

Leonard Meager
*The English Gardener: Or, a Sure
Guide to Young Planters & Gardeners, 1688*

The storm that had shot a bolt of lightning down Ruby's
chimney and destroyed her garage seemed to have been
whimsically aimed at her block. I didn't see any other
damage as I drove home, and Arnold's mother reported
that it had rained there for only a few minutes. Texas
thunderstorms are like that: half of Adams county can be
floating away while the other half is on its knees praying
for rain. Still, it was an odd coincidence that the storm
had been so narrowly concentrated, at the exact moment
Ondine was doing her thing.

The stars were out and a sliver of moon was showing
in the eastern sky when we got home. It had rained just
hard enough to erase the tire marks we'd left when we
drove out, and the headlights revealed no footprints or
tire marks in the drive. Still, I was cautious when I pulled
up in front of the dark house. It didn't take a warning
from La Que Sabe and a bolt out of the blue to make me
wish that we had installed a security light. The house *is*

isolated. The closest neighbors live on the other side of the ridge, and the lane leading from the county road to the house is a quarter mile long. Nice when you want privacy, a little unsettling if you're concerned about security.

"What are we waiting for?" Brian asked.

"Nothing." There was a misshapen shadow under the willow tree. I opened the glove box, fished out a flashlight, and shined it on Howard Cosell, grumpily aroused and resentful that he hadn't been let in to sleep behind the sofa, away from the fire ants. He lay back down, scorning to bark. So much for our trusty watchdog.

Brian turned to face me, his child's face a blurry triangle in the dark. "You're not *really* afraid of that guy with the tattoo snake, are you?"

"Absolutely not," I said firmly. "Lock the door behind me and wait in the car until I call you."

It took a few minutes to search the house, but I felt better when it was done. I had just finished checking the answering machine when Smart Cookie showed up with her clothes and the wine. We were in the kitchen when the phone rang. I grabbed for it, thinking it was Mc-Quaid.

"I just wanted to see that you got home okay," Ruby said.

"Thanks for worrying," I said.

Ruby hesitated. "Uh, China, I know it's hard for you to believe this stuff. But I really think you should take Ondine seriously."

"Maybe so," I said. I was remembering Lyle Biggs and his vision of a grave in a muddy field. And Peggy Simmons and Samuel, and the woman who had been stabbed to death by her boyfriend. The police hadn't taken them seriously—in the beginning. When it was all over, they did.

"Well, that's all I have to say," Ruby said, and hung up. I had just put the phone down when it rang again.

"Everything okay?" McQuaid asked. "Any messages for me?"

"Everything's okay," I said. I reported my conversations with Matt and Bubba (leaving out the bit about Jacoby and the knifing in New Braufels). I added the message I'd picked up from the answering machine. "Bubba says that the Brownsville police matched Clark's prints with those in the car. They apparently didn't get them off the steering wheel or the stick shift, though. He said they came from the door."

"The stick was grooved," McQuaid said, "and the wheel had a pebble vinyl cover. Neither would have taken a print." He sighed wearily. "I guess that cinches it, China. Clark's our man. That's not the name he used coming through Immigration, though."

"He must have false documents," I said. *The wrong man.* Could La Que Sabe be confused because Jeff had assumed a different name? I stopped myself. That was ridiculous. I was acting as though Ondine knew what she was talking about.

"You can get papers in Brownsville as easy as you can get a beer." He was silent for a minute, and I could picture him pulling at his lip and scowling. "I never would've believed it of him, though."

The wrong man. The prints on the gun and the prints on the car were indisputably Jeff's. What did Ondine know that we didn't? But I couldn't tell McQuaid what she had said. He'd never believe it. I didn't believe it myself—did I?

"What's on your agenda for tomorrow?" I asked, keeping my voice level.

"Checking around. Car rentals, hotels, bars, et cetera." He sounded dispirited and very tired. He gave me the telephone number of the hotel where he was staying. "If you turn up anything I need to know, leave it with the desk. I'll phone the hotel periodically to check for messages."

Maybe La Que Sabe ought to get in touch with McQuaid directly, instead of through me. I pushed aside this slightly crazy thought, and said instead, "You want me to give this number to Matt?"

"I'd rather channel everything through you. Makes for less confusion. You and Brian will be at the shop tomorrow?"

"That's the plan," I replied slowly.

McQuaid's chuckle was sympathetic. "Kid giving you a hard time, honey?"

"No," I said, "Brian's okay. It's just that—"

It was just that my old instincts were kicking in. Whether he was the right man or the wrong man, Jeff needed a lawyer *now*. He needed somebody to file a petition requiring the prosecution to turn over any exculpatory evidence the police had uncovered. He needed somebody to canvass Rosemary's neighborhood and dig up anything that might suggest other suspects. He needed somebody to start building alternative theories of the case that might be used in court.

I wasn't Jeff's lawyer. But if it weren't for Brian, I wouldn't go to the shop tomorrow. I'd start digging, and when McQuaid brought Jeff back and he hired a lawyer, I'd turn over any information I had found. But I'd promised to take Brian, and I wasn't going back on my word.

"It's just that you don't want to go to the shop tomorrow?" McQuaid asked.

"How'd you know?"

He chuckled. "I'm psychic. Are you thinking of taking off for the day to look into this business?"

"Well, yes," I admitted. "But I'm responsible for Brian."

"I hope you take that responsibility seriously," he said. "Jacoby is a snake."

I shivered. *The child is in peril. You have much to fear.* "I do take it seriously," I said.

"I wish I were home."

"I do, too." I laughed a little, teasing. "But I'm afraid I have to settle for Sheila."

"Say again?"

"She's moved in for a few days," I explained. "To help me defend the home front."

"Not a bad idea," McQuaid replied. We said a lingering good night. I put the phone down reluctantly, thinking of the way his eyes looked when he wanted me, the way his mouth felt on mine when he kissed me, the way . . .

I shook myself, went to the kitchen, and pulled out some cold chicken for sandwiches. Brian took one and went upstairs to bed, having wrangled my promise to make pancakes for breakfast. Sheila put together a salad, and we made a night of it, drinking and talking at the kitchen table until well after midnight.

The wine and late supper that had seemed like such a good idea on Tuesday night felt like a very bad one on Wednesday morning. I woke with a headache at seven, pulled on denim cutoffs, and groped my way to the kitchen. I brewed a pot of strong peppermint tea and was into my second cup when Sheila came downstairs, wearing a chic black suit with a white blouse and pearls. She looked gorgeously anorexic, irritatingly businesslike, and insufferably alert.

"God," I groaned, "I can't stand to look at you."

"It's not my fault," she said apologetically. "It's my metabolism. I'm one of those people who function well in the mornings." She flicked back her smooth ash blond hair. "I meet with the campus patrol unit at eight sharp every Wednesday morning."

"I'll bet they love you for it," I said. "The bananas are on top of the refrigerator." I paused while she found them. "I've been thinking about Curtis Robbins."

"What about him?" She poured Grapenuts into a bowl.

"If Jeff Clark didn't do it—"

"Don't tell me you're buying that bullfeathers we heard last night. Where do you keep the knives?"

"Top drawer on the left." I paused. "I'm just considering other theories that might fit the facts. How thoroughly did Bubba check out Robbins's alibi?"

She sliced banana on top of the cereal. "He interviewed the sister."

"What else did he do? Did he talk to the sister's neighbors? Did he check out Robbins's movements? What about other suspects? Did he talk to people who knew Rosemary to see if she had any enemies? A former client, maybe, who had a grudge?"

Sheila poured milk on her cereal. "I don't think he spent a lot of time on the ex-husband. The gun turned up, and he dropped Robbins in favor of Clark. The PSPD doesn't have a lot of extra manpower, you know." She perched on a stool and began to eat. "Why are you asking?"

"Does anybody know whether Robbins knew Jeff Clark?" I poured her tea and pushed the honey jar down the counter where she could reach it. "Lily Box saw Robbins at the hotel, and Rosemary claimed he was there to see her. But what if he came to see Clark, not Rosemary? What if he was in Clark's office, alone, and happened to see Big Chuck's gun in the case? What if—"

I was stopped by the ringing of the telephone. Still engaged with what if's, I answered tersely. But I was jolted into sudden awareness by a man's hard, raspy voice.

"I got a message for yer ol' man, Miz McQuaid."

"I'm not Mrs. McQuaid," I said. "I'm—"

The voice sliced me off, sharp as high-carbon steel. "I don' give a shit who you are, sugar. You live with the bastard, don' you? You tell that motherfucker I'm gonna get that kid of his."

My fingers tightened on the receiver. "Who is this?" I whispered. But it wasn't a real question. I knew.

His chuckle was harshly sardonic. "Ain't he tol' you 'bout his ol' buddy, the jailbird? Well, it don' matter none. He'll know who I am. You hang 'round the phone, baby, at home an' at that cutesy little store of yours. I'm gonna wanna hear yer sweet voice again. You tell him now, you mind?" The connection was broken.

"China!" Sheila stood, staring. "Was that—?"

I was clenching the phone. Carefully, so my hands didn't shake, I replaced it in the cradle. "The man with the snake." My stomach was churning. I felt sick.

"Hey," Brian said from the doorway, "where's my pancakes?"

CHAPTER ELEVEN

Out of this nettle, danger, we pluck this flower, safety.

William Shakespeare
Henry IV, Part I

"Brian might not even be safe at the shop," Sheila said, after I'd sent the boy upstairs to get dressed and related Jacoby's threat. "The guy sounds dangerous."

"I don't have a lot of options," I said, getting out the pancake mix. We have scratch pancakes on weekends; today was the utility version. I thought about the woman Jacoby had knifed in New Braunfels, and shivered.

Sheila took her bowl to the sink and rinsed it out. "How about if I take Brian to the campus? I can't do it tomorrow, because I have to go to Austin. But today would be fine."

"I can't ask you to take the responsibility." I added milk to the mix, broke in an egg, and began to beat it as if I were whipping up on Jake Jacoby. We might be in the middle of a crisis, but there would be pancakes.

"Why can't you?" She grinned. "If the kid gets in my face, I'll stick him with Maxine Marney, one of our patrol officers. She's a weight-lifting champion. Brian steps out of line, Maxine will settle his hash. And pity poor Jacoby, if he tries to muscle in on her territory. She's probably more dangerous than he is."

Maxine Marney had given me a ticket *and* a lecture

when I'd failed to yield to a pedestrian on a campus street. I still remembered those steely eyes. "That might work," I said.

She went to the door and raised her voice. "Get into those clothes on the double, kid. You're going to the campus cop shop."

I heard a muffled "Oh, boy!" I wiped my hands on my cutoffs and gave her a grateful look. "I don't know how to —"

"Then don't." She paused, watching me, hands on her slender hips. "Maybe you ought to blow off the shop today, too, China. If Jacoby can't get Brian, he might settle for you." She shook her head, frowning. "But if Jacoby killed Rosemary, how come Jeff Clark's prints were on the gun?"

"It's a mystery to me," I said, pouring puddles of batter onto the hot skillet. "Actually, I was thinking of letting Laurel handle the shop today. Somebody ought to check Robbins out, and his sister, too. I also thought of going up to the Springs to talk to Lily."

Sheila's mouth quirked. "You can't leave it to the cops, can you?"

"I *have* left it to the cops," I replied, and reached in the drawer for the pancake turner. "But it won't hurt to sniff around a little and see if they missed something."

After Brian finished eating, he bounced out to Sheila's car and they drove off. I called Laurel and asked her to take charge of the shop. It was a good time to take off for a day or two, with the herb conference over and the air conditioner problem solved. Then, with Jacoby's threat still ringing in my ears, I phoned the Adams County sheriff's office.

I've met my share of law enforcement people, but Sheriff Blackie Blackwell gets all the gold stars. He's intelligent and careful and he never reacts without thinking, not even when the pot's up to five bucks and he's holding a handful of aces. His father was sheriff here for something like a quarter century, so Blackie knows every inch of the county. Of course, things have changed from the days when Corky Blackwell tracked down sheep stealers and goat rustlers and Reba Blackwell cooked for the prisoners in the county jail. Blackie has drugs to deal with, and hot car rings, and undocumented aliens, and worse. But nothing gets to him. He's somebody you can depend on.

I told him about Jacoby's phone call. "Sheila Dawson is staying with us at night," I added. "She took Brian to spend the day at Campus Security. I think we've got the bases covered for today, at least, but I wanted you to know about the call." Making a threat with the intent to place any person in fear of imminent serious bodily injury is a class B misdemeanor, and a violation of the terms of Jacoby's release. Even without that business with the knife in the New Braunfels saloon, it was enough to land him back in jail.

"Thanks," Blackie said, in his flat, laconic drawl. He doesn't spare words. "Let me know when you get home this evening. And tell McQuaid we'll handle things at this end."

"Mm-m-m," I said noncommittally. I'd already decided not to tell McQuaid about Jacoby's call, just as I hadn't told him about the knifing. It would only worry him, and he couldn't do anything. I paused. Rosemary's murder investigation was Bubba's business, but Blackie is the law throughout the county. He'd know the details of the case. "Do you know how thoroughly the PSPD checked out Curtis Robbins's alibi?" I asked.

Blackie tch-tched. "You're not sticking your nose into *that?*"

"McQuaid asked me to ask," I lied.

"They checked with the sister and that was it. They got on Clark pretty early in the game."

"But the gun—the lead to Clark—wasn't found until Sunday night," I argued. "I discovered the body Thursday morning. Thursday through Sunday—that's more than seventy-two hours. The police had plenty of time to take a hard look at Robbins."

"Harris got onto Clark before the gun was found. Some woman phoned in a tip on Friday. Wouldn't leave her name. Claimed that the victim and Clark were romantically involved. Said she thought he had a reason to kill her."

My skin prickled. A woman? Lily Box, maybe? Not likely—she was convinced that Robbins was the killer. Who? "So they let up on Robbins at that point?"

"They only have so much manpower," Blackie said. "I offered a couple of deputies, but Bubba likes to run his own shop." The more likely truth is that Bubba considers Blackie his junior. There may be a fraternity of cops, but there's also a seniority.

"Do you have a name and address for Robbins's sister?" I asked.

Blackie chuckled. "Inquisitive fella, McQuaid. Wants to know every little thing."

"That's him," I said. "Nosy."

It took Blackie a minute to come up with the name, Louise Daniels, and the address, 1412 Pecan Street, in San Marcos. He added another caution.

"You watch out for Jacoby, now, you hear? That man's mean enough to steal his mama's egg money."

"I will," I said. I thanked him and hung up, thinking

how good it is to have friends. Blackie, Sheila, Ruby, Laurel. You might even count Ondine and La Que Sabe. How do people function when they have to face life alone?

It was time to make myself respectable. I went upstairs and pulled on beige slacks, a white blouse, and a pale linen jacket. Thinking about Smart Cookie, I added a strand of pearls and a gold bracelet. Too bad I couldn't do something about my hands. No amount of lotion helps, not even comfrey salve. I was back downstairs, checking my purse for car keys and money, when there was a loud rap at the door. Then another, and then the insistent ringing of the doorbell.

I froze. Jacoby? My glance went to the hallway closet, where McQuaid's shotgun was stashed behind the raincoats. I hesitated for a moment, then tiptoed to the door and peered out through the peephole. A yellow Toyota was parked in the drive, and a short, heavyset woman stood on the porch, shifting uneasily from one foot to the other. Her dirty-blond hair was crimped back with a plastic comb, her lipstick had been liberally and hastily applied, and she was dressed in an ill-fitting brownish green suit with half-moons of fresh sweat under the arms. I didn't recognize her, but I was reasonably sure she wasn't Jake Jacoby in drag.

I put the door on the chain and opened it. She was holding a thick white envelope whose size and shape I recognized. It was a summons, and the woman was a process server.

"I'm looking for Michael R. McQuaid," she said. Her voice was thin and high-pitched, with the unmistakable overtones of far West Texas. "He here?"

"He's out of the country on business," I said.

She pulled a white hanky out of her purse and blotted

her glossy forehead. "That's always the way on hot days. Hunderd an' one this afternoon, an' the AC in my car ain't worth spit." She eyed me. "You his wife?"

"No," I said. I took the chain off and opened the door. "I'm his lawyer."

"Lawyer, huh?" She pursed her lipsticked mouth. "Since when do lawyers make housecalls?" She was vastly amused by her small joke. "So when do you figger he'll be back?"

"I'm not sure," I said. I glanced at the envelope. So far as I knew, the only legal business McQuaid was involved in also involved Sally and Brian. There was no reason for me to prevaricate. "If this involves a custody action, he intends to cooperate. May I see the summons, so I can let him know the date and the particulars?"

"We-ll . . ." The woman drew it out with the air of someone who has already heard too many versions of this response.

"Look," I said, "it's too hot for you to keep driving up here from San Antonio. The minute Mr. McQuaid returns, he'll call you. In the meantime, I can at least calendar the action."

After another moment's hesitation, she handed me the papers, which were exactly what I expected: Notice of Action filed by Sally Jean McQuaid versus Michael Robert McQuaid, Managing Conservator, *in re* the Custody of Minor Child Brian Paul McQuaid for the Purpose of Modifying Original Custody Order under Section 14.08 of the Texas Family Code, to be Heard in the Court of blah blah blah.

"Thank you," I said, handing the papers back. "May I have your card?"

She dug for it. "You gonna be talkin' to Mr. McQuaid on the phone? You'll tell him I was here?"

"Of course," I lied. This made how many things I wasn't telling him? I'd lost count.

Miller's Gun and Sporting Goods is one of those hybrid places you sometimes find in small towns that are outgrowing their old ways but haven't yet totally grown into new ones. It's located on LBJ Boulevard, on the border, so to speak, between old and new Pecan Springs, between the original town and the campus. It caters to both the sportsman and the jock, which isn't as easy as you might think.

The store suffers from a split personality. The front half has been remodeled in the last few years: new tile floor, a lowered ceiling, recessed lighting. The plastic shelves and chrome racks are stocked with goodies for students with pockets full of their parents' money: Nikes and Reeboks, roller blades, weight-lifting equipment and racing bikes and jogging shorts, scuba gear, even a line of ski clothes that will make you the sexiest snow bunny in Aspen.

As you go farther into the store, however, you come to a middle section that has the feel of the seventies, sixties, even the fifties. The floor here is linoleum, there are bare fluorescent fixtures in the water-stained ceiling, and you're surrounded by racks of bowling balls and canoe paddles and wooden shelves stocked with kerosene lanterns, Coleman stoves, enamelware coffeepots, and cast-iron dutch ovens.

And if you venture to the very back of the store — a cavernous place where the walls are red brick, the floor is scuffed pine, and the lights are bare hanging bulbs with factory-style reflectors — you'll find what the *real* Texan needs to conquer the wilderness: rods and lures and minnow buckets and stringers and crawdad nets; collapsible deer stands, camouflage shirts and pants and ponchos; racks of shotguns, rifles, and handguns.

And ammunition. Miller's is the only place left in Adams County where a rancher who wants a dozen of this and half a dozen of that doesn't have to buy a full box of either. He can fill up the pockets of his ammo vest or the loops of his bandolier with number four buckshot cartridges to take a deer, or regular number four if he wants to stop by the tank at sunset and pick off a few ducks, or number eight for dove or quail along the road, or number two if he's after coyote. Somewhere on the sagging wooden shelves he might even find cartridges for a .45-70 buffalo gun, or an open box of ten-gauge cardboard-hulled shotgun shells, which haven't been available for a couple of decades. And out back, in a ramshackle building adjoining the store, he'll find an old-time gunsmith named Frank Getzendaner who'll put a telescopic sight on his rifle, sporterize his father's 8mm Mauser war relic, or put a custom hand grip on his revolver.

This is what McQuaid tells me, anyway. And as I remembered all this, it crossed my mind to wonder whether that gunsmith was the one who had customized the grip of Big Chuck's .38, and whether there was any connection between that gun and the manager of Miller's.

Curtis Robbins was ringing up an assortment of bass lures, and I got in line. He was a darkly handsome, narrow-hipped man whose jeans looked very good on him: the kind of man who makes some women want to check their lipstick and perfume. He was wearing a red polo shirt with the store's name embroidered on the pocket. Its open collar displayed a luxuriant tangle of black chest hair, and the backs of his hands were furry. At his belt hung the emblems of his trade: a heavy ring of keys and a tape measure. He laughed and talked with the customer, trading fishing stories with an easy macho camaraderie, and I could see why men thought he was a regular guy. But beneath the smile and the dark good looks, there was a suppressed nervous energy that made his movements almost jerky, as if he were holding himself in check. I watched closely, looking for signs of the domestic bully. Was this the kind of man who could beat up his wife, stalk her, and end by murdering her?

My turn. "Mornin', ma'am," he said softly. He flashed a smile, and I wondered how many women dropped into the sporting goods store just to see that smile, receive that soft greeting. "What can I get for you?"

"I want to talk to you about your wife's murder," I said. His jaw hardened, and I held his gaze, not letting it slide away. "I was the one who found her body."

He looked at me for a long moment, his jaw working. Then he jerked his head toward a half-open door in the wall behind the counter. "Let's go in there." Eyes still on me, he raised his voice to a curly-haired teenage girl in an off-the-shoulder white blouse and flounced denim skirt who was rearranging a shelf of sweats.

"I'm takin' fifteen, Julie. Cover the register. Gimme a holler if you get backed up."

The office was windowless and hot and smelled of stale cigarette smoke, but Robbins shut the door anyway. He punched a button on a floor fan, which began to churn the warm air sluggishly around my ankles, not cooling it appreciably. He motioned me to a Naugahyde uphol-stered chair against the wall, under a girlie calendar that displayed the substantial endowments of auburn-haired Miss July, who was wearing a red, white, and blue top hat and very little else. Robbins dropped into an ancient wooden desk chair and tilted it back. The office was hot enough to make me want to take off my linen jacket, but

I decided against it. Robbins might take it wrong.

"Rosie was my *ex*-wife," he said tonelessly. "We got divorced in March." He reached into his shirt pocket and took out a pack of Camels. "So you found her body? What do you want?"

"My name is China Bayles," I said. "I'm a lawyer. My partner, Mike McQuaid, is working for Matt Monroe. Mr. Monroe is concerned about allegations of his partner's involvement in your ex-wife's death. We are co-operating with the police in this matter." Having already dished up a couple of outright lies this morning, this equivocation came easily. I am a lawyer, having kept my Bar Association membership current. McQuaid is my partner, so to speak, and he's definitely cooperating with the police. Matt Monroe is McQuaid's client, and he's worried about his partner, Jeff Clark.

He lit his Camel with a cheap plastic lighter, puffing on it as if it were a cigar. "Yeah, I know McQuaid. Ex-cop, isn't he? He special orders reloading supplies here." He sat back and thought for a moment, obviously working it out. Then he said, with an attempt at carelessness, "So Matt doesn't think Clark did it, huh? He's hired you and McQuaid to hunt up another suspect, and you've landed on me."

"The police questioned you about your alibi, I understand."

"Sure, but it didn't get them anywhere. That ol' dog just ain't gonna hunt, Ms. Bayles." Still leaning back, he gave me an aggressively confident look. "I loved Rosie, in spite of her. I didn't kill her. You're wasting your time trying to pin it on me."

"How long were you and your wife married?"

He blew out a cloud of foul-smelling smoke. The tiny office was filling up with a blue haze, the upper layer filtering the light, the lower layer slightly stirred by the fan. "Five years, all told, including about six months when we were separated."

"Children?"

He shook his head. "I would've, but Rosie was against it. She even got an abortion a couple of years ago, without saying a word to me." His laugh was off-key. "The way the law is now, a woman can murder a man's baby and there's not a damn thing he can do about it."

I stared at him, feeling his hurt. Three weeks before she died, she was pregnant. At the time of her death, she wasn't. Maybe Ruby was right. Maybe abortion had been a motive for murder.

"Why didn't she want a child?" I asked, more gently.

He turned his lighter in his fingers. "Too busy to be bothered, I guess. She was never happy unless she was working. Used to drive me nuts. Not that I don't like my job, but I sure as hell don't live it fourteen, sixteen hours a day the way she did, twenty during tax season. She had something to prove, and babies would only get in the way." His hands twitched. They were big hands, the backs matted with heavy, dark hair. "At least that's how it was when she was married to me. But apparently she changed." His tone was matter-of-fact, but beneath it there was a deep hurt, and a deeper anger.

"What makes you say that?"

The words sounded as if they were wrenched out of him. "Because she was pregnant and she aimed to keep it."

"She told you that?"

"Hell, she threw it up to me. Said I'd never treated her like a woman, so she'd refused to give me the one thing that would make me feel like a man. So now she's got some other poor bastard in love with her, and she's telling me she's dying to have his kid." Each word lay the wound open wider so I could see into his heart. I could understand his bitterness, his anguish, but I wasn't sure that his picture of Rosemary was an accurate picture. Perhaps it had been his violence that had made her refuse to have his child, and she had poured herself into work to escape him. Perhaps her refusal, and her escape, had fueled his violence.

I gave him a straight-on look. "That sounds like a motive for murder."

"You bet it does." He leaned forward intently. His eyes were the eyes of a man who had carried a heavy burden for a very long time and knew he could never put it down. "I hated her enough to kill her. Came near to it. Why I didn't, lord only knows. But I didn't. Somebody else did."

"Who, then?"

He shrugged. "The police figure it was Clark. That's how come they laid off me. She was carryin' his kid, or so she said. She was killed with his daddy's gun. And now he's in Mexico. A man doesn't run if he doesn't have something to hide."

I tried a different tack. "Suppose Jeff Clark didn't kill her, Mr. Robbins. Suppose you were asked to name others—clients, acquaintances, neighbors—who might have had a grudge against her. What would you say? Where would you tell me to look, if I were looking for her killer?"

I thought for a moment he would blow off the question. He pulled on his cigarette, then stubbed it out in an overflowing ashtray. When he looked up, he'd decided to give me an answer. It was hard to tell whether he was being straight or trying to throw me off the track.

"Well, first off, you maybe ought to dig around some up at the hotel. The bookkeeper there had the hots for

Clark. She was pretty pissed when Rosemary snatched him away from her. A regular Peyton Place, that hotel."

"The bookkeeper's name?"

"Carol something. Ask Julie, out front. She's the one who told me." His mouth twisted into a bitter smile. "Rosie sure could pick 'em."

"Anybody else?"

"Yeah, now that you mention it. Look up Howie Rhodes, over in San Marcos. Real estate broker—deals in commercial land, mostly, some residential. Rosie did his books for a couple of years. The business seemed straight enough in the beginning, but when she got into it, she said things didn't look right. There was a lot of unexplained cash, and some pretty slick laundering going on. She began to think Rhodes was dealing." He paused and flicked the cigarette lighter, staring at the flame, then flicked it again.

"So? What happened?"

He pocketed the lighter. "Rosie told him she was going to quit unless he documented what was bothering her. She wanted more money, too. She felt like she was taking a big risk if she stayed on the account. She thought the IRS might be looking at him, you see. If they tagged him, they'd come after her, too, and her other clients. That's how they keep tax accountants in line." He shook his head. "You've got to give it to Rosie. She would never let herself be blindsided. Not even by somebody she was sleeping with."

I picked up on it, as he expected. "Did she often sleep with her clients?"

He flexed his fingers, opening and closing his fist. "Far as I was concerned, what she did on the side was her business. She didn't tell me. She never told me anything. She was a very private person."

I looked at Robbins, speculating about how much it would take to make this particular man turn violent. One lover, two, three? Another man's baby, when his wife had refused to have his?

"How long ago was this business with Rhodes?" I asked.

"Three years, maybe. She dropped the account when he wouldn't come clean. Sure enough, not two months later the Feds busted the guy. He pleaded, and got two years at the federal prison over by Bastrop. It made Rosie nervous. She was afraid Rhodes thought she'd turned him in. Whistle blowers get a cut, you know."

"Did she turn him in?"

"She may have. Who knows? I never checked her bank balance." He sat forward in his chair, earnest, candid. "Look. Rosie and I didn't get along, and I probably got mad and pushed her around a little too hard. But I didn't have anything to do with her death, and that's God's truth. You want to dig up some real dirt, go poke around that hotel, talk to the bookkeeper. Or flush Rhodes — he's probably out of prison by now. Either of them had more reason to want her dead than I did." The muscle in his jaw was knotted, and I had a sense of the control he was exerting over his feelings. Grief, was it, or anger, that he was trying to keep a lid on?

"One more question," I said. "How well do you know Jeff Clark?"

His lips thinned. "Clark? I don't know the man. Oh, I've seen him at Chamber meetings, and we worked the beer booth at the Pecan Festival last year. But that's the extent of it. I should buddy up to a guy who's screwing my ex-wife?"

"You haven't visited him in his office?"

He shook his head, then chuckled dryly. "I have been

up at that hotel, though. Maybe that's what you're thinking of. I took the final papers to Rosie the day the divorce
went through." That sour mouth again. "She couldn't be
bothered to go to the hearing."

And that was it. I thanked him, and we stepped out of
the smoky office. From Julie, the girl in the off-the-
shoulder white blouse, I learned that the bookkeeper who
had the hots for Jeff Clark was named Carol Connally,
and that she rented the apartment next door to Julie's
mother. Julie had walked in on a conversation one evening between Connally and her mother. Connally was
hysterical because Clark had thrown her over for Rosemary.

"Really. You'd think somebody her age would be too
old for things like that," Julie said, disapproving. She
touched a zit on her pretty, dimpled chin.

"Things like what?"

"Oh, you know. Falling in love with the boss."

"How old is Miss Connally?" I asked.

Julie rearranged the ruffles on her blouse to expose a
half inch more of tanned shoulder, seductively sliced by
the pale shadow of a swimsuit strap. She slid a moony
glance in the direction of Curtis Robbins, who was dem-
onstrating the merit of a particular tennis racket to a
pretty blond woman in the middle of the store.

"Oh, all of thirty-five," she said.

It was time I was going.

CHAPTER TWELVE

To learn humility, one must weed the Thymes.
Folk saying

Now I had two reasons to make the half-hour trip to San Marcos: to check out Robbins's alibi and to look up a real estate broker named Howie Rhodes. I accomplished the first in less than thirty minutes by the simple expedient of knocking at 1413 Pecan, across the street from Robbins's sister's house. The door was opened by a tall woman wearing three-inch heels and a black and white vertically striped jumpsuit that drew the eye up and up and up — to the Biggest Hair I'd ever seen.

To appreciate Big Hair, you have to live in Texas, which is indisputably the Big Hair capital of the civilized world. This fact was documented not long ago by the *Wall Street Journal,* which reported that something like sixty percent of Dallas women over twenty-five refuse to have any truck with stylists who won't replicate the "Dallas-do." According to legend, this towering scaffold of hair was created when one strike-it-rich Dallas socialite wanted a special hairdo in honor of the oil rig on her ranch. There's also Lubbocks's Dairy-Queen-do — outrageously loose, poufy hair twisted around and around like the swirl of a custard cone; San Antonio's derring-do, hair that's been teased and tousled and moussed until it's reckless and rash and ready to rare up on its hind legs; and of course, the dazzling let's-all-do-it bouffant of our white-haired once and former Governor Ann Richards.

Big Hair may trace its illustrious roots to Madame de Pompadour, or in more recent eras, to the smoothly back-combed pouf of the young Jacqueline Kennedy or the crowning glory of born-Texan Farrah Fawcett. But if you ask me, the greatest Big Hair of all is found on top of the women of rural Texas, who do it in garage and dining room beauty parlors with names like Hilda's Hair Hut or Rae Lee's Beauty Boudoir. They don't get their hair pou-fed and pedestaled to please their men. They do it to flip a ladylike bird to Vidal's latest Sassoon bobbsies and Di-ane Sawyer look-alikes, to assert with pride that they are who they are and that's that, thank you very much.

The woman who answered the door had that look. She was already tall, maybe five foot ten or eleven in her heels, and her height was further exaggerated by the vertical black stripes on her white jumpsuit—and her hennaed hair, which towered a foot and a half above her forehead like a Valkyrie's helmet. The total came to something more than seven feet, which for me amounts to a severe crick in the neck. I lowered my gaze to her brown eyes, which were amused.

She leaned against the door jamb. "Yeah? Whaddya want?"

"I wonder," I said, and stopped. I tried again, but couldn't seem to find my voice.

"Look, honey," she said in a kindly tone, "I know my hair is bigger'n a tumbleweed, that I'm a walkin', talkin' beehive, an' when anybody loses anything, the first place they're gonna look is in my hair." She straightened. "Does that about cover it?"

I gave her do one more appreciative glance. "Actually,"

I said, "I was thinking more along the lines of the Towering Inferno. With that color, I mean: red gold, copper highlights. Awesome."

"I like that," she said, approving. "The Towering Inferno. I really, *really* like that." She stepped back, held the door open. "You wanna come in? I gotta go to work in a half hour, but you can tell DeAnne what you said. DeAnne's my cousin. She does it up for me." She glanced at my hair, which was straight as a string and damp with sweat, and compassion softened her mouth. "She'll be glad to do yours, too, honey. She ain't proud."

DeAnne was substantial. She balanced the weight of her buttocks and breasts with a head of golden Big Hair that looked suspiciously like a Dolly Parton wig. In fact, looking closer, I could see a wisp of black hair escaping just forward of her ears, and her bleached eyebrows were dark at the roots. But fake hair or not, DeAnne's sense of humor was every bit as generous as her cousin's, whose name turned out to be Jonelle. I introduced myself, and we adjourned to the kitchen, where Jonelle turned off the sound on a small television that was tuned to a game show, and offered me a doughnut and Folger's instant in a mug that said "Don't Sweat the Small Stuff" on one side and "It's All Small Stuff" on the other.

DeAnne took a refill on her coffee and gave my hair a long, pitying look. "You really *oughta* do something," she said, shaking her head. "That gray streak down the side don't look too bad now, but you're gonna get gray all over, and then where'll you be? Old before your time, that's where." A chuckle bubbled up like champagne out of her ample chest. "Pretty thing like you, honey, you don't wanna get old."

Jonelle gave my hair a critical look. "What color would you say it oughtta be, DeAnne?"

DeAnne scrunched up her mouth and held her head on one side, considering. "I'd say chestnut. Deep chestnut with red gold highlights." She patted my hand. "Bet you've got a man that'll love you chestnut."

Jonelle wasn't convinced. She reached out and fingered my hair in a kindly way, apparently not as sanguine about the solution as DeAnne. "Well, I'll tell you, DeAnne. If this hair was on my head, I'd go to Wilda's Wig Shoppe and get Wilda to fix me up until I grew it out another oh, ten, twelve inches."

"You just may be right, sweetie." DeAnne, also examining my hair, was regretful. "There really ain't much to work with. Not yet, anyhoo. Gotta give it time."

Jonelle favored her cousin with a fond smile and spoke to me. "That's not to say that DeAnne can't fix you up right now, however bad off you are. I always say, when it comes to hair, she is a real Michaelangellinni. So much talent, you wouldn't believe. Give her your hair, and she'll whip it into shape like she was makin' a piece of art." She patted her wiry helmet proudly. "And it stays put, let me tell you, even when it rains. Even when I walk in front of the fan at the cafeteria." She made a face, as if she didn't like thinking about the cafeteria. "Luby's, over on the freeway. I used to work at the lunch counter at Woolworth's, until it closed last year."

DeAnne nodded. "Well, I for one surely do miss it." She reached delicately for another doughnut. "Since Woolworth's closed, I can't find a bottle of Evening in Paris anywhere."

"It isn't the same," Jonelle agreed sadly. "At Woolworth's, I could wear whatever I wanted, but Luby's makes all us girls wear white polyester uniforms and tennies. They don't like it if we try to be different."

I'd bet. But it was time to explain why I was there. I

glanced over my shoulder and lowered my voice, as if to be sure we weren't overheard. "I'm investigating a murder case in Pecan Springs," I said, "and I need some information."

Jonelle and DeAnne immediately forgot about Woolworth's.

"A murder case!" Jonelle breathed. "For real?"

DeAnne was scornful. "That itty bitty town? You're puttin' us on. Nothin' ever happens over there."

I raised my hand. "Swear to God," I pledged.

"I got it!" Jonelle snapped her fingers. "The woman who got killed in that truck out in front of her house." She appealed to me. "Shot, wasn't she?"

"Yes," I said.

"Drug deal, probably," DeAnne said sagely. "People are crazy for drugs these days."

Jonelle leaned forward, forehead furrowed, coppery eyebrows knitted together under her edifice of hennaed hair. Her voice was hushed. "Did Louise Daniels have anything to do with that murder?"

DeAnne stared at her. *"Louise?* Why I just did her hair last Monday!" She frowned. "No, it was Tuesday. It was the day the lightning came in and blew all my circuits. We had to go to her house to dry and comb out. It took us near an hour with that dinky hand dryer of hers. Louise has got a *lot* of hair."

I barged in as DeAnne paused for breath. "What makes you think Louise had anything to do with the murder, Jonelle?"

"Because I saw a Pecan Springs police car over there towards the end of the week." Jonelle tapped her lips with the orange-enameled tip of a finger and frowned at the Adams Funeral Home calendar hung over the wall phone. "Friday, maybe it was." She seemed to be counting days, ticking them off in the air. "Yeah, it was Friday morning, because you did me that afternoon, DeAnne. I wondered at the time why the police car was there, but I never ran into Louise accidental-like to ask, and I'm not the type to push myself into somebody's house and ask why the police are hangin' around."

DeAnne and Jonelle looked at me for an explanation of the police car.

"The police were questioning Ms. Daniels about her brother, Curtis Robbins," I said. "It was his ex-wife who was killed. On the night of the Fourth of July."

DeAnne's dark eyes grew big and round under her curly gold wig, and her eyebrows rose like the Golden Arches. "An alibi," she said, poking Jonelle's arm with a pointed burgandy fingernail. "They were asking her about his alibi, I'll bet. That's what they do on *Murder, She Wrote.* The cops always want to know somebody's alibi."

Jonelle pulled her arm a safe distance away. "Well, if that's all they wanted, they could've come to me. I'd've given him an alibi."

I looked at her. "You saw Curtis Robbins on the Fourth of July?"

"I sure as shootin' did," Jonelle said sunnily. "Him *and* his truck. He runs the sporting goods store over in Pecan Springs, and when he comes to see Louise, he always drives this truck that says Miller's Gun and Sporting Goods on the side. Well, the night of the Fourth, that truck was parked in front of my house. All night. Well, until midnight, anyway," she amended.

"You're sure of that?" I asked.

She gave me a disdainful look. "Would I lie? My boyfriend Freddy came over that night about seven, after his shift at Luby's. He's the cook there. He brought fried chicken and potato salad and banana cream pie so we could have ourselves a picnic out back and watch the fireworks when it got dark. Gladys and Ray came over from next door and brought watermelon, and we all took our folding chairs up to the roof of the garage and watched."

"What about the truck?" I asked.

"It was parked out in front of my house. That's why Freddy had to park in front of Mrs. Trower's."

"I sure hope Satan didn't take after him," DeAnne said darkly. "That Satan's a devil. Like it says in the Bible, waitin' to see who he can devour."

Jonelle turned to me to explain. "Mrs. Trower's got this big black rottweiler. He's real bad to nip at folks' trousers, so Freddy was kinda upset at having to park there. A coupla months ago, Satan took the seat out of his best polyester."

"How come Louise's brother didn't park in front of *her* house?" DeAnne wanted to know.

"Because Louise's car was parked there," Jonelle said. "It's been so dry the last couple months that her driveway cracked all to pieces. The concrete man came out last Wednesday and poured her a new slab and told her not to drive on it for a while. She says she's not going to take any chances. She's not *ever* going to drive on that slab, ever again." She shook her head. "I wouldn't either, if I had to pay what she paid that concrete man. Wouldn't be worth it, to me. I'd just live with the cracks."

"Maybe she thought she had to fix it," DeAnne said. "My sister-in-law's cousin Opal had bad cracks like that in her driveway and when she went to sell, the appraiser took off some ungodly amount of money, all on account of the driveway. Opal said if she'd of fixed it, she'd of got more for the house."

"Well, I suppose," Jonelle said judiciously. "But if you

ask me, there's a racket in there somewheres. Take Freddy, for instance. A couple years back, it hailed and the insurance man came out and told him to go ahead and get a new roof, and lo and behold, the roofer was the insurance man's brother-in-law. Course, it didn't bother Freddy too much, since the insurance company paid it."

"But that's how come insurance costs so much," DeAnne objected. I cleared my throat, feeling that we were about to get mired in health care, and God knows how long it would take to get us extricated from *that* one.

"How late was the Miller's truck parked in front of your house?" I asked Jonelle.

Jonelle took a large green plastic earring out of an ashtray and delicately inserted the ear wire into the lobe of her left ear. "Well, we watched the fireworks, and after that we went in and watched part of *Nightline.* But it was about people dying in Africa, so we stopped watching and necked for a while on the sofa and then Freddy went home. When I went out on the porch to tell him good-bye, Louise's brother was getting in the truck to drive it away. A little after midnight, maybe."

"How do you know it was Louise's brother?"

"A real detective, ain't you?" Jonelle said. "No stern untoned, so to speak." She slapped her backside with a horsey laugh, and DeAnne groaned. "Well, it was him, all right. Good-looking guy, dark-haired, fills out his jeans real nice. She introduced me to him once when he came over to fix her washing machine. You see, she'd tried to get the washing machine man to—"

"Does he visit his sister often?" I interposed hurriedly.

She gave the question some thought. "Well, no, now that you ask. Don't believe he does. Not evenings, anyway."

DeAnne was examining a hangnail on her little finger.

"Brothers don't, do they," she said, thoughtful. "Least-wise, mine doesn't. In fact, it's only on Thanksgiving and Christmas that he—"

"I'm afraid I really have to be going." I pushed my coffee cup away. "Thanks for your help."

DeAnne gave me a flamingo-pink plastic comb with "Hair by DeAnne" on one side and her phone number and address on the other. Jonelle accompanied me out onto the vine-shaded porch, dim and cool even though the midday temperature was well up into the nineties.

"It's been real nice talking to you," she said earnestly. "Some people are scornful of it, you know. Like when people from the college come into the cafeteria. They think if you've got big hair, you're a bimbo. They make tacky remarks right out where a person can hear."

"Maybe they're just jealous," I said. "Not everybody can have hair like yours."

"That's true," Jonelle said proudly. She touched a hand to her Big Hair. "That's 'cause they don't have DeAnne to do it up for them."

In my view, San Marcos isn't half as pretty as Pecan Springs, but you could probably find plenty of San Marcans who'd disagree. The town offers a river walk (you don't have to walk—you can also go tubing or canoeing), historical buildings, three golf courses, and an amusement park that features a spring-fed lake with glass-bottomed boats, mermaids, and Ralph the swimming pig, whose swine dive will knock your socks off. Some might be tempted to compare the old hotel behind the amusement park to The Springs Hotel, but I doubt that even Big Chuck, in his wildest dreams of Texas whoopee, would have imagined Ralph the swimming pig.

I pulled into an Exxon station and parked on the shady

side of the building, close to the pay phone. When I stepped out of the car, the dry, scorching air seemed to sear my flesh. It was almost too hot to breathe, and in spite of my dark sunglasses, the sun's laserlike glare, ricocheting off chrome and glass, was beginning to give me a headache. I dialed the shop first, and got Laurel.

"McQuaid called," she said. "He wanted to know if everything was all right with you and Brian." Her voice took on a slightly disapproving tone. "I said you'd just gone across the street."

After McQuaid's comment last night about taking my responsibility to Brian seriously, I hadn't wanted him to know I was playing hooky today—even if Brian was in good hands. But Laurel is a very straight-up person, without a devious bone in her body. She hates to lie.

"Did he leave a message?" I asked.

"He said he'd call back at three. He thinks he's onto something."

Onto something. Did that mean he'd caught up with Jeff? What would happen when he did?

"Have there been any other calls I need to know about?" I asked. "Matt Monroe, from the Springs? Chief Harris?"

"Nope, just McQuaid," Laurel said. "Things have been pretty slow in the store. I've been pulling weeds. Anyway, it's cooler outdoors."

"It's cooler outside than in? Isn't the air conditioner working?"

She made a disgusted noise. "It isn't. I hate to complain, but it's almost ninety in here. Customers come in and go right back out again."

"Call Harold," I said firmly. "Tell him he promised there wouldn't be a second time."

"I did. He sounded cranky, but he said he'd come over

this afternoon." She hesitated. "Listen, China, maybe we ought to call my cousin Emily. She took over my uncle's air-conditioning shop over in Lockhart after he died. I know she'd be glad to come."

"Let's see what Harold's got to say for himself first," I replied, and we said good-bye.

I paused and assessed what I'd learned that morning. Not much, when you come right down to it. But sometimes investigative work requires you to pull out the truth bit by tedious bit, like plucking grass out of a thick bed of thyme. Robbins's alibi was definitely holding, although I couldn't rule out the possibility that he had paid somebody to do the job. I once defended a tiny, fragile-looking woman who had hired a large, ugly hit man to do in her co-heir to a sizable chunk of money. On the day of the murder, she was sunning herself in Bermuda. I couldn't accept Robbins's claim to innocence just because he was in San Marcos the night Rosemary was killed. Come to think of it, how many brothers did I know — particularly good-looking ones — who spent entire evenings with their sisters? And it did seem odd that Robbins had done so on the very night his ex-wife was killed. On the other hand, it's impossible to prove a case like that unless the hired killer is caught and implicates his employer.

I glanced at my watch. Nearly noon. Brian and I needed to be back in the shop at three, when McQuaid called. The thought of Brian reminded me that I'd better check on him, and I dialed Campus Security. Sheila had gone over to Data Processing, but Brian was there. He'd just come back from patrol duty with Officer Williams, he informed me importantly, and he couldn't talk now because he had to leave right away to help Officer Marney rob the parking meters. I hung up with a chuckle.

Even if Jacoby could locate Brian, which I doubted, there was no way he was going to grab the boy away from Maximum Maxine. McQuaid could rest easy.

I flipped through the Yellow Pages, looking for the information I needed next. I found it, and went back to the bake-oven that was my car. I had rolled down the windows, but it was still hot enough to grill cheese on the front seat. I started the engine and flipped on the air-conditioning, which blasted me with hot air. Then I drove onto the street, made a rash left turn in front of a UPS truck, and pulled into the Taco Bell drive-thru. The total for my bean burrito and iced tea, including tax, came to one seventy-one. I pushed away the envious thought of McQuaid in Mexico City, no doubt dining on expense-account cabrito and flambéed plantains. This investigation, if that's what you want to call it, was on my nickel.

It took me ten minutes to find the address I was looking for, on Hopkins, close to Bugg Lane. The door sported a red sign that said Rhodes Real Estate — Helping You Find Your Place in the World in large white letters. By now, it was much too hot for slacks and much, *much* too hot for my linen jacket, which stuck to my sweaty back like Saran wrap in a microwave. But I left it on because the blouse underneath was wringing wet and I hadn't worn a bra. A minute later, I was glad, because stepping into the real estate office was like stepping into an igloo. I pulled the damp jacket against me, trying to accustom myself to what felt like a blast from the arctic but which probably wasn't more than a twenty-degree temperature drop.

There were three gray metal desks in the narrow room, two to my right, both empty, and one ten paces in front of me, opposite the door I'd just entered. This one was occupied by a woman in her mid-twenties who was simultaneously talking into a telephone, consulting a card file, and checking something in a thick multiple-listing book. She threw me an I'll-get-to-you-in-a-minute smile and motioned toward a turquoise vinyl-covered chair beside a small table littered with real estate brochures. Behind the chair was a four-foot-high green plastic barrel cactus in a terra-cotta pot. On the floor in front of the chair lay a dirty Navajo rug. On the wall beside it was a gold-framed print of an Indian woman weaving a basket. The cactus, the rug, and the print were the only decorative touches in the otherwise generic room. The windows wore white mini-blinds, the floor was scuffed green tile that hadn't been waxed in recent memory, and the dingy walls were papered with photographs of houses, commercial buildings, and ranch property.

Instead of taking the chair, I walked over to the wall nearest the desk and pretended a consuming interest in an immaculate wh brk 3-2-2 ranch w/lg frml dining, hdwd floors, WBFP, cvd patio, drapes, curtains, appliances, $77,500, MUST SEE!!!! While I contemplated the out-of-focus photograph of the wh brk ranch, I was listening to the woman, whose boy-cropped brown hair would have frustrated DeAnne no end. You can learn a lot by watching people when they're on the phone, even when you have no interest in the conversation itself.

The woman was young and pretty, with a wide forehead, thick lashes, and dark eyes. But her voice was high-pitched and harried, her mouth was pinched, and her dress — a khaki-colored shirtwaist with epaulets and a wide plastic belt — cast a sallow shadow on her face. She was explaining in a pseudo-apologetic tone, apparently to an agent from another real estate firm, that Howard had already put down a contract on eight-oh-eight Macomb and she was ninety-nine percent sure the owner had already accepted the offer, or would, within the hour. However, wasn't it *lucky?* She just *happened* to have a *brand-new* listing on the same street, only a few blocks away, and much, *much* nicer, really, a gem of a house, very sweet, with *fantastic* buyer appeal.

"Why don't you drive your client by and have a look this afternoon, Patricia? There's new floor tile in the kitchen and a lovely screened-in porch out back and a brand-new thirty-gallon energy-saver gas water heater in the utility room. Oh, and the bedrooms have all been freshly painted and the drapes dry-cleaned. I did a walk-through yesterday, and I'm sure it'll move fast. This weekend, in fact. I've sent a couple of agents by already." She paused, doodling on her desk pad. "That's right, six-twelve Macomb. The owner's been transferred and is ready to sell and I mean *really* ready, just bring her an offer and watch her jump for it." Another pause, then briskly: "Sure thing, Patricia. If I can help, just whistle. I'll be here another couple of hours. After that, you'll get my pager."

She hung up the phone, flashed me a smile that was even more superficial than the first, and held up her finger to indicate one more moment. She punched a number into the phone as if she were punching somebody's lights out, turned away from me, and spoke in a half-whisper into the phone, very angry. I moved two paces to my right, listening without shame. Some of my old habits are harder to break than others.

"Howard? You better get your ass moving on that contract on eight-oh-eight. I've had two calls on it this morning." Her voice sharpened, impatient, angry. "No, of course I didn't. You think I'm stupid or something? I sent them both to six-twelve, which is a dog, needs a lot of work, but it's our only other listing in the area. You said you'd have that contract to the owner by seven last night, and it's already noon." A pause. "I don't give a shit *why* you haven't. Just get the fuck out of that bed and *do* it." Her hang-up barely missed being a grand slam, and only because she'd suddenly remembered that I was there.

The woman's recovery reminded me of those comediennes who do impersonations. One minute they've got one face and voice, then a turn, a twist of the shoulder and a turn back, and voilà! You'd swear to God it wasn't the same person. This gal wasn't that good, and it took her several seconds to recompose her face and flush the anger out of her voice. But when she stood and spoke to me, the corners of her mouth were turned up nicely, there were fetching dimples in her cheeks, and her expression was cheerfully bland.

"I'm Linda Rhodes," she said, extending her hand. "Glad you stopped by. What can I show you today?" Her smile showed white teeth that were either the result of good genes or expensive preteen braces. She gestured toward the wall. "If you're interested in that three-two-two, I'd be glad to take you by. Rosewood school district, four blocks from the supermarket, very quiet neighborhood, lovely landscaping. You'll *love* it. Everything you've ever wanted in a house, and then some."

Linda Rhodes. Did that make her Rhodes's daughter, his sister, or his wife? I couldn't tell without asking. But the Howard she'd chewed out on the phone must be the Howard I wanted. Her tone had suggested that he was either her husband or her brother. Women don't usually talk to their fathers that way.

"My name is China Bayles," I said. "I'm looking for Howard Rhodes."

Her gray eyes slitted and her smile went away. "Junior or senior?"

A complication. There was no way to segue gracefully

into this one, so I put both feet in it. "The man I'm looking for spent some time in the federal facility at Bastrop."

Her face wrenched. She sat down and reached for a pack of Virginia Slims and a red plastic Bic. "What do you want him for?" She didn't look up and she didn't invite me to sit down.

"I want to talk to him about Rosemary Robbins."

That brought her eyes up, and fast, nostrils flaring. "That *bitch,*" she spat out. "I read about her in the paper." She had to flick the lighter once, twice, three times to get it going. "She deserves to be dead. Too fucking bad somebody didn't blow her away years ago."

Definitely a woman with a grudge. "You're Mrs. Rhodes?"

A short, quick shake of the head, eyes down again. A hard pull on the cigarette.

"His sister?"

Eyes up and flinty, jaw working. She took her time answering. Finally, she said, "I'm Howard Rhodes's daughter. Excuse me, but just who the hell are you and what business is this of yours?"

His daughter. So the Howard on the phone—presumably a late sleeper or a drunk or both—was most likely Howard Junior. Her brother.

"My name is China Bayles," I said. "I was told that your father might be able to shed some light on Rosemary Robbins's death. Can you tell me where I can reach him?"

The laugh was brittle as old glass. "Cypress Springs Memorial Gardens. Row twenty-three, plot fifteen. I doubt he'll have much to say." Her voice cracked. "The dead don't, you know."

I looked at her. Beneath her bitterness was etched a cross-hatching of fresh, raw grief. "When did it happen?"

"Three weeks ago yesterday." She leaned back in her

chair and exhaled a stream of blue smoke from her nostrils. "Time flies, whether you're having fun or not." She examined the tip of her cigarette. "Are you going to ask how?"

"How?"

She bit her lip and half turned away, but not far enough to hide the pain. "He drove into a concrete overpass abutment south of Austin at something over ninety miles an hour."

"He was alone?"

She turned and met my eyes, not flinching. "Alone, broad daylight, dry pavement, no skid marks, no blood alcohol. That tell you anything?"

It did. Some people do it with a gun, some barricade themselves in the garage with the motor running, some put the accelerator to the floor and ram the nearest solid object. The next logical question — had her father's life insurance been in force long enough for his suicide to be covered? — was not relevant to my inquiry. And since he had died more than two weeks before Rosemary was killed, he couldn't have killed her. It was entirely within the realm of possibility, however, that his death was the *cause* of hers. The woman in front of me looked angry enough to kill.

"I'm sorry for your loss," I said.

She shrugged. The grief had gone and there was only a sour resignation left, mixed with bitterness — and anger. "We'd already gotten used to handling the business without him, Howard and me. Slamming himself into the abutment didn't make a dent in Rhodes Real Estate." She darted me a venomous glance and stabbed her cigarette out in a black ashtray shaped like the state of Texas. "You want to know about Robbins? Well, let me tell you, lady. Robbins was a vampire. First she seduced him, then she tried to blackmail him —"

"Blackmail him? Do you have any evidence of that?"

"What evidence do I need? She told him she needed this and this assurance about the accounts and oh by the way it would be nice to have a raise, too. In my book, that's blackmail."

"How do you know this?"

"Because I was there when she told him what she wanted."

"You were there?"

"Well, sure. I was handling his books, wasn't I? I may have been just a teenager, but I knew enough to get the numbers in the right columns."

"What did your father do when she said she wanted more money?"

"He told her to go to hell. That's when she turned him in to the IRS. She was the reason he went to prison. I laughed when I read that she was dead." Her voice went up a notch, shrill. "Laughed, do you hear? The bitch ruined my father's life, turned my mother into an old woman and my brother into a drunk." She cocked her finger and aimed it at me as if it were a gun. "A bullet to the head is what she deserved. It's about all she was worth."

I regarded Linda Rhodes with some distaste. The picture she painted of Rosemary Robbins — seductress, blackmailer, IRS stooge — was ugly and maybe even accurate, but I couldn't be sure. Her father had killed himself. It was natural for her to blame someone, and Rosemary Robbins (who could no longer defend herself) was a logical target.

But whatever Rosemary had done, the Rhodes family couldn't blame all their troubles on her. I knew businessmen who survived a tax conviction to build a stronger business, wives who endured their husbands' disgrace with equanimity, sons who lived through their father's dishonor without becoming drunks. And daughters who were not ready to kill the cause, real or imagined, of their family's humiliation. Was Linda Rhodes harboring enough blunt, unreasoning rage to murder the woman she blamed for her father's suicide? Had she, or her brother, or the two of them working together, shot Rosemary Robbins?

"I need to know where you were on the Fourth of July," I said.

There was dead silence. Then she dropped her hand, lifted her narrow chin, and gave me a defiant smile. "That's the night she was killed?"

I nodded.

Her smile became mocking. "On the day before the holiday, my brother and I drove my mother to Houston to visit my grandmother. My father's mother." The smile shattered and her eyes suddenly, without warning, filled with tears. "She's ninety-six, in a nursing home. We had to tell her that her only son was dead, and that we'd already buried him." She struggled with the tears for a moment, then opened her drawer and began to search. After a minute she found a wadded-up tissue. She used it to wipe her eyes and blow her nose, then said, "We stayed with my aunt in Bellaire over the Fourth, and drove home on the fifth. Does that satisfy you?"

"For the moment," I said. "I'm sorry I had to ask."

I'd bet that her alibi would check out. And if the Rhodes children had paid someone to shoot the woman they blamed for their father's downfall, it would be tough to prove.

The energy of anger and grief were both gone from her face, leaving the mouth pinched, the cheeks sagging, the eyes empty. "Yeah," she muttered. She looked away, looked back, reached for the Virginia Slims and the red plastic lighter. "I heard on TV that her boyfriend killed her and ran off to Mexico. Is that true?"

"That's an avenue the police are exploring, I believe."

She leaned forward, body taut, voice bitter. "I need to know who killed her. Whether it was her boyfriend, or somebody else, I want to thank him. I can sleep nights, because of what he did." She balled her hands into fists and pressed them to her chest, as if she were holding the pain, like a knife, against her heart. "I don't have to think of her alive and happy and remember him wrapped around that abutment so tight it took two wreckers to pry him loose. I can imagine her with her head blown off." When the phone rang, I was glad. Her malice was a dark, acrid whirlpool, its vortex sucking her down and down, and me with her.

The phone rang again, and she reached for it. As she did, her face began to change, to lighten, to grow less tense. Her lips curled up in the corners, and she raised her shoulders. On the third ring, she picked up the receiver and spoke into it, a chirpy smile in her voice.

"Good afternoon, Rhodes Real Estate. Linda Rhodes. What can I do for you this afternoon?"

CHAPTER THIRTEEN

Lavender's green, riddle diddle
Lavender's blue.
You must love me, riddle diddle
'Cause I love you.

Folk rhyme

I drove back to Pecan Springs, trying to sort out what I had learned. In one sense, it amounted to nothing, *nada*, a big cipher. Robbins and Rhodes — as well as Rhodes's daughter and probably his son — had had plenty of reason to kill Rosemary, but no opportunity. The long morning and a good hunk of the afternoon had been totally wasted.

But from another point of view, I had learned quite a bit. I might not be any closer to Rosemary's killer, but I felt a good deal closer to Rosemary herself. I had seen her through the eyes of two people who remembered her quite clearly.

But how accurate were their recollections? Curt Robbins's bitter memory of his wife was colored by the unhappiness of their marriage, a marriage marred by passion and violence. Rosemary may have done what a thinking woman should do: reject the violence, put it out of her life, and find someone else who could love her gently, tenderly, who could make her happy. Linda Rhodes's memory of Rosemary was filtered through her father's conviction for tax fraud. There was no concrete evidence that Rosemary had seduced him, attempted to blackmail him, or turned him in to the IRS. In fact, she may have simply been doing what a good accountant ought to do: question the numbers the client gives her and charge more for an account that posed difficulty. I sighed heavily as I drove up the long drive to The Springs Hotel. All I had really learned this morning was how Rosemary was remembered. I wasn't much closer to the woman herself.

I had planned to talk next to Carol Connally, the bookkeeper at the Springs. I struck out on that, but the trip wasn't wasted. I ran into somebody who told me a great deal more than I might have gotten out of the bookkeeper.

Her name tag said Hi! I'm Priscilla! She was sitting cross-legged on the floor beside the file cabinet, a stack of manila folders in the lap of her floral print dress. She was probably thirty pounds overweight, a fact that her girlish dress only exaggerated. Her plain, square-jawed face would have been more attractive without the purple eye shadow and the frilly ruffle at her throat. Her expression conveyed an anxious eagerness to please and the simultaneous and almost hopeless conviction that whatever she did would *not* please.

I gave her my name. "I'm looking for Carol," I said.

Priscilla scrambled heavily to her feet and shook her head. "I'm afraid I'm the only one in the office today. Lily's in Lubbock. Her mother had surgery." She glanced at the phone on Lily's desk, where the red button was lit opposite Matt Monroe's name. "Mr. Monroe's on the phone. Maybe I can help you." There wasn't much conviction in her voice.

"That's too bad about Lily's mother," I said, shaking my head. "It isn't as if she didn't have enough on her mind, what with —" I waved my hand toward Jeff Clark's office door. "You know."

"I sure do," Priscilla said earnestly. She was wearing so much mascara that her eyelashes were little black twigs. "Everybody's in a state of turmoil, especially after the police were here on Monday. I just can't believe it was Mr. Clark's gun that —" She bit her lip and blinked hard. "It's just too awful for words."

"What about Carol?" I asked with concern. "She's not sick, is she?"

"Nuh-uh. Her sister Nancy had a baby." She bent over and picked up an armload of folders and put them on the desk. "She went to Austin to help with the kids for a few days."

"Not many sisters would do that," I said. "Do you happen to know Nancy's address?"

Priscilla's face brightened. "Oh, you're going to send a present! That's nice. *I* did, a kimono trimmed in pink and white checks. It's a girl, you know. Jennifer, if you want to put her name on the card. I think it's wonderful for mothers to get presents when their babies are born, even if . . ." She shifted her bulky shoulders. "I guess you know that Nancy isn't married. But Carol says it doesn't matter. She was just happy that the baby was healthy and Nancy was okay. And under the circumstances, I'm sure she was glad to have an excuse to get out of the office. But I do have Nancy's address. I had to get it yesterday to give to the police."

"The police have talked to Carol?"

"I don't know. I suppose so. They talked to me, and to Lily, before she flew to Lubbock. We couldn't tell them much, though. We don't know any of the facts, and it doesn't seem right to . . . well, you know." She wrinkled her nose. "Dish the office dirt."

You'd be surprised how many people think it's their duty to conceal gossip from the police during an official investigation. They confuse talking to the cops with testifying in court, where they're permitted to say only what they can swear to. As a result, the police often miss out on some very useful information which an informant may be quite willing to share with a less intimidating person in a less formal interrogative situation — like our chat just now.

"I suppose Carol has some *real* information," I said. "Especially because she and Mr. Clark used to be . . ." I let the sentence float like a dry fly on a swift current. "But you must know about all that, too," I added, giving the lure an extra tweak.

The glitter in Priscilla's eye and her voluminous sigh told me what I needed to know. This overweight, unpretty girl felt herself to have been an important, if peripheral, participant in what amounted to an office triangle: the bookkeeper in love with the boss, a rival murdered, the boss himself suspected of the crime and on the lam. She might not have many "facts," but she was dying to share her impressions, romantic as they were. It would have been unkind of me not to encourage her.

"Oh, yes, I *do* know," she said passionately. "We talked every day for the past three or four months. Carol said that the only thing that's kept her sane is being able to talk about it. And of course she felt so much *worse* after Miss Robbins was shot."

She paused, and I wondered briefly why Carol Connally had chosen this inexperienced, unsophisticated young woman as a confidante. Perhaps it was Priscilla's romantic naïveté that had invited Carol to open up to her, her willingness to accept and trust another person at face value, as she had accepted and trusted me because she thought I was nice enough to send a present to a new mother. I felt awkward about violating that trust, but I was pulled forward by the intuition that there was something important to be learned here.

"By 'worse,' " I prompted gently, "you mean — "

She twisted her mouth. "Well, like it was her fault, or something. Of course it wasn't."

"Her fault?"

"You know." Priscilla waved her hand vaguely. "Well, Carol was *very* jealous of Miss Robbins. And she was very mad at Mr. Clark for being such a snake. For breaking their engagement."

"I didn't know they were engaged."

"It wasn't formal or anything, and they hadn't set a date, but she considered herself all but engaged. She really loved him, I mean *really.*" Priscilla's eyes, brown spaniel eyes, were teary with the romance of it. "I've never seen anybody love a person the way Carol loved Mr. Clark."

All but. I wondered how many women broke their hearts over *all but.*

"Well," Priscilla hurried forward with her story, "like I say, she was already very hurt about Mr. Clark jilting her, and when she found out Miss Robbins was preggie, she just about — "

"Carol knew that?" I asked. I spoke more sharply than I meant, but Priscilla was so involved with her story that she didn't appear to notice.

"We both knew it, Carol and me. We overheard Miss Robbins telling him after she found out from the doctor. It really made Carol crazy, believe you me." The sympathy was drawn on Priscilla's face, together with an appreciation of the drama of the situation. "Wouldn't it you, if you came back from a nice cheeseburger and fries at Wendy's, all unsuspecting, and overheard some woman telling the man you loved that she was going to have his baby? Just like *All My Children*."

"I'm sure it would," I said. It wouldn't make me crazy enough to kill, though—at least I didn't think so. How crazy had it made Carol? Crazy enough to steal her ex-lover's gun and shoot her rival in the face with it? Crazy enough to wear gloves, to preserve his prints on the gun? Passionate love turns to passionate hate—the basic plot of many a murder mystery.

Priscilla was talking faster, with greater urgency, as if her story was pushing its way up out of her soul. "That's why when Miss Robbins got murdered, Carol felt like it was her fault. Not because she did it or anything like that. Carol is a very nice, very sweet person who wouldn't hurt a fly. I mean, because she *wanted* her dead. Do you get what I'm trying to say?"

Carol Connally wouldn't be the first very nice, very sweet person to kill the other woman. But I only nodded.

"Well, that's how I saw it, anyway," Priscilla said. "Like, I mean, I know *I* would've felt guilty if I said, 'I hope a certain person burns in hell,' and then that person goes and gets herself murdered."

"Carol must have been terribly shocked when she heard about it," I said sympathetically. "I can't imagine."

Priscilla bobbed her head. "Oh God, yes. Dazed, sort of. Like she couldn't really believe it. She goes, 'I'll never believe it, not in a hundred years,' and I go, 'I'll never believe it, either.' " Her chin wobbled a little and she sniffled. "It *is* hard to believe, don't you think? I mean, I never knew anybody who died, except for my grandmother and she was really old, seventy-two, and too sick to get around. I just sorta keep remembering Miss Robbins like she was, kind of pretty—" She paused, wanting to be truthful. "Well, not pretty, exactly, but nice-looking. Elegant, you might say. I would of gone to the funeral if they'd had it here." She wiped her nose on the back of her large, square hand. "Miss Robbins was always nice to me," she added a little defensively, "even though I was Carol's friend. And everybody knew how smart she was. She had to've been, to find out about the money."

"Oh, really?" I looked at her. "What about the money?"

"Well—" Priscilla glanced at the telephone set on Lily's desk. The button opposite "Monroe" was still lit. She lowered her voice and leaned forward conspiratorially. "There's a lot of money missing from the hotel accounts. Like a *whole* lot."

I stared at her. Priscilla couldn't know it, but she had just given me a whole new view of the crime. Matt had hired Rosemary to do an audit of the hotel books. If she had turned up any discrepancies, she presumably had also discovered who was responsible and had taken the information back to the person who had hired her. To Matt.

But suppose she hadn't gone to Matt. Suppose she had gone instead to the embezzler and offered her silence in return for a cut. That's what Howard Rhodes's daughter accused her of doing. And suppose the embezzler was the other owner, Jeff Clark, who'd gotten tired of splitting the hotel's revenues with his ex-brother-in-law and decided to skim a bit off the top. Had Rosemary offered her silence in return for marriage? Had she been asking, not for just a cut of the deal, but a lifetime partnership? Had she gotten pregnant—or claimed she was pregnant—to put more pressure on Jeff?

An interesting scenario. The prosecution would find it irresistible. But it wasn't the only possible scenario.

"Poor Carol," I said. "She must have been really upset when she heard about the money. If I'd been in her place, I'd be really scared that they'd suspect *me* of taking it."

Priscilla rolled her eyes heavenward. "You better believe she was scared. We both heard Miss Robbins telling Mr. Clark that there was a couple hundred thousand missing. At the very least, Carol figured she'd get fired, even though she and Mr. Clark had been been—" She held up two fingers, intertwined. "Well, you know. She thought about looking for another job, but once they checked her references, they'd find out that there'd been trouble here. And she isn't really an accountant, you know. Like she doesn't have a degree or anything. All she does is put the numbers in the books the way Mrs. Monroe taught her when she first came to work here, way back."

"And that was—"

"Ten years ago." Priscilla pulled in her breath and let it out in a puff. "That's how come this whole thing has been so hard on her. After ten years of her doing exactly like she was told, first by Mrs. Monroe and then by Mr. Monroe, and getting bonuses and everything. And then Mr. Clark leading her on to believe that he really loved her and wanted to marry her. Well, of course she had to think she was home free. I would of. Wouldn't you?"

She scarcely heard my murmured "Of course." There was a look of empathetic pain on her face as she felt in her soul the tragedy of Carol Connally's fall from grace and she spoke very fast, in the breathless voice of a witness to catastrophe. "Well, anyway, she really went to pieces. If she hadn't had to leave to take care of Nancy's kids, Mr. Monroe would've sent her home, she was in such a terrible tizzy."

I waited until she had taken a couple of deep breaths. "Having her and Lily out at the same time must be awfully hard on you," I said finally. "The work is probably stacking up."

"There's *mountains* of it," Priscilla said, her voice rich with self-pity. "Not to mention that Mr. Monroe can't seem to do much except—"

The sound of a door opening made her stop, and a sudden flush flared on her cheeks. She turned, and we saw Matt Monroe, standing in the doorway of his office, collar open, sleeves rolled up. He was scowling.

"Oh, Mr. Monroe, you're off the phone," she said, flustered.

Matt was curt. "If you've got so much work to do, you'd better get back to it, Prissy." He nodded to me. "Hello, Miz Bayles," he said, and motioned me into the office. He shut the door behind us with a resigned look.

"That girl," he sighed, wiping his forehead with a handkerchief. "You'd think she was practicing for *Hard Copy*." He stuffed his handkerchief in his pocket and strode to his desk. "I'm glad you stopped by, Miz Bayles. I was goin' to call you so you can get word to McQuaid. I just got off the phone with the bank. Jeff's been usin' that credit card down there in Mexico City—pretty freely, too." He gave a short, sharp laugh. "Running up quite a bill."

"That's surprising," I said, taking a chair opposite the desk. "If I were Jeff, I wouldn't use my cards. Not unless I wanted to be found."

Matt lowered himself into his upholstered leather chair. "He's made it to Mexico—he probably feels safe. And he *would* be, if it was just the Pecan Springs cops after him. He doesn't know McQuaid's on his trail."

"Where did the card show up?"

"Mexico City. He used it to charge the hotel and some clothes, a camera, luggage, stuff like that. *And* a plane ticket."

"I don't suppose he's flying back to Brownsville," I said wryly.

He gave an ascerbic chuckle. "You know better. I checked with the airline by phone to save McQuaid the legwork. He's gone to Acapulco. Tell McQuaid to get the next plane after him. And there's something else you should tell him, too, Miz Bayles. Seems like there's been some big-time funny business with the hotel books. From what I hear from the office help, Rosemary Robbins stumbled onto it. She went to Jeff with the news, instead of to me, like she should of." He shook his head sadly. "If Jeff was dippin' into the till and that lady found out, he was in a shit pot of trouble. She must've offered to keep her mouth shut if he married her, maybe even got herself storked to up the ante. He probably figured it was cheaper in the long run to kill her than marry her." He shook his head. "She was tough as saddle leather. *I* sure as hell wouldn't of wanted to be married to her."

"How much of this have you told the police?"

"Just that Jeff was maybe cooking the books. I don't have anything firm to tell them until I bring in an auditor, which I will, quick as I can." He gave me an apologetic glance. "I know this isn't going to make McQuaid happy, because Jeff's a friend of his. You tell him to watch himself, Miz Bayles. I sure wouldn't have said Jeff was dangerous, but now—" He shook his head, his mouth set. "This business is ugly as homemade sin."

I glanced at my watch. "He'll be calling at three," I said. Suddenly I caught myself wanting to connect with McQuaid, hear his voice, talk to him about what I had learned. Living with him, I'd gotten into the habit of telling him what was going on in my life, hearing his side, testing my responses against his. I missed it. *Dangerous dependency*, the other China whispered. *It's a good thing he's gone. You can be your own woman again.* The other China be damned. I could be my own woman and still miss McQuaid.

Matt stood up. "Well, when he calls, you tell him to hightail it down to Acapulco. Tell him to stay on the trail, even if he doesn't turn up anything for a while." He shook his head, frowning, deeply troubled. "Jeff has really ripped his britches on this one. He can run from here to Rio, and it's not goin' to solve a damn thing. McQuaid's *got* to find him. You hear?"

I nodded and left. On the way out, Priscilla surreptitiously handed me a slip of paper. I probably should have felt like a rat for having obtained Carol Connally's sister's address and phone number under false pretenses, but I didn't.

As I drove along the winding road to the campus to pick up Brian, I considered what I had learned. Connally's sister lived in South Austin. The way things stood, I probably couldn't get there before the next day. But I *had* to talk to Connally. The facts seemed to support the theory that Jeff had been stealing from the hotel's accounts, that Rosemary had found him out, and that he killed her to keep her quiet. If I were Chick Barton, it was the theory I'd use to construct the People's case.

But I could use the same facts to argue at least two different theories. Maybe it was Matt, not Jeff, who had been stealing from the hotel's accounts. But Matt would hardly have hired an accountant to examine the very books he'd been diddling. No, it was far more likely that Carol had been embezzling money from the hotel and that she had stolen Jeff's gun to kill Rosemary, silencing her and framing him, revenging herself and protecting herself in one brutal act. I remembered that it was a woman who had phoned the police with the tip about Jeff — Carol, no doubt. There were a few holes in my theory, but at least it was a beginning. If I were arguing Jeff's defense, I'd find a way to plug them.

I sighed as I negotiated the turn into the campus and drove up to the entry kiosk to wrangle a parking permit from the surly guard who doles them out as if they were Dallas Cowboy Super Bowl rings. It was too bad I couldn't drop everything and drive up to Austin tonight to question Carol Connally. But I had to pick up Brian and head for the shop to catch McQuaid's phone call. And after that, I needed to spend the evening being a *mom.* Not an ordinary mom, either, but a mom who is responsible for the safety and well-being of a small boy who is the declared target of a killer ex-con out for revenge.

Life is sometimes very complicated.

When McQuaid called me at the shop, I could hear the frustration in his voice. "I've been trucking around Mexico City all day, and I haven't been able to dig up a trace of Clark," he said. "He's vanished into thin air. I have no idea where to look next."

"I have," I said. "How about Acapulco?" It only took a minute to fill him in on what Matt had learned from the credit card company, and another couple of minutes to tell him about the situation with the hotel books. "Matt wants you to get the next plane to Acapulco. And he wants you to be careful. Clark could be dangerous."

"Oh, Christ," McQuaid said. "Anything else I don't want to hear? Any word from Jacoby?"

I pushed away the involuntary shiver that came with the memory of the cold, rough voice on the phone. For better or worse, I had already made up my mind not to tell McQuaid about Jacoby's threatening phone call that morning. What could he do? Abandon his search and fly home? Stay with the search and lay down even more stringent rules for Brian's safety, while worrying himself half-crazy?

"No," I lied. "Nothing." It wasn't an easy lie. It separated us in a way that distance couldn't. "Nothing from Bubba, either," I added. At least that much was true.

"No news is good news, I guess." McQuaid's tone was dry. "What did you do today?"

"Oh, the usual," I said evasively. There was no point in telling him that I'd staved off a process server, eliminated two suspects, and discovered two more. The eliminations only tightened the case against Jeff, which he didn't need to hear. I had nothing concrete to report about the bookkeeper, although of the two suspects, she was by far the more viable. I didn't have anything on Matt, either. I'd spent the entire day coming up with nothing. A big, fat zip, at least as far as evidence was concerned.

"Good," McQuaid said emphatically. "I'm glad you're managing to stay out of trouble. What's the kid up to?"

I glanced over my shoulder. Brian was perched on the stool behind the counter, a book in his lap. "He's studying Klingon. He bought a new dictionary when he was up at the campus today."

"At the campus?" McQuaid asked, alarmed. "I thought he was at the store, with you."

"Smart Cookie volunteered to baby-sit," I said lightly, "so I took advantage of the offer. I figured that Brian's as safe under the wing of the campus cops as he is here." Safer, actually, but I wouldn't tell McQuaid that.

"Oh," McQuaid said, the relieved father. "Yeah, you're probably right. I doubt if Jacoby could get his hands on him with Sheila around."

"Do you want to talk to him? Maybe the two of you can have a conversation in Klingon." Brian isn't the only Trekkie in the family. When there's nothing else on TV, McQuaid reruns tapes of *The Next Generation,* and he and Brian keep up a running critique on the action.

"I don't know if I can," McQuaid said. "About the only Klingon I can remember is *BortaS blr jablu'Dl'reH QaQqu' nay'.*"

"Which means?"

" 'Revenge is a dish best served cold.' " He chuckled. "You haven't heard that famous Klingon proverb? Everybody in the galaxy knows it."

"My galactic education obviously doesn't extend to proverbs," I said. "But Brian seems to have gotten as far as 'Where does one find the ice cream?' There's probably a connection there somewhere."

"Well, fetch him," McQuaid said. "I might as well display my ignorance."

While Laurel and I discussed what to do with the air conditioner (Harold was out back, working on it), Brian and McQuaid talked. Unfortunately, their conversation did not come to a happy end.

"It's not *fair* to keep me from going to the convention!" Brian cried, stamping his foot angrily. "You know how much I want to get that card."

I couldn't hear what McQuaid said in rebuttal but whatever it was, Brian wasn't having any. "You're a Marcasian slime mold!" he burst out. He thrust the receiver at me and stormed furiously out of the store.

"What's a Marcasian slime mold?" I asked.

"It would turn your stomach," McQuaid said. He sighed. "If I'd said something like that to my old man, he would have belted me. And my mother would've washed out my mouth with lye soap and sent me to my room for a month or two."

"Don't you think maybe it would be okay for Brian to go to the convention with Arnold?" I ventured. I didn't want to say it to McQuaid, but the boy would be safer there, where he was just one small Trekkie among hundreds. Here, he was out where Jacoby could target him.

"No convention," the Marcasian slime mold said sternly. "I want him home, where he's safe. Where he's in your sight every minute."

I cleared my throat. "Actually, I don't think I—"

"Look, China," McQuaid said, "I'm sorry you're stuck with the little turd. If there were any other way—"

"It's not Brian," I said. "Actually, he's behaving pretty well. It's just that—"

The other China spoke in an I-told-you-so tone. *You just don't like being responsible for the boy, do you? Admit it. It's a good thing you and McQuaid aren't married. What kind of mom doesn't want to be responsible for her child?*

"Hey, I've got a thought," McQuaid broke in. "Why don't you phone Blackie and ask him to take Brian for a day? Jacoby's not going to try anything if the kid's in the custody of the sheriff."

"Now *that,*" I said, "is an outstanding idea. I'll do it." *Of course you will,* the other China said. *You'd jump at anything to get the kid off your hands.* "Anything else?"

"Keep your sense of humor. I'll phone you tomorrow. Oh, by the way. *JIH bang SoH.*"

"Okay, I'll bite. What does it mean?"

"I love you," he said. "In Klingon."

"Bang means love?" Suddenly I missed McQuaid very much, missed laughing at silly word jokes, missed lying beside him in the early morning before the world woke up and the day's complications had to be dealt with.

"*Bang* means love," he said, and chuckled. "Klingons don't mess around." There was a silence. "When I get back, though," he said reflectively, "a little messing around would certainly be in order. Wouldn't you say?"

I would, but we didn't have time to go into it. Laurel was just coming in from the back, where she had been checking on Harold's autopsy of the air conditioner. Laurel is one-quarter Native American (her full name is Laurel Walkingwater Wiley, and her mother's mother was a Cherokee), and she almost never complains. She wasn't complaining now, either, although her face was flushed with the heat, sweat was running into her eyes, and her tee shirt was plastered to her back. Native Americans are a stoic lot.

"Harold says that what's wrong with it now isn't the same thing that was wrong with it last time," she said.

I sighed. "I suppose he wants more money to fix it."

"Four hundred," she said. "It's the compressor. He admits that it might have been bad when he did the other stuff."

"Four hundred more?" I exclaimed. "Okay, that's it for Harold. We're calling your cousin. If we've got to put in a new compressor, I'd rather pay somebody else to do it."

Revenge is a dish best eaten cold.

CHAPTER FOURTEEN

Where the yarrow grows
There is one who knows.

Folk saying

When we got home, I made Brian sit in the locked car
while I gave the house a good looking-over. But everything was locked up tight and all I found were a couple
of hang-ups on the answering machine. There was another while I was making the spaghetti sauce, but I didn't
have any reason to believe that it was Jacoby. He'd promised to phone, but he didn't strike me as the kind of man
who'd call and hang up, just to keep me on edge. Just
the same, I was a good deal more unsettled than I let on,
either to Brian or Sheila, who arrived just in time to make
the salad. Hang-ups unnerve me. I hate to pick up a telephone, say hello, and get an earful of sinister silence, followed by a dial tone.

For the most part, our evening was uneventful. Sheila
helped load the dishwasher after dinner, then drove back
to her house to pick up some clothes. Brian, still sulking
about his conversation with the Marcasian slime mold,
took Ivan the Hairible into the living room to comfort
himself with a Star Trek rerun. I went into McQuaid's
office to get out the schedule of store events for August.

Summer can be slow, so I like to schedule plenty of
activities to bring people into the shop. I plan everything

early in the year to cut down on the expense of mailing announcements, and then do a monthly calendar to hand out to customers, post in the store, and place in the newspaper. August's schedule includes a demonstration of herbal candle making by Gretel Schumaker, who runs CandleWorks at the Craft Emporium; a class on herbal pestos (basil isn't the only pesto herb); and a Lammas festival that Ruby and I will cohost. The ancient midsummer celebration of Lammas (Old English for loaf mass) consecrated the first loaves of bread baked from the new harvest. In honor of Lammas, I'll teach a class on herbal breads, while Ruby will do a class on ritual. We'll bring the two classes together for our celebration.

But before any of these good things can happen, I have to put together a flyer, which meant turning on Mc-Quaid's computer and settling down to work. I was nearly done when Brian came in and tried once more to cajole me into taking him to the Star Trek convention. He started off by telling me how much he wanted the Mr. Data card he was sure he'd find at the show, then reminded me that if he spent the day in Austin he'd be out of my hair, and finished up with the promise that if I'd let him go with Arnold, he'd be exceptionally good for at least two months.

"I can't let you go, Brian," I said.

His face wrinkled. "But China—"

"It's not me, it's your dad. He's worried about this Jacoby thing."

He flung up his arms angrily. "Jacoby, Jacoby. I'm *sick* of hearing about the guy. Nobody can be as bad as Dad says he is."

I thought about the cold, hard voice on the phone. "I wouldn't be too sure about that," I said. "There are some pretty violent people running around out there."

"My mother would let me go."

"Even after your father said no?"

"Sure. She doesn't care what he says."

"Well, *I* care. You have to mind your dad."

He scowled deeply. "If I can't go, I'll never, never speak to you again."

"That sounds like blackmail," I said.

He gave me a dark look. "I don't know why you had to stick your nose in, anyway. Dad and me were doing all right by ourselves. Dad's a good cook, and I pick up my stuff. We don't need some woman cleaning up after us."

The other China was deeply offended. *Tell him that women weren't created to clean up after men,* she said. But I settled for "I'm here because your father and I want to be together."

He raised his chin. "Well, nobody asked me what *I* wanted. So why don't you just leave?" He turned and left the room.

I stared after him despairingly. If I ever had any hope that we might be a family, I could scrap it. If Brian truly didn't want me here, he could very easily come between his father and me. Maybe I'd better think of other alternatives. I'd already gone too far in remodeling the shop to move back there. But I could stay with Ruby for a while. Or I could move into the cottage behind the shop. To be fair, I'd have to make some sort of deal with McQuaid about the lease on the house.

But that was next week or the week after. It was tomorrow I had to deal with. I called Blackie, who readily agreed to McQuaid's suggestion that he take Brian the next day.

"Have him ready at eight," he instructed. "I'll stop by on my way to the office. Any sign of Jacoby?"

"No," I said. "A couple of hang-ups on the answering machine is all."

"Any trouble, you holler," he said. "See you in the morning."

I'd been off the line for only a minute when the phone rang again. I picked it up uneasily, but it was not a hang-up. It was Ruby.

"Everything okay over there?"

"Why? Should there be something wrong?"

"Well, no, not really. I was just thinking about what La Que Sabe said last night and wondering—"

"La Que Sabe doesn't know *everything*," I said testily.

"You don't need to get huffy, China. I know you were out talking to people today. What did you find out about Rosemary?"

"About Rosemary? Well, let's see," I said. "I found out that her ex-husband thinks she was sleeping with a real estate dealer named Howard Rhodes. I found out that Rhodes's daughter thinks she blackmailed her father or blew the whistle on him for cheating on his taxes, or both. And I found out that Matt thinks she may have uncovered some accounting hanky-panky and tried to blackmail Jeff Clark."

Ruby blew out a long breath. "You're making all that up."

"I am not. It may not be *true*, but it's what I found out."

"Oh," Ruby said, relieved. "You mean, that's what people *told* you about Rosemary."

"That's what I said."

"Well, we shouldn't confuse what people say about Rosemary with the truth," Ruby reminded me sagely.

"Whose truth? We're sort of like the blind men with the elephant. Each of us knows only a little bit about her, and nobody's bit matches anybody else's bit."

There was silence for a moment. Finally, Ruby said, "Ondine started back to Berkeley this morning. But La Que Sabe left a message for you. She wants you to be sure to remember about *el río abajo*. She says it's important."

The river beneath. The place where I was supposed to find the truth about Rosemary's murder. "Remembering *el río abajo* is not exactly like remembering the Alamo," I said. "It can't be all that important if I don't know what it means. If La Que Sabe wants to get her message across, she shouldn't talk in riddles."

"Messages from channeled entities are often enigmatic," Ruby objected.

"This message isn't enigmatic," I said. "It's just plain silly. 'The river beneath.' What does La Que Sabe expect me to do? Fetch a forked stick and start dowsing?"

"Maybe you shouldn't take it so literally. Maybe she means, like, well, the river of human motivation that flows under all our actions."

"Well, if that's what she means, I've got news for her. It's not a river, it's an ocean. There's so much motivation in this case, you could drown in it."

Ruby cleared her throat. "There's one more thing," she said. "It's about the air-conditioning. I hate to complain, but it was ninety-two in the Cave this afternoon, and my customers are wilting. Can't Harold *do* something?"

"Harold's been fired," I said. "Laurel phoned her cousin Emily, who inherited an air-conditioning repair shop from her father. Emily's supposed to be there first thing tomorrow."

"Wonderful!" Ruby exclaimed. "Never ask a man to do a woman's work."

Five minutes after Ruby and I finished our conversation, the phone rang again. It was Sally. She asked to speak to McQuaid, and when I told her he wasn't there, to Brian. Her voice was edgy and almost hysterical, and I wondered whether she was on some kind of medication. McQuaid was right — she didn't seem emotionally stable. I wasn't sure it was a good idea for Brian to talk to her, but she *is* his mother and who am I to say no? I yelled up the stairs to Brian that his mom was on the line and hung up the downstairs phone when I heard him pick it up.

A few minutes later, Sheila arrived, wearing sleek black pants and a slithery top that made her look like Batwoman and carrying a bag of lavender cookies from Pam Neely. Inspired, I made some lavender-mint tea punch. I took a plate of cookies and some punch upstairs to Brian, put them beside his door, and told him they were there. I didn't get any answer.

Downstairs again, I went over for Sheila what I'd learned in the course of the day.

"Sounds like a soap opera," she said, when I'd finished relating Priscilla's narrative. "So now we know Clark's motive. Are you ready to admit that he's guilty?"

"I'm not trying to defend Jeff Clark," I said, not entirely truthfully. "All I want to do is find out the truth — for Rosemary's sake, if nothing else."

"Very noble," Smart Cookie muttered. "What's next?"

"Blackie's keeping Brian tomorrow, and I'm driving to Austin to talk to the bookkeeper, Carol Connally."

Sheila cocked her head. "Austin, huh? It just so happens that I'll be there. I've got a 1:30 meeting with the UT campus security staff. How about lunch? We could do Katz's."

"Sure," I said. "I'm hoping to to see Connally in the

morning. I have a feeling that there's a lot more to be known about this situation."

How much more, I couldn't have guessed.

Sheila left at seven-thirty the next morning, with a promise to meet me at twelve-fifteen for lunch at Katz's Deli, at the corner of Sixth and Rio Grande. I went upstairs and put on a lightweight khaki suit, ivory blouse, and brown pumps. Blackie showed up twenty minutes later to collect Brian, who was delighted to go off with the sheriff but still pointedly refused to speak to me. Wearing his Captain Kirk jersey and Mr. Spock ears, he shouldered his gear bag and loped out to the sheriff's white Jeep Cherokee. The sheriff lingered to talk to me.

Blackie Blackwell is a dry, quiet man about my age, with a square jaw, solid shoulders, and a Marine Corp haircut. But beneath his dispassionate intelligence and singleness of purpose, there's a compassionate heart. Even people who don't trust cops trust him. Blackie's a widower with no children, but he's an expert on kids. He's a scoutmaster and the uncle of three boys—two in high school and one a year older than Brian—who frequently come to stay with him.

"Kids go through phases," he said, when I told him that Brian was giving me the silent treatment. "Don't sweat it, China."

"The thought has occurred to me that Brian needs more mother than he's getting," I said ruefully. "Maybe he *should* spend more time with Sally. But she's pretty unstable right now. I don't know if he could handle that."

Blackie grinned and patted my shoulder. "Kids are resiliant. He'll survive, and so will you. A few more years, and you'll forget that there ever was a day like this." His mouth tightened. "Anything new from Jacoby?"

"Not a word," I said. "What have you heard?"

He shook his head. "Nothing. The guy's layin' low. You be careful, China. He's a mean SOB. I'm glad that Dawson woman is staying with you." He chuckled. "According to Bubba, she's a first-class lady. Number one on his list."

"Which list is that?" I asked innocently, and got another grin.

"He's taken to her like a hog to persimmons," he said. "Gladys better watch out." He sobered. "And you watch yourself, you hear?"

I promised to be careful, arranged to retrieve Brian late that afternoon, and waved good-bye. Blackie returned my wave, but Brian stared straight ahead, his folded arms resting on his gear bag. I was obviously not number one on *his* list.

Blackie's car had barely disappeared down the drive when I was out the door and into the Datsun. My first stop was the shop, where I was to meet Emily, the air-conditioning repair person, at eight-fifteen. She proved to be a slim, attractive young woman with a competent, no-nonsense air, brown hair held back with a blue headband, and thoughtful gray eyes, very much like Laurel's. She was wearing a red jumpsuit, sneakers, and a hip-slung leather belt that held screwdrivers and pliers and such. Her style wasn't exactly haute couture, but it bolstered my confidence.

Emily looked down at the air conditioner. "I'll give it a good going over and get back to you this afternoon," she said. "If it really is the compressor, it'll be more economical to replace the unit than replace the part. You can pour a lot of dollars into repairs, but the efficiency will never compare with units on the market today. And there's never any guarantee that the darn thing won't de-

velop a different problem tomorrow. Of course, that's
what keeps some repairmen in business."

"I know," I said, thinking how happy Harold was to
keep on patching this one. After the compressor, it would
have been something else. I glanced at her with a suspicious thought. "You aren't in the air conditioner sales
business, by any chance?"

"Nope." She grinned cheerfully. "I just repair them.
But I can make some recommendations if it turns out that
you want to buy a new one."

I left Emily to her work, went inside to check with
Laurel on shop business, and got back in the car and
started for Austin, the AC going full blast. It wasn't even
nine yet, but the sun was blistering and the sweat was
already pouring off me.

I've always wondered how much of Texas's growth has
depended on air-conditioning. It may be a post hoc argument to suggest that Austin and Dallas and Houston
and San Antonio began to mushroom because people discovered how to stay cool in the summer, but it is certainly
true that the greatest urban expansion in the state's history took place after the invention of refrigeration.
Through the early part of this century, Austin was a
sleepy little town cuddled into an elbow of the Colorado.
In the thirties, it leapfrogged the river and pushed a mile
south to Oltorf Street. By the early seventies, it had
sprawled six miles north to Research Boulevard and three
miles south to Ben White, and the upscale villages of
West Lake Hills and Bee Caves had grown up to the
west. Now, the city spills southward past Onion Creek
and northward into Williamson County to merge with the
town of Round Rock. The metroplex encompasses more
than a million souls, and it's still growing. I wonder how

many of those million souls would pack up and head north if the air-conditioning quit.

The residential area where I was headed — Travis Heights, named in honor of the commander of the Alamo who faced up to Santa Anna — lies on a promontory just south of the river. Bounded on the west by Congress Avenue and on the east by I-35, its shady, hilly streets are a hodgepodge of small cottages, duplexes, and two-story frame houses with garage apartments.

The house I was looking for was on Mission Ridge, a block-long street between Kenwood and Chelsea. The small white cottage could've used a coat of paint, and the lower half of the screen door was covered with splintered plywood. Somebody had planted yarrow beside the porch, but the bed was weedy and full of deadheads, and the grass was trampled to dust under the tire swing in the pecan tree out front. The doorbell wore a note that invited me to knock, please. I did, several times, but there was no answer, and I didn't hear anything inside. I went around to the back and repeated the effort, unsuccessfully. Maybe I should have called first, after all. Disappointed, I glanced at my watch. Just after nine. I'd come back in a half hour.

In the interim, I had a different kind of business to pursue. I got back in the Datsun, drove a couple of blocks to South Congress, and made a left, then a right on West Mary. Two blocks west, I came to The Herb Bar — after Thyme and Seasons, my favorite herb shop. Connie Moore, the owner, gave me a welcoming grin and a lift of her hand, and when her customers finished their purchases and left, we talked shop. I admired the collection of wreaths for which The Herb Bar is famous, asked questions about the way Connie puts together her catalog and handles her mail order business (something I've been thinking of developing), and picked up a dozen copies of a popular book that she and Janette Grainer wrote: *Natural Insect Repellents*. The book, which describes botanical repellents and insecticides, was my excuse for dropping by, if I needed one. My customers are always asking for it.

When I stepped up onto the porch of the Mission Ridge house forty minutes later, I knew someone was home. A lipstick-red Toyota van, so new that it still carried dealer's tags, was parked on the gravel drive. Inside the house, I could hear the insane cackle of a cartoon show. Carol's sister had three children, four now, with the baby. The place must be a zoo. How under the sun does she do it? I wondered. I can't handle *one*.

A moment after my knock, I saw a face peering out of the window next to the door. Then the door was taken off the chain and opened, cautiously. The dark-haired woman was small-boned and very thin, with prominent cheekbones, a sharp nose and chin, and a deep crease between heavy brows — not a pretty face, especially when it was pulled into an anxious frown. Her white tee shirt had a picture of chile peppers and announced that she was a red-hot mama. It was stained with what looked like grape juice and hung loosely over grubby jeans. A toddler hid like a shy forest creature behind her, clinging with jellied fingers to her jeans and peeking between her knees.

"Yeah?" Her voice was raspy. Her blue eyes, the irises startlingly light, caught mine and slid quickly away.

"I'm looking for Carol Connally."

"She's not here," the woman said briefly, and began to push the door shut.

"But that's *you*, Aunt Carol!" a little voice piped helpfully.

A smile flickered at the corner of the woman's thin

mouth and she stopped pushing the door. "Blabber-mouth," she said reprovingly, over her shoulder. To me, she said, "What do you want?"

I had thought about various ways to approach this woman. She'd been at the hotel for ten years, long enough to figure out how to manipulate the system. She'd also gotten close to her boss, either because she genuinely loved him or because she was taking out insurance. With the possibility of her guilt in mind, I had given some thought to cover stories. But after trying out two or three different explanations for my visit, all of them as obviously phony as a three-dollar bill, I'd settled for playing it as it lay, starting with the truth and trusting my instincts.

"My name is China Bayles," I said through the screen. "I want to talk to you about what happened at the hotel."

Her lips thinned and her eyes became apprehensive. "Are you from the police?" There was an unmistakable tremor in her voice.

"No," I said, and acted on my hunch. "I'm a lawyer. Priscilla told me that you were worried about . . . well, things. She had the idea that you might want to talk to a lawyer and suggested I drop by."

Her eyes flicked across my face, my khaki suit, brown pumps, shoulder bag. "What kind of lawyer?"

"I worked as a defense lawyer for fifteen years," I said. "If you think you might be in some kind of trouble, it could pay to get some legal advice." I opened my purse. I carry my Thyme and Seasons business cards, of course, but I also have a few cards that have just my name and phone number. I gave her one.

Over the din of the television, I heard a childish "Oh no!" and a loud wail. In the tone of a practiced tattler, a child called, "Tommy spilled his orange juice!"

Somebody—obviously Tommy speaking in his own defense—countered with, "Marcie made me do it."

"I did not, you stupid!" Marcie retorted righteously. "You were trying to balance it on your nose. Now just look. It's all over Aunt Carol's brand-new sofa!"

"Anyway," the criminal said, conceding his crime, "there was only a little bit."

With a sigh, Carol Connally opened the door and stepped back. "You'd better come in," she said.

We picked our way through the messy living room, which was littered with children's games and books and electronic toys, some obviously quite costly. I glanced from the large sofa, where Tommy had spilled the orange juice he'd been balancing on his nose, to the wall of television and stereo equipment that filled one whole end of the room. The van, the sofa, the entertainment center— all new, all expensive. My hunch got stronger.

At Carol Connally's direction, I brushed bread crumbs off the cane seat of a kitchen chair and sat at a glass-topped table on which was a toaster, a drippy jar of strawberry jam, and several more-or-less-finished bowls of cereal and glasses of milk. She poured me a mug of coffee and offered me a doughnut from a bakery box. I said no, thank you.

"You don't like doughnuts?" The child who spoke was an elfish girl of about eight, probably the same one who had pointed out that Aunt Carol *was* Aunt Carol and who had ratted on the orange juice juggler. She asked her question gravely, with a curious tilt of her brown head.

"I do like doughnuts," I said, also gravely. "I've already had my breakfast, though."

"Can I have her doughnut, Aunt Carol?" It was an unrepetant Tommy, in jockey shorts and no shirt, with an orange juice mustache under a runny nose.

"Wipe up the orange juice Tommy spilled on the sofa,

Marcie," Carol Connally instructed, handing a wet dish-cloth and a roll of paper towels to the older girl. "No doughnuts for you, Tommy," she said to the little boy, who was probably five. The tenderness in her voice soft-ened her refusal. She put one on a saucer and handed it to him. "But you can take this one to your mother. She's nursing the baby. Cream?" she asked me, putting a coffee mug in front of me. She opened a large double-door re-frigerator and took out a carton. "It's milk, actually. We ran out this morning, and I had to load the kids into the van and go to the supermarket before Nancy got up." Her words came out in hurried jerks, as if this kitchen-talk were a way of avoiding a different subject.

"I stopped by earlier," I said. "I guess that was while you were at the store."

I accepted the milk and sweetener, while Marcie took the clean-up equipment and Tommy carried off the doughnut. The only one left was the smallest child, a little girl of about two, who had stood behind Carol Connally's legs. Now she was hiding behind the kitchen door, one round blue eye peeping owlishly around it, a one-eyed wraith. I wondered if she thought she was invisible as long as she stood behind something. Carol Connally put her cup on the table and sat down, with an audible sigh.

"They must be keeping you pretty busy," I said.

"Do you have kids?"

I shook my head. "I can't imagine living with four un-der the age of—what is it? Eight?"

"Marcie's seven," she said. In the sharper light, I no-ticed that there were dark circles under her eyes and fine lines around her mouth. Weariness or worry or both? She looked at me over the rim of her coffee mug. "Prissy talks too much. What did she tell you?"

Sitting here watching this small, thin woman going

about the everyday task of caring for her sister's children, it was hard to visualize her putting a bullet through Rosemary's cheek. But I'd known murderers who looked innocent enough to fool a jury. Anyway, there was the van out front, the toys and the sofa and the entertainment center, and who knows what else—not the kind of things you buy on a bookkeeper's salary. And her obvious nervousness. She was so fidgety she could hardly sit still.

I answered her question honestly. "She said that Rosemary Robbins discovered a shortage in the hotel accounts. She said you were worried that you might be accused of stealing the money, or that you'd be fired. Or both."

She put down the mug with a thump. Her nails were bitten short. I wondered if she was an ex-smoker.

"Is that true, Carol?" I asked after a minute. "*Are* you afraid you might be accused?"

"Mama wants a cup of coffee," Tommy said. He was followed by Marcie, with a dripping dishcloth and a wad of used paper towels. "I'm supposed to bring it to her."

"You're too little to carry coffee, Tommy," Marcie said authoritatively. "You'll just spill it, like your orange juice. And you might spill it on the baby. *I'll* take it to Mama."

Carol pushed back her chair and got up. "I'll take it to her, kids. You go watch cartoons." Without a word to me, she poured a cup of black coffee and left the room with it. But the children didn't leave. They stood staring at me as if I were an alien from outer space. A Klingon, maybe. Outside, in the next yard, somebody started up a lawn mower.

"Have you ever seen a baby?" Tommy inquired.

"One or two," I admitted.

Tommy wrinkled his nose. "Jennifer's ugly. She cries all the time. And she pukes. *I* never cried when I was a baby. Mama says." He put one hand into the front of his jockey shorts and his thumb into his mouth.

Marcie snatched at both hands. "You're just jealous 'cause Jennifer smiled at *me*," she said.

Tommy's lower lip went out. "That wasn't a smile. She was just goin' poop in her pants." The thumb sneaked back into the mouth, but Marcie was holding the other hand.

Marcie retaliated. "Well, *I* get to change her diaper and you don't. An' I don't suck my thumb. So *there*."

I interrupted this sibling conflict with "Your mother is very lucky to have both of you to help."

Marcie was smug, Tommy looked doubtful, and behind the door, Junie made a sad little noise.

"She's lucky to have all *three* of you," I amended.

"Junie doesn't help," Tommy said. "She only makes messes."

"Not as messy as your orange juice," Marcie said.

Carol came back into the room carrying a folded disposable diaper. "If you'll go watch cartoons and let me talk to this lady," she said, "I'll take you to Barton Springs after lunch." She put the diaper into a bulging plastic trash bag beside the back door.

There was a chorus of jubilant oh, boys! and Marcie and Tommy dashed into the living room. Junie sidled out from behind the door and followed them. Her diaper was coming down and something brown was smeared on her right leg.

"Marcie," Carol called, "clean Junie up and change her Pamper. And find her a clean shirt." She sat down again. "I don't know *what* Nancy's going to do when I go back to work." A shadow crossed her face and the corners of her mouth got firmer. "But I'm not going back to the hotel. And I'm not staying in Pecan Springs, either. I've decided to apply for a job with the State, here in Austin.

I'm moving in with Nancy and the kids."

"It might be a little crowded," I said, looking around.

She tossed her head. "We've found a new place out in Westlake Hills. A real big four-two, with a yard and a fence. The kids can go out to play without somebody having to watch all the time."

I gave her a direct glance. "What are you afraid of back at the hotel, Carol?"

She dropped her eyes, not answering. After a moment, she took a knife from one of the plates, scooped a dribble of strawberry jam off the table, and scraped it onto a saucer. "Why did you come?" she countered.

I sipped my coffee. "Because I'm not as sure as the police are that Jeff Clark is a killer."

"Jeff." His name escaped her lips involuntarily, in a shuddery sigh heavy with grief and pain.

"Priscilla told me that you and he were close," I said, watching her. Whether or not she had killed Rosemary, she had some kind of guilty knowledge. Perhaps it wasn't significant, or even relevant. But *she* thought it was, and she was afraid — for herself or someone else. For Jeff?

She hadn't been crying, but tears had suddenly appeared in her eyes. "I worked there for a long time before we got to be friends. Then I started staying late, and sometimes we'd talk. Just friendly stuff. You know how it is. And then he came over to my house and we — " She closed her eyes, remembering. When she opened them again, they were full of loss. "I loved him more than I ever loved anybody." Her fingers were trembling and she pressed them together around the cup. "He loved me, too. I know he did. Until *she* came along, anyway. I knew the day he brought her into the office that there'd be trouble."

"Wait a minute," I said. "I thought *Matt* hired Rosemary."

She shook her head. "It was Jeff."

"I suppose it was you who called the police and told them about Rosemary and Jeff."

Her mouth went tight and she sucked in her breath, as if she were trying to hold in an explosion. "I wanted to hurt him. I thought—" She swallowed. "But that was before."

"Before what?" I asked gently.

She pressed her lips together and turned her head away.

I put my hand on her thin wrist. "Look, Carol. Rosemary is dead, and the police believe Jeff killed her. Regardless of how you felt about her, or about them, it's important for the truth to come out. The only way that can happen is for everybody who's involved to tell what they know."

There was a tic at the corner of her eyelid, and she brushed her fisted hand across her cheek. Her voice was raspy. "But what if . . ." She stopped and tried again. "What if the truth could . . . get me in trouble?"

I leaned forward and put my hand on her arm. "If you know something about the embezzlement or the murder but you're afraid you'll incriminate yourself by talking to the authorities, I may be able to help. Or put you in touch with someone who can."

She moved her head stiffly. Her pupils were dilated and the color in her cheeks had faded. "What if I was scared of . . . being killed?"

I was a little surprised. "If it's Jeff you're afraid of, you can stop worrying. He's in Acapulco."

She looked at me. Her lower lip was trembling and she caught it between her teeth.

"He drove to Brownsville and left his car at the airport," I said, wanting to be reassuring. "He flew to Mexico City, paid for a hotel and some clothes with his credit card, and then went on to Acapulco. A friend of mine, Mike McQuaid, has gone down there to find him and bring him back."

Her hands came up to cover her face. "Oh, God! Poor Jeff!" Her voice was despairing. "I wish, oh, I wish . . ." She began to cry, long hard sobs that shook her shoulders. "Why did he have to get involved with her? Why couldn't he just be content for us to go on like we were? I didn't want anything from him, not like she did. She wanted everything. Him, a baby, the hotel—" She got up and found a paper towel to blow her nose into. "And now he's gone. He's gone, and I'll never see him again!"

I stood, too, and came close to her. "I know you care for him, Carol. If you have *any* information that will untangle this mess or help us find him—"

She wiped her eyes with a corner of the paper towel. "Can you guarantee I'll be okay?"

"The safest thing for you to do," I said carefully, "is to tell what you know, either to me or—"

"You can't guarantee."

"If you know anything that will bring Jeff back—"

"*Nothing* will bring him back!" She turned away, her shoulders heaving. "I—I'll think about it. I can't right now. It's too—" She swallowed, trying to get hold of herself. "I have to talk to Nancy first. I have to . . . to *think*. Maybe I didn't really see what I thought I . . . Anyway, I don't know what it means. Maybe I'm all wrong."

And that was all she would say. Whatever she knew, she wasn't going to talk about it this morning, at least not to me. And I was sure that Bubba Harris wouldn't have gotten as much out of her as I had.

She turned and led me through the living room, avoiding Tommy, who was pushing a fire engine across the floor, making siren sounds. Marcie was lying on her back with her legs draped over the back of the sofa, singing the words to a Barbie commercial. Junie stepped out from behind a chair and followed us. When we reached the door, the little girl attached herself to her aunt's legs and peeked out at me.

I turned to face Carol. "It's not going to get any easier, holding onto it like this," I said. "It will only make you more and more unhappy, and prolong Jeff's agony, wherever he is."

Her eyes were bleak. "Nothing can do that."

"Please, call me when you're ready to talk about it," I said. "Do you still have my card?"

She didn't say yes or no. She just stood there, her shoulders slumped and a look of almost unbearable misery on her face, with Marcie pretending to be Barbie, Tommy pretending to be a fire truck, and Junie pretending to be invisible.

CHAPTER FIFTEEN

On rosemary:
Grow for two ends, it matters not at all,
Be't for my bridal or my burial.

Robert Herrick, 1591–1674

Katz's Deli (Katz's Never Kloses) is famous for its kosher tacos, blintzes, and knishes. Marc Katz, the owner, used to drive a yellow cab—a *long* yellow cab. When he quit cabbing to open a restaurant, he had the cab gutted, then sliced in half lengthwise like a loaf of Jewish rye, and mounted above the second-floor windows on the Sixth Street side of his deli and bar. There's a yellow cab inside, too, painted on a blue wall opposite the door. On the other walls are pictures. Hillary's is there, "Katz's is Kool," scrawled on it. So is Michael Jordan's: "Katz's is a slam dunk." Bette Midler's, over the dining room door, says, "You don't have to be Jewish."

The dining room—with a high, pressed-tin ceiling painted black and white walls decorated with the work of local artists, a large plastic marlin, and neon—held a motley crew. There were authoritative businessmen looking like godfathers in black suits with lots of clean white cuff showing, chic businesswomen in big-shouldered jackets and short skirts with lots of thigh showing, and laid-back hippie types in frayed denim cutoffs, Birkenstocks, and Armadillo World Headquarters tee shirts. The waitpersons were formal in white shirts, black slacks or skirts, and ties. The tables held bottles of Heinz catsup and jars of Ba-Tempte Mustard. Katz's is a blend of uptown and funk.

Smart Cookie was seated at a table beside the window. As I sat down, she put aside the menu she was studying. "What did you find out from the bookkeeper?" she demanded.

"She knows something."

Sheila made an impatient noise. "So what does she know?"

"She won't say. She's scared." I didn't have to look at the menu Sheila handed me. "Bagle with lox, cream cheese, onion, and tomato," I said to the waiter who appeared at the table. His long brown hair was pulled back in a ponytail. "And iced tea."

"Iced tea for me, too, and a turkey reuben," Sheila said. "What *did* she say?" she asked me, as the waiter went away.

I unfolded my napkin onto my lap (a large cloth napkin, which is my idea of the napkins restaurants ought to use). Outside the window, a red, white, and blue Capital Metro bus stopped to disgorge a young man with a guitar case. On the side of the bus were the words "Clean Machine. Fueled by Natural Gas." Austin is that kind of city.

"She said . . ." I stopped, considering. "Well, it wasn't actually what she *said* that makes me think she knows something. It was more like what she *didn't* say." I frowned. There was something, though. Carol had said something that I should have paid more attention to, but I couldn't quite remember what it was.

"Oh, for crying out loud," Sheila said disgustedly. "You know who you sound like? Ruby. You sound *just* like

Ruby. Do you know how *irritating* it is when people talk that way?"

I gave Sheila a juridical look. "I have deposed enough criminal defendants during the course of my career to know when the subject under interrogation is concealing important facts or suspicions. It is my opinion that Carol Connally possesses knowledge of criminal misconduct which she believes relevant to this inquiry. She appears to be constrained from revealing this knowledge by a deep-seated fear that such a revelation may be self-incriminating and may place her in physical danger."

Sheila started to say something, but I shook my head and she subsided.

"This witness actually conveyed very little factual information to me during our conversation this morning, but I am confident that she will have something to say in the very near future, and that when she does, it will alter our fundamental understanding of this case." I paused. "Does that answer your question, Ms. Dawson?"

"I'm sorry," Sheila said humbly.

"You ought to be," I said. I took a long pull on my iced tea, which had arrived while I was orating. "You should grovel. You should wear sackcloth and ashes."

"That's a seriously good line of bull." Her tone was chastened. "I mean, I'm impressed."

"It was either learn how to talk that way, or forever eat the other guy's courtroom shit," I said. "But I'm sure glad I don't have to do it for a living any longer. It corrodes the soul."

"So what do you think she knows?"

"Could be any one of a number of things. She could know who took the money. Or she might have taken it herself, all or part of it. Her sister is unmarried and has four children, but the house is equipped with a floor-to-ceiling entertainment center, a huge double-door refrigerator, and a new sofa with a large orange juice stain. *And* there's a new Toyota van in the driveway and enough toys to stock a play school. But with all of that, I don't think she's a murderer."

The waiter arrived with our food, trying hard to pretend that he hadn't heard the last sentence. "Is everything all right?" he asked uneasily.

"Wonderful," Sheila said with enthusiasm, looking down at her reuben: turkey pastrami on grilled Jewish rye, smothered in hot sauerkraut and melted swiss.

"Great." I said. I glanced up at the waiter's worried face. "We're writers," I added. "We're plotting a murder mystery."

"No kidding," he said. "I always thought it'd be fun to write one of those things. If I did, I'd put Katz's into it. A lot of very weird people come in here." His glance included us among the very weird. "You putting Katz's into it?"

"That's why we're here," I said. I looked down at my bagel, slathered with cream cheese and heaped with bright orange salmon. "Among other things."

"My name is Luther," he confided. "You gonna put me in it too?"

"Absolutely," I said.

"Like, wow, man," Luther said happily, and went away.

"An orange juice stain?" Sheila asked.

"Forget the orange juice," I said. "Carol and her sister are also planning to move to Westlake Hills, where I'll bet you can't touch a rental for under nine hundred a month."

Sheila began on her reuben. "So she's been taking the money and giving it to her sister?"

"Some of it, none of it, who knows? It might be that she knows who *has* been taking it, and she's getting paid to keep her mouth shut." I layered purple onion slices on top of the salmon. "Or maybe she just likes to spend her earnings on her sister's kids, and what she knows has nothing to do with the embezzlement. Maybe it's got to do with the murder." Something was nagging at me, something I'd noticed when I was talking to Carol, but hadn't followed up on. Something about Matt—

"But if she knows who shot Rosemary, what's keeping her from going to the police?"

"She's afraid—which translates into being afraid of somebody."

"Jeff's in Mexico. She can't be afraid of *him.*"

"Exactly," I said. I picked up my bagel and bit into it. Heaven.

"But you don't *know* that what she knows is connected with the murder."

"Right," I admitted with my mouth full. "It's my guess that she'll eventually tell us what's bothering her, but not if she's pushed. *Especially* not if she's pushed. I left my name and phone number."

"Well, maybe she'll call," Sheila said, in a tone that implied she wouldn't.

I suddenly remembered what it was I'd forgotten. "Oh, yeah," I said. I put down my bagel. "Carol also said it wasn't Matt who hired Rosemary. It was Jeff."

Sheila tilted her head. "Of course it was. I told you that the night we met Ondine at Maggie's."

"You did? I guess I forgot. But if Jeff was taking money, why would he hire somebody to audit the books? It doesn't make sense."

"No, I guess it doesn't," Sheila said.

We applied ourselves to our sandwiches and the conversation lagged. When we had finished, I looked at my watch. "Too bad you've got that meeting, Smart Cookie. There's something I'd like to do back in Pecan Springs, and it would be better if we could do it together."

She made a face. "As it happens, the meeting was canceled. Yesterday, in fact. Only nobody had the presence of mind to call and save me a trip. What is it you want to do?"

"I'd like to get into Rosemary's house and have a look around. I still don't feel I know very much about who she really was. Everybody I've talked to seems to have it in for her in one way or another."

"It happens all the time. People justify the crime by putting the victim in the wrong. Like, she deserved to get raped because she was wearing a short skirt. Or she was asking to get killed, walking down that dark street."

"Yeah," I said. "Lawyers are famous for that trick. Defend the criminal by criminalizing the victim. The hell of it is, it works."

"Right." Sheila pushed her chair back. "The system sucks."

Luther appeared with the check. "Good luck with your murder," he said.

"Yeah," I said. "Thanks."

I'm not keen on breaking and entering. This is not to say that, driven to desperation, I have not done it in the past and would not do it in the future. But it's the sort of thing hard-boiled, brash PI's do in murder mysteries, and it almost always leaves me cold. I'm probably being too squeamish, but if I got caught at it, I know what would happen. Among numerous other indignities (such as being strip-searched, fingerprinted, photographed, arraigned, tried, and eventually found guilty), I'd be disbarred, sure as God made little green apples. And while I don't expect to practice law again, I egotistically (and prudently) prefer to remain an officer of the court. Which means that I have to keep my nose clean, or at least as clean as other lawyers keep theirs, which probably isn't saying a whole hell of a lot.

By the time Sheila and I had made our separate ways back to Pecan Springs and joined forces at her house, I had a plan. We talked it over for a few minutes, then I drove both of us downtown to Bubba's office.

The Pecan Springs Police Department is on one corner of the square, in the basement of an old stone building that houses City Hall on the main floor, the mayor's office on the second floor, and bats in the belfry. (Honestly. They're Mexican freetails, a great boon to civilized life in Adams County. They come out at night and gobble up tons of mosquitos. Their nitrogen-rich guano makes terrific fertilizer, as any serious Central Texas gardener will testify.)

I parked diagonally in front of the building, let Sheila out to do her errand, and sat with the windows rolled down, watching idly as MaeBelle Battersby, the latest in a venerable line of meter persons employed by the PSPD, went about her work. Idly, that is, until MaeBelle stuck a ticket under the windshield wiper of Pauline Perkins's husband's blue Oldsmobile, which was parked next to me.

"Hi, MaeBelle," I said.

She bent over to peer inside the car, and brightened. "Well, hidy, Ms. Bayles. How's the herb bidness these days?"

"Flourishing," I said. "How's it with you?"

"Busy as a hound in flea season," she said happily. "I've given out three tickets in this last block."

"I've been noticing," I said. "Do you happen to know whose Oldsmobile that is?"

She looked at it without curiosity. "Cain't say as I do," she said. "All I know is the meter's expired." She looked at the car's front end, frowning. "Got a real low right front tar, too."

"Yes," I said. "Well, if I'm not mistaken, that car belongs to Darryl Perkins, who just happens to be married to Pauline Perkins, who just happens to be—"

"Oopsie," MaeBelle said, and hastily retrieved the ticket. "Mebee I just better walk up to the second floor and tell the mayor that her right front tar's real low on air. As a curtsey."

I grinned. "I'm sure she'd appreciate it," I said. "She'll probably even give you a couple of dimes for the meter." The mayor's husband runs a used car dealership. It's not easy to guess whether a car with an expired meter near City Hall comes from Darryl's lot, but it's a basic job skill that every meter person before MaeBelle has had to learn. A prerequisite to extended tenure and optimal career enhancement, you might say.

A few minutes later, MaeBelle came back, fed coins into the meter, and bent over to look in my window.

"*Gracias*, Miz Bayles," she said, and patted my shoulder. "You need a favor, you let me know, y'hear? I never fergit a friend."

"Don't mention it," I said. MaeBelle went on to the next block, and Sheila came up the steps from the basement. She was carrying a key with a large yellow tag.

"Voilà," she said triumphantly, brandishing the key. She got into the car. "Or words to that effect."

"Did Bubba give you any grief?"

She laughed. "Are you kidding? I gave him the spiel, and he said he'd hate like hell for me to get into any kind of trouble with the IRS, and handed me the key. After all, I *am* a fellow police officer. He knows he can trust me."

I grinned. Sheila's story, as we settled on it after we got back to Pecan Springs, was that Rosemary had been doing Sheila's taxes, late, and was almost ready to file when she was killed. Sheila needed to get her taxes straightened out, and the only way she could do it was to retrieve her material from Rosemary's office. And to do that, she needed the key and Bubba's permission to enter Rosemary's house, which (like The Blue Beast) hadn't yet been turned over to the next of kin.

Of course, Sheila's taxes were already filed, and it wasn't her material we were after. I wanted to see if I could find something, anything, that the police might have missed—some clue to what had been going on at the hotel, some idea of the relationship between Rosemary and Jeff, some *concrete* fact that might make sense of the cobwebs of belief and innuendo that still obscured the truth.

But before we went to Rosemary's, I wanted to make a quick swing past the shop. Thyme and Seasons is a couple of blocks from the square, so it only took a few minutes to get there. It took even less time for Laurel to give me a rundown on the morning's business, and for me to ring a total on the register. It wasn't bad, considering that it was July.

"Did McQuaid call?" I asked. He'd only been gone since Monday, but it felt like a month. I caught myself wishing he was back. I'd like to hear his take on Carol Connally.

Laurel shook her head. "Haven't heard anything from him," she said. "But Mr. Monroe called, from the hotel. He said for you to tell McQuaid that the bank hasn't picked up any charges since Mexico City—whatever that means."

"If McQuaid calls here," I said, "give him the message. He'll understand. And tell him I'll be home after I pick Brian up at the sheriff's office. Has Emily come up with anything on the air-conditioning?"

Laurel sighed and fanned her face with her hand. All the doors and windows were open and there was a breeze, but the shop was still pretty hot. "The compresser is a dead duck," she said. "She'll call you tonight, at home." She looked down at her khaki shorts. "I hope you don't mind my shorts. I went home at lunchtime and changed. It's too hot for jeans."

"No problem," I said. "I guess we'll have to get a new unit. Any other good news?"

A smile quirked Laurel's mouth. "Your mother called. She'll call you tonight at home."

I muttered something under my breath.

"What was that?" Laurel asked in an innocent tone. "I didn't quite hear."

"I said I think I'll take Brian to the movies tonight."

Laurel pursed her lips. "Well, she *is* your mother."

"Just because she's my mother doesn't mean she's my *mother*," I replied obscurely. Now that Leatha's sobered up and married a man who actually pays attention to her (something my father never did), she thinks the only thing that will bring her total happiness is a warm and loving relationship with her only child. But I am as unskilled at being a daughter to my mother as I am at being a stand-in mother to McQuaid's son, and I continually disappoint her by not being as warmly responsive as she would like.

I left Laurel watering the plants out front, and Sheila and I drove to Rosemary's house. The cicadas were still droning like a flock of buzz saws, the cuckoo was still mildly sardonic, and the neon-yellow crime scene tape was still strung across Rosemary's drive.

"When's Bubba going to release the house?" I asked as we got out.

"The cousin's coming in next week," Sheila said. "Normally, he wouldn't hold onto it this long, but nobody was pressing for access. Anyway, the tape discourages vandals." We walked to the front door of the stone-and-cedar house and used the key to open it and go in. Legally.

I had been inside Rosemary's office at the back of the house, but not the house itself. From the expensive and well-kept exterior, I could guess what it would be like: plush carpets, high ceilings, chandeliers, lovely (and expensive) furniture. I was right. The house was all that, and more.

But as Sheila and I walked from room to room, I became more and more uneasy — an uneasiness threaded through with a strong sense of déjà vu. Rosemary's house took me back to the upscale condo where I'd lived when I practiced law in Houston, working eighty-hour weeks, too busy to do more than sleep and change clothes and take a bath in the house where I was supposed to live. Looking around, I sensed that her life was as empty as mine was then, and as lonely. I couldn't help hoping that her relationship with Jeff had lightened that loneliness.

But if it had, there were no signs of it. There were, in fact, few signs of Rosemary herself. There was nothing in this lovely house that whispered her name, nothing that suggested that she had been a unique person, a *real* person. Oh, there was furniture: sofas and tables and chairs and lamps and so on, all in harmonious and stylish colors and sizes and fabrics, as if they had recently come out of a furniture showroom, decorator-designed, color-matched. But the rooms were as bland and generic as a suite at the Hilton. There wasn't a family photograph to show that she'd belonged to someone, or a piece of craftwork to show that she'd enjoyed making something, or even a cheap souvenir to show that she'd been somewhere. The signature of an individual, the unique touches that say "This is China's house, this is where her soul lives" or "Sheila went to the Cayman Islands once on vacation" or "Ruby absolutely adores Southwestern art"—these were absent. The house suggested that Rosemary used her home the way travelers use hotels, leaving nothing but accidental traces behind. There wasn't even enough of Rosemary to haunt the place.

The impersonal quality of the house was intensified by the oppresive silence and the stale, stuffy air. The thermostat in the hall showed the temperature to be ninety, but I shivered. Sheila and I might be here with the permission of the police, but in a deeper sense we were trespassers, violators of a private space that belonged to the dead, searchers for secrets that the living might have no right to find.

Sheila caught my glance. "Sobering, isn't it?" she said quietly. "What do you suppose she did in her spare time?"

"Maybe she didn't have any," I said. In front of me was a living room sofa that bore no indication that Rosemary had ever sat on it. Even the fireplace looked as if it had never been used. "Her ex-husband said she worked fourteen hours a day. That doesn't leave much time to get a life."

Sheila shuddered. "Let's make it snappy, huh? This is depressing."

The house offered luxury living for one: kitchen, living room, spacious master bedroom, small guest bedroom, office, garage. Sheila took Rosemary's bedroom, the living room, and the kitchen. I took the rest.

The guest bedroom at the end of the hall was obviously used for storage. Pieces of extra furniture, suitcases full of out-of-date clothing, boxes of college textbooks, winter coats — things that would go into the basement if Texas houses had basements, which they generally don't. I checked the dresser drawers, the closet shelves, under the bed. There were no financial records, no journals, no personal papers, nothing related to her death or to her real, unique life. Everything in this room could have been owned by *anybody*.

After ten minutes, I closed the door and went through the kitchen and into the office. Of the whole house, this room seemed to remember Rosemary most clearly, and all because of one simple, playful thing: a balloon. In one corner was a conference grouping of floral-print loveseat, beige chairs, and a table. In another corner was a workstation of desk, computer, file cabinets, and shelves. Everything was orderly, everything was ordinary, except for the balloon that made this room special and unique: a large, silver, heart-shaped balloon on a long string, with curliques of red paper ribbon dangling from it. Hand-printed on one side of the heart, in big red letters, was the name Rosemary. On the other side was the name Jeff. The whole room seemed to organize itself around that balloon. It made me smile.

I began with the desk. On it was a telephone and answering machine, an appointment calendar, a neat stack of papers. I replayed the messages on the answering machine. There were a half-dozen calls from people who apparently hadn't heard of her death. Several were from clients, one was from the *Enterprise*, reminding her to renew her subscription, two were from Snider's Jewelry, reminding her to pick up the ring she'd had engraved. I jotted down the names and numbers of the callers, disappointed that there were no personal messages.

While the answering machine was playing, I went through the desk drawers. From a Bills to Pay file in the top drawer, I learned that Rosemary hadn't yet made the July mortgage payment of $977.17, and that she still owed the Pecan Springs Electrical Co-Op $112.42 for June electricity. The Pecan Springs National Bank statements in the second drawer showed that she had a balance of just over $3,200 in her personal account, something less than $4,700 in her business account, and $4,300 in savings. If she was stashing money in another account in a different bank, the evidence for it wasn't here.

But something else was. Behind the bank statements was a Paid Invoices folder. In it was insurance paperwork and a bill, stapled together. The bill was from Dr. Gina Steuben, OB-GYN, for a D and C, performed on June 11. A dilation and curettage — not an abortion, but a surgical procedure that would finish what nature had started: a miscarriage. I glanced at the appointment calendar on the desk and turned back a page to June. Yes, there it was. Friday June 11 was marked with a small penciled "dr," and a light line had been drawn through Saturday and Sunday — days she probably wanted to take it easy.

I stared at the notation for a moment, wondering how Rosemary had felt when she wrote it. Had she been relieved, or full of sad emptiness when she learned that there wouldn't be a baby? How had Jeff felt? I glanced up at the balloon, wondering whether he had given it to her when she told him that she was pregnant with his baby — or when he learned there wouldn't be a baby. Was it a celebration, or a reassurance that whatever happened, the two of them would go on together? But the balloon was fully inflated, which suggested that she hadn't had it more than a few days before she died.

Going back to the calendar, I could see how carefully Rosemary had parceled out her time. She spent ten working hours a week at the hotel, the rest with other clients. When I turned to July, I noticed something else: beginning with last Saturday, July 7, the nine days through Sunday the 15th were marked through in a straight line, and the little letter J was neatly penciled at the beginning of the line.

I looked at it thoughtfully. If this were my calendar, my life, that marked-off time would mean a vacation, and J was the person I planned to be with. Had Rosemary and Jeff intended to go away somewhere together? But if that was what they'd meant to do, something had gone dreadfully wrong. She had died on the eve of their going, and he had fled alone. I was filled with a sense of sad futility. What had happened to bring them to this end? Was Jeff responsible, as everybody thought? Or had someone else intervened? The image of Carol Connally rose up in my mind, and I found myself questioning my intuition of her innocence. Had she learned that they planned to go away together and killed Rosemary to keep that from happening?

Still feeling the weight of Rosemary's unfulfilled plan, I turned to the file cabinet to the right of the desk. The alphabetized manila folders in the drawers contained copies of clients' tax forms, working notes, calculator tapes, computer printouts. I found one marked Bayles, another Dawson, a third McQuaid, and pulled them out. Sheila could get Bubba's permission to take them — no point in leaving them for the executor to handle. The files were the only interesting items in the cabinet. There was nothing pertaining to the hotel accounts and nothing in any way personal. No letters, no diary.

On the left side of the desk was a Macintosh, a printer, and a small copier. I considered the Mac for a minute. I had an old Apple IIc at the shop, but it was primitive in comparison. I couldn't even find the power switch on this one. I'd seen a Mac in Sheila's office, though; I'd ask her to have a look at Rosemary's computer files.

That was it for the desk. I got up. I was about to check out the closet when Sheila came in.

"Find anything?" I asked, not hopefully.

She shook her head. "A two-year-old card from the cousin in Tulsa. A Steven King thriller. Clothes in the closet, makeup in the bathroom, a grocery list on the re-frigerator door, TV dinners in the freezer. No diary, no photographs, no love letters. This place has about as much personality as a nun's cell." She paused. "What did you find?"

I pointed to the balloon.

"Ah," she said thoughtfully, and her mouth relaxed into a half-smile. "So it wasn't all work and no play. She took a vacation from numbers every now and then."

"Speaking of vacations," I said, and showed her the markings on the July page of the calendar. "What do you think? A fishing trip à deux?" I paused strategically. "Does it make sense to you that a man would murder a woman he's planning to spend nine days with?"

She made an indelicate noise. "Oh, come on, China. Men murder women they spend their *lives* with. And vice versa."

"Well, sure. But if I planned to kill somebody, I wouldn't do it before we were supposed to leave on a fishing trip. I'd do it *during*. I'd push her off the boat and claim she fell overboard or something like that. I sure as hell wouldn't kill her in her driveway and leave the body *and* my father's famous gun for the cops to find." I flipped the calendar back to June. "Here's when she ended the pregnancy. There's a medical bill in the drawer. She had a D and C."

Sheila's "Oh" was thoughtful. "So it was a miscarriage."

"That's what it looks like. I wonder if she was terribly upset about it. I would have been."

As I heard myself saying the words, I felt it: Rosemary's loss, the emptiness, the sadness when she realized that there wouldn't be a baby after all. And Rosemary and I were about the same age, which meant that the clock was running out for her, just as it was for me, just as it was for so many of us who had been single-minded about our careers. There wouldn't be many more fertile months. I'd been on the pill for years, but if by some accident I'd gotten pregnant with McQuaid's child and miscarried . . . Yes, I could feel Rosemary's loss. But whose grief? Mine or hers?

Sheila asked me something that didn't register. "What?" I asked.

"Who was the OB-GYN?" she repeated.

"Oh. Somebody named Steuben."

"That's a coincidence. Gina's my doctor, too." She paused. "I'm overdue for a Pap. Maybe she won't mind talking about Rosemary. I'd like to know why she had to have that D and C."

"She's not supposed to tell you."

"Sure. But women do chat. And there's a certain vulnerability about lying on your back with your legs spread, with her peering into your insides. I doubt if she's likely to feel threatened by my questions."

I gave her a grin. "I wonder how a male investigator would handle that one. Would you take a look at the Mac?"

While Sheila sat down at the computer, I went through the closet, which turned out to hold nothing but supplies. There was only one more place to check. I walked through the searing afternoon heat to the curb and took a handful of mail, most of it junk, out of the mailbox.

But it wasn't all junk.

Among the litter of Wal-Mart flyers and Publishers' Clearinghouse Sweepstakes announcements, I found a thick envelope that bore the return address of a San Antonio travel agency. In it was an American Airlines plane ticket in Rosemary's name, from San Antonio to Mexico City on July 7, to Acapulco on Tuesday July 10, and back to San Antonio on July 15. With the plane ticket was a confirmation from the Mexico City Hilton for the nights of July 7–9 and the Acapulco Hilton for July 10–14. The rooms were reserved in the names of Mr. and Mrs. Jeff Clark.

I stared at the confirmation form for a moment, the fuzzy picture in my mind becoming clearer. Then I went back to Rosemary's office, dialed Snider's Jewelry, and asked for Delia Snider, the owner. What Delia told me brought the picture into even sharper focus.

The ring that Rosemary had bought was a man's wedding ring. The engraving she had ordered said, "For my husband, Jeff, my heart and my life."

CHAPTER SIXTEEN

Saturn Incense

2 parts Sandalwood
2 parts Myrrh
1 part Dittany of Crete
a few drops Cypress oil
a few drops Patchouly oil

Mix thoroughly and store in a tightly capped jar. To burn, light a charcoal tablet (available where incense is sold) and place it in a censor. Once the block is glowing, sprinkle a half-teaspoon or so of the incense on the block. It will immediately begin to burn and in doing so, release fragrant smoke.

Scott Cunningham
The Complete Book of Incense, Oils & Brews

An hour later, Bubba was once more in possession of Rosemary's house key and I had retrieved Brian from the custody of the sheriff, who reported that there was still no sign of Jacoby anywhere in the county, and that Brian had been a model of deportment.

The fact that Brian had enjoyed the sheriff's office didn't seem to change his attitude toward me, however. He was communicating only in grunts and head shakes.

"Did you have a good day?" I asked cheerily. "What did you do?"

A sullen nod and a shrug, nothing else.

I tried again. "The sheriff says you helped the dispatcher. Was it fun, working with the radio?"

Another nod, then a turn to the window that said, as loudly as words, that he didn't want to talk to me.

I was frustrated and more than a little irritated. And saddened, too. This was McQuaid's child. If I loved McQuaid, I ought to at least manage to stay on speaking terms with his son. The sadness was exacerbated by the memory of Rosemary's loss. Like Rosemary, I had very little time left to have a child. But even if I could get pregnant, I didn't want to. My hands were full with the shop, with my life. If I stayed with McQuaid, Brian was the only child we'd ever have. The knowledge made the silence between us more dispiriting.

Sheila arrived a few minutes after we did. I changed into shorts and a tee, and we adjourned to the kitchen to do something about supper. We settled on ham sandwiches, salad, and cold cucumber soup, from a favorite recipe collected by Fannie Couch, who writes the recipe column for my newsletter and does a live call-in show called *Fannie's Back Fence* on KPST-FM.

While we worked, we talked. It was clear to me from what we had discovered at Rosemary's house that she and Jeff had planned to be married and take a nine-day Mexican honeymoon, and that Jeff had concealed their intentions with the cover story of a fishing trip to South Padre.

Sheila acknowledged that my explanation made a certain sense, but she put a different spin on what we found.

"The evidence that they planned to get married is *Rosemary's* evidence," she said, slicing the last cucumber lengthwise. "She bought the ring and made the hotel reservations. Maybe the whole scheme was her idea. Maybe when she discovered that Jeff was fiddling the books, she offered him a deal: her silence in return for a wedding ring and a community property share of everything he had. She had the leverage to get it, too." She seeded the cucumber and popped it into the blender. "So he shot her, hopped in the car, and drove to Brownsville, then simply followed the itinerary they'd worked out." She turned the blender on.

"What about the balloon?" I asked.

"What about it? Anybody can buy a balloon and write names on it with Magic Marker. Maybe she was engaging in some wishful thinking."

"It still doesn't make any sense to me," I said. "Jeff would have to be crazy to kill her in her driveway and toss his father's gun where it was sure to be found."

"Lots of killers are crazy." She turned off the blender. "Anyway, who's got a better motive? You eliminated Curtis Robbins and that Rhodes woman over in San Marcos, and you said yourself that you don't think the bookkeeper did it. Who's left?"

"How about Matt Monroe?"

"I suppose it's possible." Sheila went to the refrigerator for buttermilk. "But if Matt killed Rosemary because she had the goods on him, why would *Jeff* run? More to the point, why would he turn over his half of the hotel to Matt? That makes about as much sense as hip pockets on a hog."

"Hip pockets on a hog?"

"Sure." She poured buttermilk into the blender. "Haven't you ever heard that one? It was my granddaddy's favorite put-down. That, and 'It does about as much good as pushing a wheelbarrow with rope handles.' "

I finished slicing the ham and began to layer it onto the

bread. "Too bad you didn't find anything in the computer files," I said.

"Yeah." She flipped the blender on for a few seconds, then off again. "There could be something there, but if it is, it's in the numbers, and I'm no accountant." She glanced up. "Do you have any mint? Cucumber soup isn't the same without it."

"There's some growing down by the creek," I said. "I'll send Brian." I went to the foot of the stairs and yelled. No answer. I yelled again. Nothing.

"Little twit," I muttered under my breath, and took the stairs two at a time. "Brian!" I banged on his door. No answer. "Hey, Brian, I need you!" I shoved the door open. The room was empty. Einstein clung to the drape, eyeing me malevolently. Ivan the Hairible sat stoically in his terrarium. There was no sign of Brian.

Downstairs and through the house I went, calling, first with irritation, then with anger, and then, inescapably and irrevocably, with fear.

Sheila came to the kitchen door with a tomato in her hand, and saw the look on my face.

"Brian's gone," I said frantically.

"Maybe he went to play at the creek," she said.

The two of us dashed through the yard and hurtled down to the creek, calling. There was no sign of Brian. Then we ran back through the yard and up the drive into the lane. That's when we saw the first drips. Dime-sized, heart-stopping splashes in the dust. Drops of blood.

"Brian!" I cried. But the only answer was the brilliant trill of a cardinal.

We broke into a pounding run down the quarter-mile length of dusty lane, following the bloody trail. Finally, we reached the road. There were no more drips.

And no Brian.

• • •

The first county car came screaming down the lane ten minutes after I dialed 911. Blackie arrived seven minutes later. He and the two deputies searched the premises and followed the bloody trail to its stopping point, and then came back to the house.

"You're sure he just didn't decide to go see one of his buddies?"

I shook my head numbly. "His bike is still in the garage, and the nearest friend lives two miles away." That was Arnold. I'd already called to be sure he wasn't there. "Anyway, he knows he's not supposed to leave the house. And there's the blood." *The blood.* My heart was a clenched fist, throbbing, painful.

"Since when did knowing he wasn't supposed to do something keep a kid from doing it?" Blackie asked. "But we have to go on the premise that Jacoby's got him." He added, as if to ease my fears, "That's standard procedure now. We treat every missing child report as if the child is in immediate danger. Chances are, he's not."

I nodded, hardly hearing. My hands were clammy and my breath was ragged. If I'd taken better precautions, if I'd watched Brian more closely, if I hadn't been so busy talking to Sheila—

"What was he wearing?"

The question brought Brian to my mind: a small, vulnerable boy with a wide grin and freckles. With the image came the painful recollection that when I'd seen him last, he wasn't speaking to me. If Jacoby had taken him, if I never saw him again, that memory would haunt me the rest of my life.

"The same thing he had on when he was with you." I blinked to keep the tears back. "Jeans. A Star Trek jersey. Oh, and Mr. Spock ears."

Blackie nodded. "Shouldn't be too hard to spot him in that getup. I'll need a good photograph, without the ears." He stepped off the porch and went to his county car to put out an APB for a small boy with large pointed ears and a man with a snake tattoo, and then dispatched one of his deputies to collect drip samples for lab testing. I found the photograph to give to Blackie. I gave him one of Jacoby's mug shots, as well.

A half hour later, a dozen men — neighbors, volunteer firemen, off-duty police — began to gather in the yard to search the rugged area between Limekiln Road and the old quarry, flooded now, on the theory that Brian might have wandered off in that direction. I couldn't believe that's what had happened, but I was too restless to simply sit and wait.

"I'll go with the searchers," I said.

Blackie shook his head. "I want you by the phone. Brian may call. Or Jacoby — if that's who we're dealing with here — may make a ransom demand."

"Ransom?" I didn't believe it for a second. Jacoby didn't take Brian because he was after money. He took the boy because he wanted revenge. My blood felt cold and thin. But the mention of the phone reminded of something else, and I looked at the clock. It was nearly 7:30.

"McQuaid's supposed to call in a couple of minutes," I said. My throat was so thick I could barely speak. "I've got to tell him what's happened."

"Hang on," Blackie said. He put a hand on my arm. "McQuaid can't do a damned thing but worry. Let him get a night's sleep. If the boy hasn't shown up, we can tell him tomorrow."

"The sheriff's right," Sheila agreed, as the two of us went into the kitchen to make another pot of coffee.

"When McQuaid calls, I'll tell him that you and Brian went to a movie. Should I tell him about what we found today? The plane tickets and the hotel reservations, I mean."

"I guess so," I said dully. "Whatever you think."

When McQuaid phoned from Acapulco a little later, Sheila took the call in his office. I stood by the kitchen window, leaning my cheek against the glass, separated from McQuaid by a gulf of evasions and half-truths and outright lies, separated by the fact that he had been right about Jacoby while I had been arrogantly self-confident, and wrong.

"He's been working Acapulco all day and hasn't found a trace of Jeff," Sheila said, coming into the kitchen. "I told him what we found. You're supposed to call him." She gave me a half-smile. "He says to tell you he loves you."

Matt, Jeff, Rosemary—they seemed a thousand miles away, farther even than McQuaid. I sank down in the rocker and dropped my face in my hands. "How am I going to tell him, Sheila?" I asked bleakly. "It's exactly what he was afraid of. And it's *my* fault for not being more careful!"

Sheila knelt beside me, pulled my hands down, and made me look at her. "It's not your fault Brian's gone, any more than it's McQuaid's fault for going off to Mexico, or my fault for letting Jacoby walk in and kidnap the boy while I was running the blender in the kitchen." Her voice toughened. "It *happened*, China. That's all. Don't beat yourself up about it."

"I know," I said. "But the thing is . . . the thing is that I've never been able to show Brian that I care about him, Sheila. That I *love* him—" I doubled up over the sudden, agonizing pain in my stomach. The tears were flowing. I could taste salt on my tongue.

Why couldn't I just have said that to him? Hey, Brian, I love you. I want you here with us, Brian. Not with your mother, just *here*, with the rest of the circus, Einstein and Ivan and Howard Cosell and Khat and your father and me. Such a simple thing, and I didn't do it, couldn't do it. It was the same thing with McQuaid, too. There was something lacking in me, in my soul, something not deep enough, somehow, not *caring* enough. I suddenly felt swamped with sorrow for my own lack, for what I had missed. For what *they* were missing, because of me.

"Brian and McQuaid—" I choked out. "Both of them, they deserve more than I have to give."

"Stop it!" Sheila stood up, her voice sharp, clear, like a knife, slicing through my pain. "Life isn't a soap opera, China. We do what we can. We give as much as we can. And we say, 'There it is, that's it, guys. That's all I can do, that's how much I have to give, and it's got to be enough, damn it.' "

"But what if it *isn't* enough?"

She looked down at me, her eyes warm and cool at the same time. "Come on, China. When you give all you have, you've given it *all*. When you do all you can, you've done your best. Nobody can expect any more."

I stared at her. A tear dripped off the end of my nose. "It can't be as simple as that."

"Hey." She smiled a little. "I'm your friend, would I lie to you? Now quit feeling sorry for yourself and get your ass in gear. Work will help."

Get your ass in gear. Where had I heard that before? This time, though, the other China didn't have a smart remark to make.

● ● ●

I won't say that I didn't fall back into that numbed state of dazed sorrow and self-pity a half-dozen times that night, but it was never quite as bad as it was when Sheila yanked me out of it.

For one thing, I had an idea. Southwestern Bell had made caller identification available in our area just the month before. If the system could be installed and if either Brian or Jacoby called, the originating number would be displayed on my telephone. A long shot—but if it worked, it might give us an idea of where to start looking.

Blackie called the telephone company and pulled strings to get an immediate installation. Immediate meant something over three hours. That's how long it took to get an off-duty technician to make the necessary connections in the local phone company office. Not bad, considering that the tech had to be pulled away from the softball game she was umpiring.

And the work *did* help, too. Because we wanted to keep the main telephone line free, I unplugged McQuaid's fax machine and used that phone to call the rest of Brian's friends. All I got was "Sorry, I haven't seen him," but at least I had checked. I also sat down at the computer and made up a Missing Child flyer. If Brian hadn't turned up by morning, it would be ready to go to the copy shop first thing.

But what helped most of all was Ruby. She heard the news from a female deputy who stopped to use the bathroom at the 7-Eleven store where Ruby had gone to pick up an emergency pack of Tampax. Talk about synchronicity. Twenty minutes later, she was on my doorstep, a six-foot-tall carrot in orange tunic and skinnies, wringing her hands.

"Oh, God, China," she said raggedly. Her eyes were filled with tears. "I'm so sorry. What else can I say?"

"Don't say anything else," Sheila told her practically. "Come in and have supper with us. We've been too busy to stop for a bite. Sandwiches and cucumber soup. I can guarantee the soup. I made it."

I smiled crookedly. Smart Cookie is tough and hard as any cop, and I'd hate to run into her at midnight in a dark alley. But food comes to her mind in a crisis, just as it does to most women. What is there about sandwiches and soup that soothes the soul?

Ruby followed us into the kitchen. "I called Ondine before I left home," she said, "long distance in California. She's going to consult La Que Sabe. Maybe we'll hear something before the night's out. Meanwhile, I've brought this." She held up a flat box for us to see.

"A Ouija board?" Sheila demanded. "Brian's out there with a nut case, and you want to commune with spooks? Who knows what's next?"

Ruby gave her a defensive look. "Well, we have to do something while we're waiting for the phone to ring, don't we? We can't just sit around and stare at one another. I thought this would take China's mind off—" She bit her lip, obviously not wanting to say something that would upset me.

Sheila got the soup out of the refrigerator and ladled three bowls full. "We could play poker."

"Poker's better than Ouija?" Ruby turned to me, solicitous. "What do *you* want to do, China?"

I wanted to get in the car and drive up and down streets and roads, looking for Brian, but that was a waste of energy, and anyway, I had to stay by the phone. I wanted McQuaid to walk in the door and put his arms around me and hold me, but that wasn't going to happen, at least not tonight. I wanted to tell Ruby to stop treating me as if I were slightly dysfunctional, but that would be rude.

"Let's go with Ruby's idea," I told Sheila. I got out the plate of ham sandwiches and set it on the table. "I don't think I can concentrate well enough to play poker."

"There's nothing more mindless than a Ouija board," Sheila agreed.

So after we ate, Ruby cleared off the coffee table in the living room, lit some incense, and whispered something magical over her Ouija board as she laid it out. But nothing much happened, whether it was because Sheila kept making scornful remarks or because the spirits were offended by the frequent ringing of the telephone. A half-dozen people phoned in the space of a hour: a reporter from Channel Seven in Austin, our neighbors on Limekiln Road, the chairman of McQuaid's department at CTSU, Blackie with a no-progress report. There were no calls from Ondine or La Que Sabe and none from Jacoby or from Brian, whose voice I wanted most desperately to hear. I wouldn't even mind if he'd come into the room screaming, "You're a Marcasian slime mold!" —as long as he *came*.

A few minutes before ten, I suddenly thought of Sally. Keeping the situation from McQuaid didn't pose much of a problem, since it was unlikely that the news of one little boy's kidnapping would be carried in the Mexican media. But San Antonio was another story. Sally might learn about Brian from the ten o'clock television news. I was angry at myself for not calling her sooner.

When I dialed her number, though, I got a crisply metallic voice saying in computer-chip syllables, "This number has been disconnected." And when I called San Antonio information for her new number, I got another metallic voice, informing me that as far as the phone company was concerned, there was no such person as Sally McQuaid.

"She's probably gone unlisted." Ruby pushed the planchette toward me. "Smart Cookie's too skeptical to do any good with Ouija. You try, China."

"Yeah, China." Sheila laughed shortly. "Ask Ouija for Sally's phone number."

"I'm no good at right-brained things, Ruby," I said. "I'm a left-brain person."

Ruby was patient. "*Everybody's* brain has two halves, China. Even yours. Give it a try. You might not get anything, but it'll be good for your right brain to get a little exercise."

I did get something, though. It was odd, the sensation of that flimsy little plastic thing tugging, almost, against my reluctant fingers. I didn't for a minute believe that there was anything to it, of course. But Ruby believed. She started writing down the letters the minute the planchette veered toward one.

"*G,*" she said excitedly. "You're onto something! You're connecting!"

Sheila scowled. "Stop pushing that thing, China. You'll just get Ruby all worked up."

"I'm not pushing," I said. "It's moving by itself."

Ruby sat forward on her chair, eyes wide, pencil poised over her notepad. Her orange hair seemed to be charged with electricity. "What's that? A *U*? Way to go, China! *G,U.* What's next?"

"Guppy?" Sheila guessed. "Gullible?"

Ruby's excitement ran out pretty quickly, because the silly little plastic piece was only interested in three more letters, an *R,* a *P,* an *S,* and then it quit. Or I quit, or something. The whole thing was stupid, anyway. I shouldn't be wasting time with something as foolish as a

Ouija board, when Brian was out there in the dark somewhere, held captive by a man who'd already killed two people and had nothing to lose.

"G-U-R-P-S," Ruby muttered, squinting at what she had written. "Gurps. It must be a clue to Brian's whereabouts. Maybe it's a town."

"Maybe Ouija doesn't know how to spell," Sheila said. She pushed the board away and stood up. "Or maybe that first letter was supposed to be a *B*, which would make it burps, which is exactly what I feel like doing. Who wants coffee?"

"I'll make some herb tea," I said. "I'm wired enough already. And maybe I'll have another cup of that cucumber soup."

"Sheila," Ruby said, "you are even more left-brained than China, if that's possible. We're going to have to work on you." She looked at me. "Where's your atlas? I want to check out Gurps. I'm sure it's a town."

But there wasn't any such town in Texas or Louisiana or Oklahoma. When Ruby looked in the dictionary and the encyclopedia, there wasn't any such word. And the telephone directory offered Gurny and Gurski, but no Gurps. So she trailed after us back to the kitchen, where I got the soup out of the refrigerator, put the kettle on the Home Comfort stove, and made chamomile and catnip tea, sweetened with honey, for Ruby and me. Sheila made coffee for herself.

The doorbell rang a little after eleven, sending my pulse into double time. But it was only the telephone technician, who had made the appropriate connections in the telephone company's computer and had come to install the caller ID box. A little later, the phone rang and Blackie's number appeared on the Band-Aid–sized LCD panel. He was phoning to say that he was turning the office over to the night shift, but he'd stick close to the phone. His voice sounded weary.

"Go to bed and get some sleep, China," he said. "It'll make the time go faster." It sounded like a good idea, if oversimplified.

Ruby took the Missing Child flyer, promising to drop it off at Quick Copy the next morning. She also promised to pick up my photos of the herb conference, which I'd left at Fox Foto, next door to the copy shop.

"Try meditating," she instructed as she headed for the door. "Count your breaths. It'll calm your mind."

"Which side of my mind?" I asked. "Right or left?"

"Both." She hugged me. "When Brian calls," she added, with her normal optimism, "give him my love and tell him to come home safe. When Ondine relays something from La Que Sabe, I'll let you know." And then her optimism failed and the tears came to her eyes. She hugged me again. "I've got some Saturn incense that I keep for emergencies. Sandalwood and myrrh and dittany of Crete and borage, with cypress oil and patchouli oil. It's supposed to help you banish demons and bad spirits — you know, Saturn stuff. I'll burn some and visualize Brian being free."

Sheila headed upstairs to take a shower. "Forget all that shit about meditation and incense," she said. "It's worth about as much as that Ouija board nonsense. Try a good stiff shot of that Jack Daniel's I brought."

I turned off the lights, opened the window, and sat in the rocker, my hands in my lap, my eyes closed, trying to follow Ruby's instructions. Inhale-exhale, one-two. After a while I realized that my monkey mind wasn't going to stop swinging from tree to tree in the clamoring jungle of my thoughts, so I took Sheila's advice instead.

I climbed the stairs with a strong nightcap in one hand and the caller ID box in the other, to plug into the telephone by my bed in case Brian called during the night.

He didn't. La Que Sabe didn't call, either. And in spite of the whiskey, I lay wide awake for a long time, my eyes staring and gritty. My brain told me that guilt and sorrow wouldn't accomplish anything, that I should just do what had to be done minute to minute and let go of the wish that I'd done things differently. But my heart wouldn't let that happen.

And so I lay awake in the dark, wishing I hadn't evaded the truth so often with McQuaid, wishing I'd told Brian I loved him, wishing I'd hugged both of them a little harder, a little more often.

CHAPTER SEVENTEEN

I Borage bring alwaies courage.
                John Gerard
                John Gerard's Herbal, 1633

Blackie woke me at seven with another no-progress report. I answered groggily, brushed the sleep out of my
eyes, and carried the caller ID box downstairs to the
kitchen, where Sheila was making coffee. She was dressed
in white shorts and a red shirt with the tail out—hardly
her work costume.

"I'm not going to work," she said in answer to my question. "I called in and told them I'm taking a personal day."

"Thanks," I said. She had turned on the portable television, and Channel Seven in Austin was broadcasting
Brian's and Jacoby's photos and a plea for information.
I turned away, not wanting to look. "What do you suppose iguanas and tarantulas eat?"

We debated the question and decided to experiment
with raw hamburger and lettuce, which I took upstairs
and left in a saucer near Einstein's drape and on the floor
of Ivan's terrarium. Einstein no longer looked malevolent,
just lonely. Tarantulas are even more inscrutable than
iguanas, but I thought Ivan looked lonely, too. Just being
in Brian's room made my heart hurt, and I didn't linger.

It was a morning for telephoning, on McQuaid's fax

line so I wouldn't block incoming calls. Just after eight, I called Matt and reported what Sheila and I had found the day before. He didn't seem surprised.

"I guess none of this is important any longer as far as you're concerned," he said. "After what happened to your kid, I mean. I saw it on the TV news last night." His voice was tight. "I wish to hell I'd never sent McQuaid off on that wild-goose chase. If he'd been here, this might not've happened. You tell him to hightail it on back."

Blackie and I had talked about this. After my wakeful, remorseful night, I'd voted for calling McQuaid first thing this morning. Blackie wanted to hold off until evening, and I had finally given in.

"The sheriff says to give it another twelve hours," I said. "If Brian hasn't turned up by tonight, I'll ask McQuaid to get the first plane out tomorrow morning."

"Fair enough," Matt said. "Anyway, I've about decided that Jeff's gone for good. We'll probably never hear from him again."

My second call was to McQuaid's hotel in Acapulco. I breathed much easier when he didn't answer the phone in his room, and left a message with the switchboard. I hung up, feeling glad that I hadn't had to talk to him and guilty for feeling glad.

The third call was to Justine Wyzinski, a lawyer in San Antonio. Justine and I had been friends at law school at the University of Texas. Well, not friends, exactly — more like friendly enemies. The other law students called her The Whiz because she always came up with the right answer faster than anybody else. They called me Hot Shot because I tried like the very devil to beat her. After a couple of years of this competitive craziness, we both made Law Review, which blunted our rivalry and allowed us to relax into a wary friendship. I called on The Whiz a few months ago when Dottie Riddle got into trouble over her cats. I called her now, when *I* was in trouble, and sketched out what had happened. With The Whiz, you don't have to fill in a lot of details. She gets the picture very fast.

"I need you to locate Brian's mother for me," I said. "I have to talk to her as soon as possible." I gave her Sally's name and the only address I had. "Her home phone's disconnected, and she's quit her job."

"The news has been on TV, I take it."

"Yes," I said. "It's probably in the newspaper, too. But she'd call me the minute she heard, and she hasn't called. See what you can do, would you?"

"No sweat, Hot Shot," The Whiz said briskly. "I'll find the mom, you find the kid. Fair trade, no charge. Okay?"

"Okay," I said, and hung up with a sigh, wishing I could be more like The Whiz. She has the great knack of reducing the problem to its simplest terms and making the solution seem easy.

By the time I finished with this string of telephone calls, Ruby had arrived with the Missing Child flyers from Quick Copy, my herb conference pictures from Fox Foto, and a bag of jelly doughnuts from the Doughnut Queen.

"Did you hear anything from Ondine?" she asked.

I shook my head. "Did you?"

"Not a word," she said. She held up the bag of jelly doughnuts. "Breakfast, anybody?"

Ruby and Sheila and I installed ourselves at the kitchen table and plotted the morning's strategy. It was not quite as complicated as the landing at Normandy, but almost. Ruby would drop off flyers at the newspaper and radio stations and with a dozen friends, who had agreed to post them in all the small communities in the area and take them to the local radio stations. Sheila would use Mc-

Quaid's computer to go on-line with Internet's Missing Child network. I would stay by the other phone, which had only rung once in the last hour, with a call from the *Enterprise.*

It rang again and I grabbed for it, my heart pounding. Jacoby wasn't the kind of man who would just *take* Brian. He'd have to call and brag about it, have to make it hurt even more. But when he called, he'd give away his location. Surely this was him. Please, God, make it be him.

But the number on the LCD was the shop's number and it was Emily on the line, calling to say she was sorry about Brian and to ask what to do about the air-conditioning.

"Work it out with Laurel, would you?" I said. "I really can't think about it right now."

I hung up the phone and tuned back into the kitchen-table conversation. Sheila was telling Ruby that she had a friend who worked with the Runaway Hotline, who might know something about the best way to search for missing children. Ruby was telling Sheila that her cousin JoAnne once coordinated a search for a little girl whose father took her to Canada instead of to the circus, where the mother thought they were going.

As they talked, I reached for another jelly doughnut, and was momentarily distracted by one of the photographs Ruby had brought back from the photo shop. It was the picture I'd taken on Saturday morning: a group of smiling herbalists standing between the new fountain and a very crooked rosemary. The photo was perfect for a "What's Wrong With This Picture" caption in a gardening magazine. The rosemary had been stuck into the ground at an angle, so hastily and incompetently planted that the burlap root wrap was still intact. It could even be seen above the surface of the soil, bunched around the plant's trunk and held in place with a wire. Somebody really ought to dig up that poor rosemary and straighten it. I tucked the photo into my purse, with the thought that it would remind me to ask Matt to have it replanted.

"Well," Ruby said finally, "I guess I'd better get going." She looked at me. "You'll be all right?"

"I'll be fine," I said. "As fine as I can be, anyway." I hugged her as she headed out the door, the flyers under her arm.

"Have courage, China," she said, and touched my cheek. "We'll get these posters up this morning. Somewhere, somebody's got to have seen them. Maybe we'll get some news this morning."

But the morning wore on, and there wasn't any news. Sheila and I cleaned house (a woman's antidote for worry), made a batch of Brian's favorite cookies, and listened for the phone. Every time it rang I rushed to answer it; every time it rang I was disappointed. At noon, we fixed sandwiches and ate a few of Brian's cookies. I was washing up the dishes when the phone rang again. I looked at the LCD. It was not a number I recognized, so I started copying it as I reached for the receiver. I almost didn't recognize the voice, either, because it was so tense and raspy. The caller was Carol Connally.

"I need to see you." I could hear the clamor of children's voices in the background, and she raised hers over the din. "I've been talking things over with my sister. She's convinced me that I can't go on with my life until I get this thing settled."

"We've got a family emergency here," I said. "I need to leave this line open. Let me hang up and call you back on another line." I went into McQuaid's office and dialed the number I had copied down. Carol picked it up immediately.

"I can't go into this over the phone," she said, when I asked her why she'd called. "You'll have to come to Austin."

"I can't," I said bleakly. "My son's been kidnapped. I have to stay by the phone."

"Kidnapped!" she exclaimed. "You mean that was your kid I heard about on TV this morning?" She paused, suspicious. "Wait a minute. I thought you said you didn't have any kids."

"I live with his father," I said. "That makes him my son."

It was an epiphany for me. For the four years McQuaid and I had been together, I'd always thought of Brian as *his* son, a kind of weekend rent-a-kid whose antics livened up the picnics and kept things from getting too serious. But now he was *my* son as well, and the recognition brought raw, sharp pain. I loved him, I was responsible for him, and I didn't know where he was or even whether he was still alive. All my muscles were knotted up, and my throat hurt.

She sounded resigned. "Well, I guess if you can't come here, I'll have to tell you over the phone. The thing is, it sounds so unreal, like I'm making it up. Sometimes I think maybe I am. Like maybe I dreamed it, and it didn't really happen." Her voice was thin, reedy. "Maybe you don't want to hear it anyway, with this kidnapping thing. You must be crazy with worry. I know I'd be, if somebody grabbed one of these kids. Maybe they're not technically mine, but I love them like—"

"Please, Carol," I said. "I don't have a lot of time."

She cleared her throat, seeming to pull herself together. "It's about Jeff."

"You don't have to be afraid of him," I said patiently. "I told you. He can't hurt you. He's in Mexico."

Her sigh was long and trembling. "I'm not afraid of Jeff," she said sadly.

And then she told me what she'd seen on Friday night when she was working late, and I understood what had happened. Not all of it, by any means. There were still a couple of big holes and quite a few little ones that had to be plugged, but I knew the basic outlines. The question was, where did I go from here?

I was still sitting at McQuaid's desk, trying to reconstruct the narrative sequence of events in my mind, when the phone rang in the kitchen. I jumped up, but before I took two steps, Sheila was yelling.

"China! China, it's Brian!"

I ran. In a few seconds, I was snatching the phone from her fingers. "Brian! Where *are* you? Are you okay?"

His voice was a whisper, as if he didn't want to be overheard. "I'm scared, China. Come and get me. I want to come home."

"I'm on my way, honey," I answered fiercely. "Where are you?"

"I'm at the—" There was a sudden scrambling noise and Brian gasped.

"No, don't!" he cried fearfully. "Oh, no, please, don't hurt—"

The connection was broken.

"Brian!" I cried helplessly. "Brian!"

Sheila was waving a scrap of paper. "I've got it! I've got the number, China!"

The prefix was 512, which meant that Brian was calling from somewhere within driving distance. I dialed it with shaking hands. The female voice that came on the line was crisply efficient. "Town Lake Hotel."

Town Lake? That was Austin. A *hotel?* I was momentarily blank. "Uh, do you have a guest by the name of Jacoby?"

"Transferring to Guest Registration," the voice chirped, and my ear was filled with Musak. I sat with my jaw clenched, clutching the receiver as if it were a lifeline keeping me from going over the falls. A young and less efficient male voice, noticeably Texan, drawled "Howmi help ya?"

"Jacoby," I said. What was his first name? "Jake. Jake Jacoby. Do you have a guest by that name?"

More Musak. "Sorree, there's no Jacoby registered here." The voice was blithe.

My stomach turned over. "Look," I gritted, "this is an emergency. My eleven-year-old son just phoned me from your hotel. He's wearing a maroon Star Trek jersey and Mr. Spock ears, so he shouldn't be too hard to spot. Have you seen him?"

The voice chuckled. "Have I *seen* him? Ya don't know what's happenin' here this afternoon, ma'am?"

"No," I snapped. "What's happening there?"

"A Star Trek convention, that's what. This place is jammed with kids in maroon jerseys and pointy ears."

Sheila called Blackie while I pulled on clean jeans, found my sandals, and ran a comb through my hair. I grabbed up my purse, and Sheila and I ran out to her yellow Mustang. When we got to the intersection of Limekiln Road and I-35, Blackie roared up behind us with his light bar flashing and siren shrieking. The Jeep Cherokee passed us as we got onto the interstate, and Sheila pushed the Mustang hard to stay with it. I picked up Sheila's mobile phone and dialed the Cherokee.

"Thanks for responding so fast," I said.

"I've alerted the Austin PD," he replied tersely.

"They'll have two uniforms waiting for us at the hotel."

"Good. That means we can split up. Sheila and I will look for Brian, while you and the cops can go after Jacoby."

Blackie cleared his throat. "The Austin police agreed to treat this as a kidnapping, China, but I've got to tell you, I have my doubts. Brian called from the hotel where they're having the convention. It sounds to me like the kid just took off and caught a bus."

"But there was *blood*," I objected. "A lot of it. We all saw it. If Brian wasn't hurt, where did it come from?"

A moment of silence. "The lab report came back this morning," Blackie said finally. "It wasn't real blood. It was fake."

My heart flopped. I was remembering how I'd been conned by Arnold's nail-through-the-finger trick. I'd almost had the kid in the emergency room before I realized it was a mail-order gag. But still, something inside me couldn't accept the idea that Brian had faked a kidnapping.

"Look," I said. "I can imagine Brian hitching a ride to the convention with one of his buddies, but I can't believe he'd stay away all night without letting me know where he was. And there's the phone call. He was scared. I could hear it in his voice. *That* wasn't faked."

"We'll see when we get there, I guess," Blackie said, and broke off.

"What was that about?" Sheila asked, her eyes intent on the road. The traffic was heavy on the six-lane highway, but Blackie's light and siren were clearing the fast lane ahead. The Mustang was doing eighty-five.

I told her about the fake blood.

"Shit," she said.

"Yeah," I said. "But I don't believe Brian faked it. He wouldn't *do* that."

"Then who?"

"Jacoby?"

"Maybe," she said doubtfully.

"There's something else," I said, and told her about Carol's call. That kept us busy until we swung off I-35 onto Riverside and Sheila had to pay more attention to driving than to talking. In a couple of minutes, we were hanging a right onto Congress, crossing the bridge, and making two more quick rights under the hotel canopy, where an Austin police car was already parked, waiting. Two uniformed officers got out just as we drove up. Blackie, Sheila, and I consulted with them briefly, and then we separated. Sheila and I went into the main lobby, while Blackie and the police went through a service entrance.

The Town Lake is an older hotel, remodeled often over the years, the lobby resplendent now with imitation Persian carpet, dark paneling, overstuffed sofas, and crystal chandeliers. A sign directed us to the rear foyer, where I was brought up short by a six-foot-tall full-color cardboard stand-up of Lieutenant Worf with some sort of weapon aimed at my chest. Recovering, I was greeted by a scowling, flesh-and-blood Worf with walnut ridges on his brown forehead and lots of dark facial hair. He was wearing a gold and black jersey with a spiffy gold sash spangled with medals and ribbons. He was seated behind a table, taking money.

"Fifteen dollars," he said in a guttural voice, and growled "please," apparently out of respect for human niceties.

"I don't want an admission ticket," I said. "I'm looking

for my son. He's been kidnapped." I pulled out Brian's photograph.

"No kidding." The Klingon grimace might or might not have been a smile. "Fifteen bucks."

Sheila's face hardened. "I'm a law officer," she snapped, pulling out her official ID. "This is a police emergency." Unfortunately, her identification showed that she was a campus cop. The Klingon smiled again, showing strong, malevolent teeth.

"And I'm the security officer of this starship, lady. Fifteen apiece, or we'll beam you back to your home planet."

I pulled out my wallet. "Let's stop wasting time," I said, and took out a ten and a twenty. The transaction resulted in two large lapel buttons, numbered, two boarding passes, and a forty-page convention guide. As these items were being assembled, the Klingon male was joined by a Klingon female, wearing a gold leather jerkin with a metal pentagram hanging around her neck, a short black skirt, black stockings, and black leather gauntlets studded with bits of silver.

I thumbed hastily through the guide. "If I were an eleven-year-old kid," I said to the Klingon, "where would I be?"

I was assuming that Brian wasn't bound and gagged and locked in a closet—in which case, we would have to do a room-by-room search to find him. That would mean a warrant, which would mean even more time. My breath caught as I remembered the fear in Brian's voice when he was pleading not to be hurt. Had we already run out of time?

The Klingon scratched his rippled forehead, amiable enough now that we had paid up. But it was the female who spoke up. "Is he a trader?"

I was blank. "A trader?"

"Like, you know, cards."

Cards! Of course! Only a few days ago—only a few? it seemed like a century—Brian had been in hot pursuit of a Mr. Data hologram card.

"If he is," the Klingon male said helpfully, "the dealers' room is that way." He jerked a heavy hand to the left. The back of his hand bore the tattoo of a coiled snake.

I stared at it, jolted by a new idea. Was Jacoby a Klingon? Was that why he had brought Brian here? It seemed to fit with what little I knew about his personality. It—

But Sheila was grabbing my arm. "Let's check out the dealer's room."

The first door down the hall to the left opened onto a ballroom-sized space filled with rows of tables that were spread with a chaos of intergalactic merchandise: sweatshirts, books, cassette tapes, weapons, toys, starship replicas, Trekker costumes, jewelry, and so on. It was peopled by a bewildering assortment of aliens, Druids, Starfleet personnel, and small children in Halloween costumes.

"God help us," Sheila breathed.

"Let's hope so," I said. "Otherwise, we may never find him."

Sheila and I stopped at the first card dealer's booth and I took out Brian's photograph.

"I'm looking for this boy," I said. "He's wearing a maroon jersey, Spock ears, and he's trying to find a Mr. Data holgram card."

The card dealer affected the Captain Picard look: a completely bald head. He was wearing skintight black pants and a black tee shirt that said, Beam me sideways, Scottie. No one here knows which way is up. He glanced at Brian's picture and shrugged.

"Maybe yes, maybe no," he said. "Half the kids in town

are chasing that card." He moved his head to the left. "Try the corner booth. I heard they had one."

Three trading card booths later, we found a dealer who had sold Brian a card — not a Mr. Data hologram card, but a Lieutenant Yar 3-D image card.

"It was around ten, right after I got set up," the dealer said, handing my picture back. He grinned. "Kid's got smarts. Knew the book value on that card. Wouldn't pay a penny more." I wondered how many kids without smarts had paid the dealer's inflated price.

"Did you see who was with him?" Sheila asked. "A big, heavy man with a snake tattoo on his neck, maybe?"

He grinned. "There are a lot of guys around here with snake tattoos, but I didn't see anybody with the boy." He glanced from one to the other of us. "What's the matter, d'ya lose him?"

"Yes," I said soberly. "We think he's been kidnapped. He disappeared last night."

The man shrugged. "Not to make light of your problem," he said, "but kids play a lot of scams to get to the convention. Last year, one boy stowed away in the back of a delivery van up in Lubbock. Parents like to killed the little rat when they finally caught up with him down here." He grinned comfortingly. "Chances are your boy just climbed out the window and lifted his thumb. You tried the video rooms?"

The sign outside the third-floor video room announced that it operated twenty-four hours a day. Inside, my eyes took a minute to adjust to the flickering dark. The room contained a dozen mostly empty chairs, a large-screen television and VCR, and three semirecumbent bodies in various stages of wakefulness. "She was aroused by your power," intoned one odd-looking galactic freak on the screen to a furry humanoid topped by a helmet that might have come from the Third Reich. "You took her to the edge. What is this ability that you have to attract and hold women? Tell me, so I can have it, too."

That was enough. There was no Brian in the room, and definitely no reason to hang around. "The Trouble with Tribbles" was showing in the next room, to a much larger audience, but Brian wasn't there, either. Back in the hall, I thumbed frantically through the guide. Where else could he be?

"How about the game rooms?" Sheila asked. "I saw a sign that said they're on the fifth floor."

The first game room was filled with intense Storm-troopers, exotic galactic maidens, and a couple of bearded dwarves, gathered by threes and fours around tables filled with cards. A smudgy blackboard on the wall announced that the players were advancing to the third round of Krentl, apparently the name of the game they were play-ing.

A man with a badge that said Games Master came up to us. I showed him Brian's picture, and he nodded.

"Yeah, he was here until a little while ago, as a matter of fact. Did okay in the first round, but got blipped in the second. Second round's the hardest. Krentl's set up that way." He drew his finger down a page of names until he came to Brian's, penciled in Brian's childish hand. I stared at it and swallowed hard. "He clocked in at ten and out at ten-thirty," the games master added.

"Was he alone?" I asked. "Was there a big, ugly guy with him?"

The games master shrugged. "Who's to say? There are always spectators. Most of them are big and ugly." His eyes went to a young woman in green body paint, a harem skirt, and a low-cut bodice. "Not all, though."

"Where else should we look?" Sheila asked.

"You might try Gurps," the games master said. "Some of the younger players prefer it because it's—"

"Gurps!" I exclaimed. Sheila's mouth had fallen open.

"Yeah. Next door."

Out in the hall again, I stared at the sign. There it was, in big red letters crayoned on white cardboard. GURPS. The skin prickled at the back of my neck.

"That *is* what the Ouija board said, isn't it? Gurps?"

Sheila's eyes were slitted, her lips pressed together. She didn't say anything. She just nodded.

The door to the Gurps game room was open. It, too, was full of round tables, and the tables were full of players, many of them youngsters in the costumes of various galactic cultures. I scanned them quickly, searching for—

"China!"

And then I was kneeling with my arms open and he was bounding out of his chair, scattering cards, rushing to me, throwing his arms around my neck and burying his face against my shoulder, sobbing.

"Oh, China, I thought you'd *never* come! I didn't want to stay. I tried, but I couldn't get away. Please believe me."

"It's okay, Brian," I whispered, and held him tight. "It's okay, son."

Sheila's hand was in her purse, her feet wide apart, her shoulders braced for action. She was scanning the room. "Where's Jacoby?" she asked sharply.

Brian looked up. "Who?"

"The man who brought you here," I said. I stood up and pulled Brian quickly behind me. "Where is he, Brian?"

"It wasn't him," he said, "it was—" He suddenly

screamed and ran out from behind me. "No! Oh, don't, please!"

And then I saw the woman and my heart turned over. She had raised the window and was straddling the sill.

"Stop that woman!" I yelled. "She's jumping!"

A Romulan commander with patent-leather hair and winged black brows reached out and grabbed the woman's arm. "Stay where you are, lady," he growled. "That's gravity out there."

Sheila was shaking her head in bewilderment. "Where's Jacoby?" she asked again. "And who the hell is *she*?"

"She's my mom," Brian said, and began to cry.

CHAPTER EIGHTEEN

As for Rosmarine, I lett it runne all over my garden walls, not onlie because my bees love it, but because it is the herb sacred to remembrance, and, therefore, to friendship; whence a sprig of it hath a dumb language that maketh it the chosen emblem of our funeral wakes and in our buriall grounds.

Sir Thomas More
1478–1535

Fifteen minutes later, Blackie, Sheila, and I were sitting in the hotel coffee bar with Brian, having a late lunch and trying to make sense out of what had happened over the past couple of days. Little by little, question by question, the pieces were beginning to fit together.

Desperate to get to the Star Trek convention and chase down the Mr. Data hologram card, Brian had accepted his mother's offer to pick him up on Thursday evening and take him to Austin so that he could be in the dealer's room the minute it opened Friday morning. They had cooked up the arrangement on the telephone Wednesday evening. Sally would park out on the road and wait, and Brian would simply pick his moment to walk out.

"I didn't mean to scare you," he said, his freckled face pinched and white. He pushed his hamburger away, half-eaten. "Honest, I didn't, China. I was going to call you the minute we got to the hotel and tell you not to worry."

"What about the stuff that looked like blood?" Blackie asked. He put both elbows on the table and leaned forward, his voice stern. "It sure looks like you wanted to convince everybody you'd been kidnapped."

"Blood?" Brian sounded confused.

"That red stuff that dripped on the drive," I said.

Brian bit his lip. "It dripped on the drive, too?" He blinked hard, as if he were trying not to cry. "That was an accident. Arnold gave me this stuff he made. Karo syrup with red food coloring and catsup in it. It was in a plastic baggie and I stuck it in my gear bag and forgot about it. I didn't know it was leaking until Mom started yelling at me about getting it all over the seat of her car." He looked at me, anguished. "It was totally fake, China. I never thought it would really *fool* anybody!"

Sheila rolled her eyes at me and the corners of Blackie's mouth twitched.

"Forget the fake blood," I said. "So how come you didn't call?"

Brian's chin quivered. "Because when we got to the hotel, Mom wouldn't let me." His voice broke and he swallowed. "I asked and asked, and first she said I could, as soon as room service brought us something to eat. Then after we ate she said I couldn't call because things were going to be different from now on. I was supposed to live with *her*, because that was the way you and Dad wanted it. Now that you guys were together, I was just in the way. You didn't need me. *She* needed me a lot more. She did, too. I could see how much she needed me."

I put my arm around his shoulders. "That's not the way it is, Brian. With us, I mean. You're *not* in the way."

"I'm not?" His eyes looked lost in his pale face.

"No, you're not," I said firmly. I pushed his hamburger back toward him. "What did she say after that?"

He took a bite of his burger. "She said we weren't going to waste money going to court. We were just going away. California maybe, or Alaska, maybe even Europe. We were going to have different names, and I wasn't supposed to tell anybody who we really were. If I did, everybody would be very upset at her, and they'd put her in jail." He swallowed. "She said before she let that happen, she'd kill herself."

I tightened my arm around his shoulder. Blackie muttered something under his breath.

"That must have been pretty tough," Sheila said.

Brian nodded, struggling against the tears. "I tried to call home last night, but the line was busy. When I finally got hold of you, she caught me. She went out on the balcony and started to climb over the railing. That's why I hung up."

"She probably didn't really mean to jump," Sheila said. "She was just trying to scare you."

"I figured that." He put the burger down and wiped his nose with the sleeve of his jersey. "She wasn't, like, well, thinking straight. I mean, I didn't think we could do all the stuff she said. Mom isn't . . . well, I just couldn't see her in Alaska, with the snow and the bears and everything. I thought I ought to go with her, just to keep her from freezing to death or getting eaten by a polar bear."

So it isn't just dads and moms who have a hard time drawing the line between holding on and letting go.

"So what did you say to her?" I asked gently.

"Well, I said I'd go, and she said we should check out. But I said I wanted to play the games first. I was hoping you'd figure out where I was and come for me."

"For a kid, you have a lot of courage," I said. I hugged him. "I love you very much."

He leaned his head against me. "What's going to happen to her?" He looked at Blackie. "Will she have to go to jail?"

"Your father will have to decide whether to press charges," Blackie said. "Right now, the Austin police have her in custody. A doctor will talk to her, too, and maybe put her in the hospital for a day or two. She was a little upset."

That was an understatement. Sally had smashed the Romulan in the face with a Coke bottle, pushed a small purple elf off a chair, and tipped over a table. She might have gone on creating general havoc, but she was collared by an impassive young Vulcan and a beefy Boraalan in a silver jumpsuit. Somebody called hotel security, and a few minutes later a security officer had come, with Blackie and the Austin cops right behind.

Brian looked up at me. "Will she be all right, China?"

"I don't know," I said honestly. "It depends, I guess. On a lot of things." I could see that some good might come from what had happened in the last couple of days. No judge would turn a child over to an emotionally un-balanced woman who had kidnapped her child and held him by threatening suicide. Under the circumstances, Sally's lawyer would advise her to drop the suit. And she would be forced to get counseling.

I touched his face. "The important thing right now is that you're safe. Have you had enough adventure for one weekend?"

He managed a smile. "I guess. But I still didn't get my Mr. Data hologram card." He looked across the table at Sheila. "It's a very big hotel. How did you guys know to look for me in the Gurps room?"

Sheila cleared her throat. "Superior detective work," she said. Ruby, no doubt, would have another explana-tion.

At that moment, a man came over to the table. He was dressed in a Next Generation tee shirt with a dragon stick-on tattoo on one cheek. He gave Brian a questioning look. "You the kid who was looking for the Mr. Data card?"

"Yeah," Brian said eagerly. "You got one?"

"Matter of fact, I have," the man said, "back in the dealers' room. Just picked it up not half an hour ago. Thirty-five bucks."

"Thirty," Brian said.

The man scowled. "Thirty-two."

"I gotta see it first," Brian said. He looked at me. "Can I?"

"Have you got thirty dollars?"

His face fell. "Not anymore, I guess."

"How much do you need?" I asked with a sigh. I opened my wallet. "Will twelve dollars do it? That's all I have."

"That's great," he said. "Thanks!"

I gave him the money and stood up to let him out. "Ten minutes," I said. "And then beam yourself back here."

He hugged me and was gone.

Blackie laughed as I sat down. "All's well that ends well, I guess."

"It hasn't ended yet," I said.

"Right," Sheila said meaningfully. "You'd better tell him about Carol's phone call."

It took me five minutes. At a certain point in the narrative, I handed him the photograph of the crooked rosemary bush I had stuck in my purse. He stared at it, incredulous. "Say that again," he demanded.

I repeated what Carol had told me, added my interpretation, and described what needed to be done. When I finished, there was a silence. Finally he gave a long, low whistle.

"Puts a whole new face on things, doesn't it?" Sheila asked.

"You bet," he said grimly, handing back my photograph. "Does Bubba know?"

"Not yet," I replied. "I guess that's the next step. That, and having a face-to-face talk with Carol." I glanced at Sheila. "That's a job for Sheila and me, though. Bubba wouldn't get to first base."

Blackie gave me a crooked grin. "Better leave Bubba to me."

So that's how it was decided. Blackie would take Brian back to Pecan Springs and drop the boy off at the county jail before he went to talk to Bubba. Sheila and I would talk to Carol. After that—

"Hey, I *got* it!" Brian said, coming toward us, waving a trading card.

"Terrific," I said. "You ready to go?"

"Yeah," he said. He looked up at me shyly. "Thanks for the twelve bucks, Mom."

Sheila and I spent the next hour in Nancy's kitchen, talking to Carol over cups of coffee and butterscotch rolls left from the kids' lunch. After a while, Nancy came to join us, with her baby at her full, heavy breast.

Carol didn't want to do what we asked. "I'm afraid," she said. "If it doesn't work—"

Nancy broke in. "You have to," she said. "You'll never have any peace in your heart until you've told it."

"I *have* told it," Carol objected. "I told her." She pointed at me.

Sheila leaned forward. "That's not good enough," she said. "You've got to tell the police."

"Okay," she said finally, red-eyed. "I'll do it."

I stood up, feeling sticky from too many butterscotch rolls. "I need to make a couple of phone calls," I said.

We caravanned down to Pecan Springs in two vehicles and went directly to Judge Porterfield's house, where Nancy and the kids waited in the van while Sheila and I took Carol inside. I introduced Carol to Judge Porterfield and Bubba Harris, who arrived just as we did. She told them what she had seen, and I showed them my photograph. Bubba looked as if he didn't believe us, in spite of having already heard most of the story from the sheriff, but the judge didn't have any problem. She thought about it for, oh, maybe all of thirty seconds before she signed the search warrant.

So that's how Sheila and Bubba Harris happened to be standing on either side of Matt Monroe in the herb garden at the hotel later that evening, with Judge Porterfield and me. All of us were watching Hector Gomez dig up the crooked rosemary bush. It was still very hot, but the newly installed fountain played a cooling melody of cascading water and the sun was sinking into a rosy puddle of clouds on the western edge of the Edwards Plateau. At the edge of the lake a frog harrumphed hollowly, and somewhere in the cedars and live oaks a rain crow chuckled a sardonic greeting.

"I still don't understand what all this is about," Matt said with nervous bravado. He glanced at Gomez, who was lifting the rosemary, its burlap root wrap still intact around the unopened ball of soil. "You guys are crazy as fucking bullbats. I'll fix your wagon. I'll sue your asses!"

Judge Porterfield looked sternly at Matt. The red silk rose trembled at the throat of her white dress. "You cut that out, Mr. Monroe." She wagged her finger at him like a third-grade teacher at a recalcitrant small boy. "It's hot an' we got work to do, an' you're not makin' it any easier with your foul mouth. Now you hush up."

Hector Gomez, sweating from his exertion, continued to dig. After a few minutes, he straightened up.

"Mebbe you'd better check this out, chief," he said, and stepped out of the hole. Bubba squatted down and studied something intently. Then he dug at the loose dirt with his fingers. In a minute, he got out a pocket knife, worked a little longer, then stood up.

"Have a look, judge," he said loudly, into Miss Porterfield's good ear.

"What is it?" the judge asked, bending forward to peer into the hole. "What am I lookin' at?"

"It's not a what," Bubba said. "It's a who."

I stepped forward. The sweetish odor of decomposing human flesh told me I had been right. Bubba had cut open the plastic garbage bag that wrapped the body of Jeff Clark.

"I still don't see what you're tryin' to prove," Matt Monroe said desperately. Sheila had her hand on his arm.

The judge wheeled on him. "Mr. Monroe, you have been slicker than a slop jar. But you had just better shut your mouth, because anything you say can be held against you in a court of law. You got that?"

The rain crow gave one last bitter chuckle and fell silent.

But the excitement wasn't over. Late that afternoon, I had picked up The Beast, no longer an official crime scene, and driven to the county jail to bail out Brian. Then, feeling like a mother on car pool duty, I had driven him to Ruby's, where I dropped him off. Now, I went to pick him up and sketch out for Ruby the details of what had happened.

"Stay for coffee," she urged. "I want to hear *more.*"

"It's late," I said. "I have to get home and put in calls to McQuaid and The Whiz. And I need to stop at the store and see what kind of progress we've made on the air conditioner. I didn't have time to check with Laurel before she closed."

The lights from Maggie's Magnolia Kitchen spilled out onto the street when Brian and I drove up Crockett. All the street parking in front of the shop was taken, and I remembered that Maggie was hosting a wedding rehearsal party that night.

"I guess we'll park in the alley out back," I said, and made a right onto Guadalupe. A flare of auto lights close behind me caught the mirror and I blinked.

"I think I'll come in with you," Brian said in a small voice. "It might be kind of creepy sitting in the truck, thinking about that woman getting killed right here." He patted the seat beside him.

I made another right into the alley. "I don't want you to stay in the truck," I said. I pulled in beside the stone guest house at the back of my lot, turned off the lights and the ignition, and dropped the keys into my purse. "Come on. Let's —"

The lights had turned into the alley behind us, illuminating the cab of the truck with a bright glare. Suddenly an old Ford scraped around us in the narrow alley and braked to a hard stop at an angle, in front of us. The lights went off and the darkness closed around us like a heavy curtain.

"Brian," I said urgently, "get down!"

"What?" Brian asked, startled. His door was half-open. "What are we —?"

"Just get *down,*" I snapped. I yanked him back into the truck and shoved him onto the floor, pulling his door shut and locking it. Ahead of us, a car door had slammed, and heavy footsteps were crunching on the gravel. I locked my door and began to grope in my purse. Why hadn't I kept the keys in my hand? I couldn't pull forward, but I could've put the truck into reverse and—

"Is it a robber?" Brian's whisper was terrified. "Is it that Jacoby guy?"

"I don't know," I said, fumbling desperately. "Stay down." If only I'd brought the gun. I might not have to use it, but it could have been a deterrent. My fingers closed over something the size of a pocket flash. The air conditioner was off and and the sweat was beginning to run down my face and neck and trickle down my back, sticky and warm. Warm like blood. I suddenly had a vision of Rosemary lying on her back on this seat, a bullet through her head. Brian made a whimpering noise. No, it wasn't Brian, it was *me.* I was whimpering. I tightened my throat. McQuaid hadn't been paranoid. He'd been *right.*

There was a rapping on the door. "Roll down the window," a raspy voice growled. "I wanna talk to you."

"No," I said.

"I ain't got no gun," he said. "I ain't gonna hurt you. I bin waitin' for you. I just wanna talk." His laugh was high-pitched, too shrill for such a big man. I could see the ominous hulk of him, silhouetted against Mr. Cowan's back porch light, which had just gone on across the alley. Mr. Cowan, who is eighty-something, is a one-man Neighborhood Watch.

"What do you want to talk about?"

"Stop stallin'. Roll it down."

"McQuaid isn't here. He's in Mexico. If you want to

get even, he's the man you want."

The laugh was short and sharp. "I'll do that. But right now, I'm gonna fix you and that kid of his." He moved his head to peer around me. "I see you found him. Where was he? Out shootin' pool with his buddies?"

Beside me, Brian stiffened. "I was *not*," he said indignantly. "I was with—"

I cut in. "You knew Brian was gone?"

"Course I knew." Jacoby was deeply injured. "I watch TV, don't I? Didn't make me feel good to see my face plastered all over the TV screen, did it? Made me feel like a criminal. What kinda crap is McQuaid tryin' to pull, anyway? Puttin' me away once wasn't enough for him?"

"McQuaid didn't have anything to do with this. And I'm sorry about the TV coverage," I added sincerely. "I really thought you were the one who—"

"You're gonna be sorrier." His voice was bitter. "I lied. I got a gun right here." He brandished it. "You gonna roll this window down, or do I gotta blast a hole in it?"

The hot stillness closed around me, smothery. I took my right hand out of my purse and with my left, began to roll down the window.

"No, China!" Brian whispered.

"Hey, that's more like it," Jacoby said, pleased. He leaned forward and I could see the glint of light along a barrel, could smell garlic mixed with cheap booze on his breath. I raised my right hand slowly, my heart in my throat. "Now we kin talk friendly-like," he said. "I bin waitin' a long time for this."

As my hand cleared the top of the window, I pulled back hard on the trigger. It was point-blank range.

"Yiii!"

Jacoby staggered backward, dropping his gun, flinging

both hands up to his face. I leaned on the horn as he fell to his knees, clawing at his eyes and screeching, a raw, horrible scream that even the blast of the horn couldn't drown out.

Across the alley, Mr. Cowan's door opened, and I let up on the horn. "What's that racket out there?" he cried. The old man's quavery voice was accompanied by a shrill yapping. "Shut up, Miss Lula. I cain't hear a gol-durned thing with you barkin' like a idiot."

"It's me, Mr. Cowan," I yelled. "China Bayles. I've got a murderer out here. Call 911, please. Quick!"

Mr. Cowan's door slammed. Jacoby was on his hands and knees, trying to crawl in the direction of his car. Tears were streaming down his face and he was wrenched by spasms. I scrambled out of the truck and grabbed up the gun.

"On the ground!" I shouted.

Jacoby collapsed and rolled over, hands digging at his eyes, groaning. Brian jumped out of the truck.

"Wow," he said. "Just like on TV. What'd you blast that guy with, China?"

I held up the small metal cylinder McQuaid had given me. "The mother of all hot peppers," I said.

CHAPTER NINETEEN

There's rosemary, that's for remembrance. . . .

William Shakespeare
Hamlet

"El río abajo?" McQuaid asked, turning away from the barbecue with a fork in his hand. "What the hell is that?"

"It means underground river," I explained, setting the tray of foil-wrapped sweet corn ears on the table next to the barbecue. I surveyed the red-gingham–covered table, set for six with my Aunt Tullie's colorful Fiesta Ware. The weather had turned blessedly cooler, it was Sunday night, and Blackie, Sheila, and Ruby were joining us for a picnic.

"I know what it means," McQuaid said. He turned a piece of chicken. "What does it *mean?*"

Sheila lifted her glass to Blackie for a refill of before-dinner white wine. "The Edwards Aquifer," she said. "You know, where we get our water. The fountain that Jeff had put in just before he was killed—the water is tapped from an artesian spring. The pipe for the fountain runs in a trench. The dirt was already loose there and it was easier digging, so that's where Matt put the body. Alongside the pipe. *El río abajo.* Where La Que Sabe said to look."

"You don't really believe that stuff, do you?" Blackie asked, setting down the wine bottle.

Sheila reached down to fondle Howard Cosell's ears. He sighed and sank to the ground in a paroxysm of utter bliss.

"Of course she doesn't. She's too intelligent." McQuaid flipped one of the chicken halves. "Now's the time to put the corn on," he said to me. "The chicken will be ready in about twenty minutes."

"If she doesn't, she should," Ruby said emphatically, tripping across the grass with the veggie plate. "La Que Sabe knew where the body was buried, and Ouija told us where to find Brian—playing Gurps."

"Not so fast, Ruby," Blackie said. "As I understand it, China and Sheila located Brian without giving a thought to that Ouija thing. They didn't have a clue where he was."

Ruby gave him a knowing smile and tossed her carroty head. She was all in green this evening: oversized green checked shirt with the sleeves rolled up, green and white striped leggings, green sandals, even green paint on her toenails and fingernails. She had spent all afternoon, she told me, cleaning up the mess the storm had made of her garage and talking to the insurance adjuster. In the end, she'd get a new garage. A bonus, as it were, for hosting La Que Sabe.

"They didn't *need* a clue," she said. "Ouija predicted where they'd find Brian, and when they got there, there he was. It's the same with *el río abajo.*" With that indisputable logic, she picked up her glass. "Might I have a refill, please?" she asked sweetly.

Sheila chuckled, I grinned, and Blackie poured.

McQuaid sat down on the picnic bench. "Let's take it from the top," he said. "There are a few things I don't have straight yet. Matt killed Rosemary to keep her from marrying Jeff. Right?"

I sat down beside McQuaid and leaned against his arm. He ruffled my hair affectionately and pulled me closer. We hadn't discussed our differences since he got back because we'd been so glad to see one another. The other China had wanted to slug it out, lay down the law about curfews, and make a clear statement about personal freedom, but a good opportunity hadn't presented itself. That might be just as well, actually. Maybe the best thing is to just sort of muddle along, telling the truth as much as possible, lying only when we have to, and trying to be smart enough to learn from our mistakes.

"Actually, he had two reasons for killing Rosemary," I said. "The first reason was her discovery that he'd been skimming the accounts."

"Wait a minute." McQuaid frowned. "Matt said *he* hired Rosemary."

"Matt lied," I said. "It was one of his many lies. Jeff hired Rosemary because he thought something was wrong with the accounts. Carol mentioned that fact the first time I talked to her, and Sheila and I even talked about it. But it didn't make sense until some of the other pieces began to fall into place. Rosemary uncovered Matt's theft and reported it to Jeff. That was one motive for her murder."

McQuaid grunted. "The other, I suppose, was the hotel itself."

"Yes. Matt was the beneficiary of Jeff's will. If Jeff married Rosemary, that would change. In the event of his death, his half of the hotel would go to her, not to Matt. Taken together, it was a powerful combination of motives for a *double* murder."

"But that's the puzzling part," Ruby said. She took the lawn chair next to Sheila, kicked off her sandals, and propped her bare feet on Howard Cosell. He rolled over to expose his belly, all four paws in the air, a foolish, doggy grin on his face. "Matt went to a lot of trouble to make everybody believe that Jeff was still alive, somewhere in Mexico. But somebody has to be *dead* before you can inherit their money. If Matt wanted the hotel, why did he do all that?"

"Because his plan got screwed up," I said. "He intended to make Jeff's murder look like a suicide. Man goes berserk, kills fiancée with father's famous gun, then shoots self."

"Not a bad plan, actually," McQuaid reflected. "The gun was exactly the kind of weapon somebody might use for a ritual murder-suicide."

I nodded. "But Jeff did not go gentle into that good night, as the poet says. Matt and Jeff struggled for the gun. Three shots were fired, two of them in places where you couldn't or wouldn't shoot yourself."

"I'm surprised the gunshots weren't heard," Sheila said, slapping at a mosquito. "The fight happened at the hotel, in Jeff's office. When Bubba used Luminol on Jeff's desk and on the floor, he found the bloodstains Matt thought he'd wiped up."

"It was the Fourth of July," Blackie reminded her. "If anybody heard shooting, they'd think it was firecrackers."

Flames flared up in the barbecue and McQuaid got up to squirt some water on the coals. He sat back down again. "So Matt took Jeff out and buried him under the rosemary bush?"

"Not that night," I said. "Of course, if he'd been successful in making the death appear to be a suicide, he would simply have left Jeff slumped over the desk, where Lily would find him on Thursday morning, along with the gun. Rosemary would have been found at about the same time, shot by the same gun. With both Rosemary and Jeff dead, Matt would be home clear, with the hotel in the bag."

"I guess that's where he had to improvise," Blackie said.

I nodded. "Until he came up with a better idea, he wrapped Jeff in garbage bags and stashed him in the back of the hotel's walk-in freezer. It's one of those old-fashioned coolers, about as big as a boxcar, and there's a lot of stuff in there. He could be reasonably certain that nobody'd find the body before he'd figured out what to do with it, and with the gun."

"How do you know that?" Ruby asked curiously. "Did he tell you?"

Blackie shook his head. "He's not talking," he said. "It's only on TV that the accused spills the beans when he's caught." He gave a short laugh. "In real life, the lawyer shows up and tells the criminal to keep his damn mouth shut and let the prosecution build its own case."

"So how *do* we know about the freezer?" Ruby demanded.

"There was a commotion about it when I was at the hotel on Thursday. Matt insisted on keeping it locked, even though that meant a lot of extra work. And when Harold came out to repair the freezer on Friday evening, he saw something big wrapped in black plastic."

"Bubba found bloodstains in the cooler, too," Sheila put in. "They're being checked for a match with Jeff's blood."

I went on. "After the body was temporarily disposed of, Matt must've stuck Jeff's car someplace—his garage, maybe—and then worked out an alternate plan. Nobody was looking for Jeff, of course, because he'd told everybody he was going fishing at South Padre. The trip was a cover to conceal his and Rosemary's wedding trip to

Mexico. That part of it is in Jeff's journal, which turned up after a more thorough search of his house."

"That journal's going to be a big help to Chick Burton," Blackie said. "It pretty much nails the prosecution's case."

"What does it say?" Ruby asked.

"That Jeff hired Rosemary to confirm his suspicions that Matt was stealing money out of the accounts," I said. "That he loved Rosemary and had been pleased about the baby and disappointed by the miscarriage. That they planned to marry, take a short honeymoon, and come back and blow the whistle on Matt. If they had lived to do what they intended, Matt would have been finished."

Ruby sat up in her chair and tucked her feet under her. Howard Cosell looked up at her sadly, then struggled to his feet and went to lie down under the picnic table. "So how did Jeff's body get into the herb garden?"

"The freezer broke down on Friday afternoon," I said. "Matt was in a panic. He hauled the air-conditioning repairman away from his supper." I grinned wryly, remembering what Harold had said about Matt having something in the freezer he didn't want thawed out. "Harold didn't stock the parts to fix the freezer, and Matt couldn't even be sure that the thing could be repaired. So he had to bury the body. The trench for the fountain piping had been dug and the pipe installed. All he had to do was widen the trench, put Jeff's frozen body into it, and cover it up. Then, because the rosemary hadn't yet been planted and he didn't want anybody else digging in the area, he stuck it into the hole. The trouble was, he didn't take the time to unwrap the burlap around the roots and he put the bush in crooked. I doubt if he even realized what a botched-up job he'd made of it."

"He really *did* botch it up," Sheila said. "His plan, I mean. Without a body, Jeff wasn't dead. And unless Jeff was dead, Matt couldn't inherit the hotel."

"I guess that's where I came in," McQuaid said. "Matt phonied up a quit claim giving himself Jeff's share of the hotel. Then, very late on Friday night, he drove Jeff's Fiat to Brownsville. Before he left town, he slung the gun out the window, at a spot where he knew it would be found."

"How do you know that?" Ruby asked.

"The part about the gun? I'm guessing. But we do know that he drove the car to Brownsville, because the Brownsville PD turned up somebody who saw him park it — a panhandler, looking for loose change. Matt gave him a ten, which impressed the hell out of the guy. It was good for a weekend drunk."

"And the Mexico gig?" Sheila asked.

"Piece of cake," McQuaid said. "All he had to do was hire somebody to use Jeff's plane ticket to Mexico City, spend a night in the hotel, and run through a couple of hundred dollars on Jeff's credit cards."

"Was the money actually spent," I asked, "or did Matt lie about the calls from the bank?"

"Bubba's still checking on that," McQuaid said. "What we do know is that when he'd made all the arrangements, Matt took the bus back here. We know that because Bubba turned up a bus driver who remembered him. Matt told everybody he'd gone to San Antonio for the day."

"Which totally pissed Lily off," I put in. "She hadn't planned to work that weekend."

McQuaid nodded. "Then he sent me down there to find the Fiat and the quit claim, which was just as good as a dead body."

"Hiring you to look for Jeff made his flight seem a lot more real," Blackie said. "Not only that, but it deflected suspicion from him. It was clever sleight of hand."

"Yes," Ruby remarked wisely, "but La Que Sabe knew. She told China that you were following the wrong man. She said to look for the man who wears a snake. That was Matt Monroe, of course. His boots were made of snakeskin."

McQuaid gave me a quizzical look.

"I'll tell you later," I murmured. "If you really want to know."

"I'm still not quite clear about Carol Connally," Blackie said. "Where does she come into the picture?"

"She was hired about ten years ago by Jeff's sister Rachel," I said. "Carol had never done any bookkeeping and had no idea of the significance of some of the procedures Rachel taught her. You see, Rachel had her own private account and was siphoning money into it."

"Stealing from her brother, in effect," Sheila put in. "It wasn't hard, because Jeff only looked at the year-end summaries she prepared, not at the account books themselves."

"That's right," I said. "After she died, Matt carried on his wife's scheme. But Carol's no dummy, and she caught on. To insure her continued cooperation, he opened an account in her name at the bank and every now and again he'd drop some cash into it. You know, a bonus."

"He bought her," McQuaid said.

"*And* set her up to take the fall," I added. "In case his moonlight requisition ever came out." Khat walked off the porch and came over to the picnic table. He jumped up onto my lap and began to knead my leg with his claws, not very carefully.

"Poor Carol," Ruby mused. "She must have been really torn up after she and Jeff got close. On the one hand, she was taking money from the hotel, from *him*, and on the other, they were lovers."

"I'm not sure how close they actually were," I said, stroking Khat's warm fur. He purred throatily. "Carol admits that her hopes for marriage were mostly wishful thinking. But however he felt about her, she certainly loved *him* very much. She was distraught when she found out about him and Rosemary."

"But back to the night of the murder," McQuaid said. "Carol Connally saw Matt with Jeff's body?"

"Not the night of the murder," I corrected him. "It was Friday night, the night the freezer broke down. Carol was planning to take a couple of days off to be with Nancy and the new baby, and she was working late. She quit about eleven. She got as far as the parking lot when she realized that she'd left her checkbook on her desk. When she went back to get it, she glanced out the window and saw Matt wheeling a room service cart into the herb garden, where he'd already dug a hole. The cart was covered, but Carol said she had an intuition about what was under the tablecloth. By Monday morning, she was certain she'd witnessed Jeff's burial. She was sick with grief, afraid she'd be charged with embezzlement, and absolutely petrified of what Matt might do if he found out what she knew."

Blackie wore a speculative look. "If Jeff's body had never turned up, Matt might have gotten away with murder. With two murders, in fact."

I put Khat on the ground and got up to check on the corn. "The verdict isn't in yet, though," I said. "Chick Burton's got plenty to do before he's ready to go on trial. A sharp, aggressive defense attorney could poke a dozen holes in—"

"China!" Three voices spoke in reproachful unison.

I assumed an innocent look. "The corn's done. Are these chickens ready?"

McQuaid got up to check. "They look done to me," he said. "Where's the plate?"

I brushed off a bug and handed it to him. "Better call Brian. He's playing by the creek."

McQuaid raised his voice. "Get up here, Brian. On the double."

Sheila got up and stretched. "Well, at least you don't have to worry about Jacoby." The cayenne had put him out of action long enough for the police to arrive and cart him off. Bubba hadn't even thanked me for corralling Adams County's most-wanted fugitive.

"Are you kidding?" McQuaid barked a short laugh and began forking chickens onto the plate. "How long before Pardons and Paroles turns that psycho loose again? And where do you think he'll show up the minute he gets out?"

It wasn't something I wanted to think about. One problem at a time.

Brian came up the path from the creek. He was mud from head to toe, and grinning.

Ruby wrinkled her nose and shrank back. "Ugh," she said. "What's that?"

Brian was holding a small, wet turtle, head and feet tucked reclusively into its shell. "His name is Simon," he said. "I saw Garfunkel down there, too, but he got away." He tucked the turtle casually under his arm and fished in his pocket, pulling out a fistful of snails. "I found these under a rock. Simon might want them for a snack. I'll put them in the refrigerator."

With the snails in one hand and a cloistered Simon under his arm, Brian started in the direction of the kitchen. Howard Cosell got to his feet and blundered after him. Under the mistaken belief that a gourmet treat was in the offing, Khat flicked his tail and stalked after Howard Cosell.

"Put a lid on those snails," McQuaid called after him. "I don't want to find them in the salsa."

I closed my eyes briefly. What happened to those days, those halcyon days of solitary bliss, when everything in my refrigerator was docile, edible, and dead?

McQuaid kissed my cheek. "It could be worse," he said gently. "Simon might have been a snake."

I shuddered. It was true. Simon might have been a snake.

Well, that about sums it up.

But it doesn't, of course. Certain parts of this story are inexplicable. They resist summation and explanation. But as Ruby often reminds us, there are more things in heaven and earth than are dreamed of in our philosophies — or explained by our science. She helps me remember that the universe is a vast and puzzling place, and that our corner of it is very small. From the pinpoint of that perspective, who am I to try to explain La Que Sabe or a storm aimed at one city block or five nonsensical letters on a Ouija board? Captain Kirk and Mr. Spock never had any trouble accepting the fact that the universe is a surprising place. Why should I?

And there's Rosemary. I know more about her now than I did when I found her body sprawled on the seat of The Beast, but not much more. I still don't know whether she did in fact sleep with her clients or blackmail them or both, whether she loved Jeff Clark as much as he loved her, whether the pregnancy was an accident or part of a deliberate scheme. Like all of us, she must have had regrets about the past and hopes and dreams for the future, but she didn't leave enough evidence behind to tell me what they were.

And Jeff. I saw his body, I know he's dead. But the

fiction of his flight was so compelling that it's still hard for me to believe what I saw. Like Rosemary, like so many crime victims, he goes into death unmourned, with nothing to mark his passing except for the abruptness, the violence of his death.

And what of the man alleged to have killed them? In a few months, the People will summon Matt Monroe to be judged for the capital murders of Rosemary Robbins and Jeff Clark. The prosecution will establish motive and opportunity, reconstruct the crimes, present the scientific evidence, call the expert witnesses. The defense will move to suppress the evidence, deplore the police handling of the investigation, question the expert witnesses' credentials, attack Carol Connally's credibility, and construct alternate theories of the crime — all in an effort to cast doubt on the prosecution's case. If Matt Monroe is found guilty, his lawyers will appeal, and appeal, and appeal. It may be a decade before he's brought into that grim room at Huntsville, strapped to the gurney, and executed — if the Supreme Court has not once again curtailed the implementation of the death penalty. And in all these months and years, the public's attention will be focused on the accused, on the killer. He will be the star of the courtroom drama, the victims only minor characters who are remembered, when they're remembered at all, in flashback; as pieces of evidence, rather than people.

Perhaps that's why I was so compelled to learn what I could about Rosemary, and why I was so frustrated by how little she left behind. Perhaps that's why Sheila and Ruby and I and a dozen of her other clients will gather briefly next week to replant the rosemary bush in the herb garden at the hotel, and to place a small plaque there with her name on it, and Jeff's.

Remembering isn't much, but it's all we can do.

RESOURCES

For readers who want to explore the many mysteries of herbs, there is a wealth of books, magazines, and newsletters available. For this book, I consulted the following:

Rosetta E. Clarkson, *Green Enchantment*. (Collier Books, 1940.) A classic history of herbs and gardening. Clarkson's pages on rosemary are full of interesting folklore. She points out that it symbolized remembrance at weddings and funerals, that it was used to cure headache and heartache, and that it grew so prolifically in Southern France that it was used for firewood.

Scott Cunningham, *The Complete Book of Incense, Oils, and Brews*. (Llewellyn Publications, 1989.) This book gave Ruby the idea for her Saturn incense. It is a magical cookbook that brings together many traditional nonculinary uses for herbs.

Madalene Hill and Gwen Barclay, *Southern Herb Growing*. (Shearer Publishing, 1987.) Another magical book. It has everything China needs to know about growing rosemary (and 130-something other herbs) in Texas, or any of the other hot, humid southern states. Besides propagation, cultivation, and harvesting, the book suggests garden designs, gives tips for using herbs, and offers a treasury of recipes from Hilltop Herb Farm, which Madalene Hill established more than thirty years ago.

Eleanour Sinclair Rohde, *The Old English Herbals*. Reprinted by Dover Publications. Written in 1922, it is still the best available history of the development of herbal writing. The author covers all the great herbalists, from the tenth-century Anglo-Saxon manuscripts to the seventeenth-century stillroom books.

Jeanne Rose, *Herbs & Things: Jeanne Rose's Herbal*. (Perigee Books.) A marvelous compendium of herbal lore, interpreted in Jeanne Rose's unique style. Many wonderful formulas, frolicks, and informative tidbits, along with drawings, funny pictures, and quotations like this one from Ivan Petrovich Pavlov: "Life is a constant struggle against oxygen deficiency."

A Book of Thyme and Seasons. Referred to in several of the chapter headnotes, the book exists only in China's mind, at this point. *China's Garden*, however, is a real newsletter, published four times a year by China Bayles and her friends. In it you'll find sage lore, thymely tips, savory recipes, and a potpourri of information about Pecan Springs and the China Bayles mystery series. For a sample copy, send $2 and your name and address to: China's Garden, PO Drawer M, Bertram, TX 78605. Not coincidentally, you may also write to Susan Wittig Albert at that address.